S0-AYS-411

DEACON

KIT ROCHA

This book is a work of fiction. The names, characters, places, and incidents are products of the writers' imaginations and are not to be construed as real. Any resem-blance to persons, living or dead, actual events, locales or organizations is entirely coincidental.

DEACON

Copyright © 2017 by Kit Rocha
All rights reserved,
including the right of reproduction
in whole or in part in any form.

Edited by Sasha Knight
Cover Artwork by Gene Mollica

ISBN-13: 978-1975628734
ISBN-10: 197562873X

*to the people who went before us
and took the hardest punches
so we'll never have to*

one

Six weeks of extra practice had honed Ana's skills. An hour of warm-up had loosened her muscles and primed her body. Adrenaline surged as she balanced on the balls of her feet, watching Deacon for the first hint of movement. A twitch of muscle. A shift in expression.

Any indication he was going to attack.

Anticipation crawled up her spine, twisting as the seconds dragged on. Deacon was a blank-faced wall of muscle two feet in front of her, his seemingly unprepared stance a trap that had ensnared plenty of new recruits. If Ana took a swing at him, he'd move, and with more speed than a man his size had any right to possess.

She'd ended up flat on her back more than once after falling for that trap, her pride stinging as she endured the knowing laughs of her fellow Riders. It didn't matter that they'd all ended up in the same position—*they* were men. They were allowed to get their asses kicked.

Ana couldn't afford to fail as often as they did.

Deacon stretched his neck slowly, first to one side and then the other—and waited.

He was testing her patience—or was it her courage? Maybe *that* was his goal—to see if she'd put pride and aversion to humiliation before her training.

Either way, she'd lose. With Deacon, she always seemed to. Might as well get it over with.

She shifted her balance just enough to suggest an attack was coming, a feint most of the other Riders would have bought—and had, at some point. But she knew as soon as she launched her real attack that Deacon hadn't.

He moved, a blur of tattooed skin and flexing muscles, and the fight was over before it even started. Her back hit the thick mats so hard it drove the air from her lungs, but even that discomfort was mild compared to the burn of frustrated embarrassment.

She'd let him get in her head. *Again.*

Deacon leaned over, bracing one hand on his knee and holding the other out to her. "That was good."

Yeah, so good she'd ended up flat on the floor with the wind knocked out of her.

She bit back the need to slap his hand away and snap at him not to patronize her. The only thing worse than failing as a girl was looking like a bad sport about it. She let him haul her to her feet before *calmly*—oh, so *very* calmly—saying, "Not good enough. I want to go again."

"No."

Ana flexed her fingers. Spreading them wide and focusing on the gentle pull of muscles kept her from balling them into fists. "I need the practice." *Obviously.*

"You've been practicing plenty. You're up here with Ashwin nearly every day." Deacon went still, then inclined his head. "Consider this a different sort of lesson."

She couldn't stop her embarrassed flush. "What lesson is that?"

He said it like it was a universal truth, with a tiny shrug and a crinkle between his eyebrows. "Not every fight can be won."

Each Rider faced that truth—if not before they joined, then during initiation, when they stood in front of their own portrait on the memorial wall in the temple. An outline that would be painted in upon their death, just like the others that surrounded it, all the dozens of portraits of Riders who had already died.

Maybe *that* was the lesson she'd embrace. Riders spent their lives too easily. There was nothing smart about throwing yourself against a brick wall until it broke you. *Smart* was retreating until you could find another way around the damn wall.

Ana forced herself to relax and nod. "All right."

Deacon's expression didn't change. "No argument?"

Another trap. Strange how she could see it, recognize the wisdom of silent obedience—and still not manage to hold her tongue. "Nope. Sometimes you just can't win a fight...yet."

"*Yet,*" he echoed, crossing his arms over his massive chest. "Explain."

She shrugged. "I didn't lose. I withdrew. Fight's not over until you're dead. Sometimes something's important enough to die for. But sometimes you need to pull back and regroup."

He shook his head, reached for a clean, folded towel, and held it out to her. "Now you're deliberately twisting what I said. Not every fight can be won, Ana. When you're my age, you'll see the truth of it."

When you're my age. Like he was some ancient, tottering grandfather and not a man who'd barely broken a sweat tossing her around. She took the towel and wiped her forehead, wishing he *was* ancient.

If his wise and ancient years would slow him down, just a little, maybe she could dump him on *his* ass for once.

The flush of embarrassment was gone, drowned by a fresh wave of anger. Anger at him, sure—Deacon was a patronizing son of a bitch who couldn't stop treating her like a little girl playing dress-up. But that was nothing compared to her anger at herself.

Deacon was the brick wall she couldn't stop throwing herself against, no matter how emotionally bruised it left her. She knew better by now. She was never going to win his approval.

And fuck him for making her want it.

"You're learning a lot from Ashwin. Maybe we should make those informal training sessions formal. Get everyone in the room."

The compliment was meant more for Ashwin than for Ana, but at least it didn't sound patronizing. She let it smooth the edges off her anger as she started to pace in a loose circle to keep her muscles from tightening up. "Everyone could benefit from his lessons. Hunter's already working with him. So is Gabe, but only with blades, I think."

"Don't forget Reyes." The words were flat, almost sardonic, but Deacon's eyes twinkled.

Ana had gotten this far for one reason—anger never overtook her sense of humor for long. She huffed out a laugh and stretched her left arm until the pull turned into a satisfying burn. "Yeah, I don't know if we can call flirting with Kora until Ashwin is ready to pick a fight with him a comprehensive training plan. I mean, sure, the rest of us like watching them go at it... but structure is good, too."

"Careful, or I'll put you in charge of organizing it."

"You just want me to have to put up with all the bitching about extra training."

"When have you known me to give a shit if they complain?" Deacon draped his towel around his neck and eyed her appraisingly. "No. You need a project."

Ana tamped down the first rush of excitement and stretched her other arm. Deacon could think she'd be good at it—or he could want to give her a job that kept her busy at the compound and off the front lines of every fight. "I have a project," she reminded him finally. "My dad's information network."

"You need a project that's *yours*," he corrected. "But the information is too important to set aside, and his contacts trust you. You'll have to do both."

"I can handle it." The words were reflex. "I'll talk to Ashwin and see what the options are. I'm sure he can teach us a lot more than just brawling."

"He's Makhai," Deacon said simply.

A year ago, Ana had barely understood what that meant. The Base's most elite soldiers were more myth than reality to the people who'd grown up in the sectors. She'd listened to stories about grim, terrifying men with psychic powers who could make you disappear from your own bed behind a locked door while your family slept nearby, oblivious.

Ashwin didn't have psychic powers, just highly enhanced genes and the kind of brutal training Ana couldn't wrap her head around. Her father had never gone *easy* on her, for sure—she'd been practicing marksmanship by shooting bottles and discarded pottery to earn spending money from the time her hands were big enough to hold a gun.

But after she finished, her father would join her as they sorted through the broken shards for pieces the mosaic artists could use in their work. He'd crouch next to her, picking through the pieces of glass so she wouldn't cut her fingers, and tell her stories about her namesake, Santa Adriana, daughter of the Prophet, who had personally attended Ana's birth to bless her first breath.

He'd tell her stories of the world beyond Sector One, beyond any of the sectors. He'd tell her stories of the world before the Flares, and how quickly it had all changed when the lights went out.

"You've always gotta be ready, babygirl." Every time he put her in the dirt during training, he'd haul her back to her feet with those words. William Jordan hadn't been ready for the world to end when he was twelve years old. He'd fought through those dark years to survive, fought until the fighting made him hard. But when he'd pushed Ana, she could always feel the love behind his toughness.

Ana didn't think Ashwin's training had involved a lot of love, tough or otherwise.

Maybe that made her excitement over what he could teach her a little morbid, but Ashwin didn't mind. If anything, he seemed to relish the chance to pass on his hard-won skills. So she would accept Deacon's project, and poke and prod her fellow Riders until they were all benefiting from Ashwin's tutelage.

If Deacon thought that would distract her from the front lines, he'd be sincerely disappointed.

two

Sector Three had flourished since the end of the war. Everywhere Deacon looked, repairs and construction dotted the once-ravaged streets, turning the desolate landscape into something vibrant and alive. It was good to see something new arising from the ashes of destruction.

Not that the war had torn the sector apart—that was a pre-existing condition. Though nearly two decades had passed, he could still remember the day those first bombs fell, the final move in a deadly power play between the Council in Eden and the collective in charge of the electronics factories in Three. The collective had pushed back against production quotas that meant horrific conditions for its workers, banking on the fact that the city needed the technology they produced too much to risk losing it. And the city had responded by blowing every single factory in Three right off the fucking map.

The message couldn't have been clearer if they'd carved it into people's hearts—*you are* all *expendable.*

In the years that followed, Sector Three was a wasteland, a slum within the slums, the kind of place where a person could get knifed in the street in broad daylight and folks would barely notice. They had their own problems to worry about. More than once, Deacon had stood at Gideon's side as the man agonized over whether the time had come to overstep his authority and take over Three, just to stop the suffering.

Then Wilson Trent, the self-proclaimed leader of Sector Three, had decided to be the one to overstep. Despite the fact that he couldn't even handle his own business, he made an ill-fated play for Sector Four, so all Gideon had to do was sit back and let Dallas O'Kane take care of the situation.

And he had. He'd taken Sector Three for his own and started rebuilding. When the conflict between the sectors and the city had boiled over into war, they'd all been stronger for it.

"It could have been faulty wiring." Lucio ran a hand over his short hair and tilted his head at an exposed power box as they passed by a building. The metal frame was crumpled on one side, and it hung askew on the chipped brick. "Maybe someone fell asleep with a lit cigarette. Or left something flammable too close to a heater."

"In this heat?" Deacon snorted. "I don't think so."

Lucio relented. "Just speculation. Possibilities. We can't know until we get there."

"It's bad." Deacon spoke without thinking, then shrugged at Lucio's sharp look. "It must be, for Six to call us." She might be an O'Kane, more than willing to reach out to the gang's contacts for assistance, but she was also a proud woman, the leader of a sector in her own right.

She wouldn't ask for help if she didn't need it. Which meant the situation wasn't just bad—it was potentially deadly.

They cleared the end of a narrow alley, and Lucio cursed under his breath. "There it is."

The smoke from the fire had cleared, but the scents of charred wood and burned plastic still hung thick and choking in the air. It was a squat building surrounded by others like it. They were untouched, but the top floor of this particular building had been reduced to a smoldering shell.

A grim-faced brunette leaned out of what was left of a window. "Hey, Deacon," she called. "Watch your step on the way up. Bren says the stairs are solid, but shit's still hot."

"Thanks, Six." He pushed through the front door and almost recoiled. The smell was exponentially worse inside, acrid enough to burn his eyes as well as his nose as he made his way up the stairs.

"You smell that?" Lucio asked as they reached the burned-out hull of the top floor.

"All I smell is charcoal."

"Right," he answered absently, then wandered into the ruined apartment, straight past Bren and Six without another word.

Six watched him pass, shrugged, and turned to Deacon. "Thanks for coming over."

"No problem. We're here as long as you need us." He nodded to the man standing stoically at her side. "Bren."

Bren nodded back, a quick jerk of his head. His expression was even more severe than usual, and the hair rose on the back of Deacon's neck.

"The fire was easy enough to put out," Six continued. "But I need to know what happened. If it was a freak accident or..."

"You suspect it wasn't?"

She hesitated. "I don't wanna sway you one way or another. You should just look."

The next room over was worse, like opening a giant wood-burning stove and walking right into the middle of it. There was an old iron bedstead in the center, reduced to not much more than a charred lump of mattress and springs poking up everywhere.

Except for the dead man on it.

Lucio looked up from where he knelt beside the ruined bed. "He definitely wasn't bound."

No, the man's stiff arms were still raised in the air, clenched into fists, the eerie picture of someone ready to fight. "Struggle?"

Lucio followed Deacon's gaze. "No, that's the fire. Pugilistic attitude. The heat coagulates proteins in the muscles, makes them contract like that. It happens even to the dead."

"Was he?" Bren asked shortly. "Dead?"

"When the fire started? I hope so." Lucio went back to peering under the iron frame. "Because it started right here on the bed."

Six exhaled roughly. "How can you tell?"

"Fire burns upwards. So we have *that*." Lucio gestured to the ceiling. It had burned clear through so that blue sky peeked through the roof in a spot above their heads. "But under the bed..." He rose and heaved the frame aside with a grunt.

The wood beneath the bed was mostly untouched, edged with a clear border of burned flooring in what looked like puddles. But what caught Deacon's eye was a flash of white and blue as a card that had been tucked into the bottom of the frame fluttered to land face-down on the floor.

A playing card. Deacon's blood was ice, but he reached for it automatically, before anyone else—like he was the only one who could handle what he knew he'd find when he flipped it over. Then he did, and the ice solidified, crystallizing in his gut until he wanted to puke.

It was just a normal card, the kind you'd find at any poker game or blackjack table. The king of hearts, staring blankly, one arm thrusting a sword through his head.

The suicide king.

Six frowned and leaned over his shoulder. "That's weird."

Six might not know what it was. Lucio might not. But Bren had served in Eden's Special Tasks force, so there was no hiding what this meant. "It's a message," Deacon murmured through numb lips. "Your friend was murdered. Professionally."

Bren took the card and turned it over between his fingers. "It's a mercenary group called the Suicide Kings," he explained. "I've heard of them, but I've never seen one of their kills."

Lucio glowered. "Makes sense. The fire was destructive but contained with surgical precision. It didn't spread to other buildings, or even downstairs. They knew what they were doing."

"They always do." Deacon turned to Six. "You should find out what your friend was up to. The Kings don't work cheap. If someone hired them, it wasn't over a personal beef. This was business."

"Shit." She sounded more resigned than surprised. "Okay. Laurel's been needing a new job, so I'll set her on it. We'll keep you guys in the loop."

They kept talking, words that tumbled around in a haze that Deacon couldn't quite catch. His attention kept drifting back to the card in Bren's hand, like a ghost in the room that only he could see.

Gideon would probably say that ghosts were like that—elusive things that showed up when you least expected them and shook you to your core. Otherwise, it wouldn't be a proper haunting, would it?

"You know how to reach us." Lucio held out his hand.

Six grasped it. "Thanks for the help. If anything else catches fire, now we know who to call."

"Once the flames are out, you got it."

Deacon couldn't take a breath until they were outside, away from the death and the soot that seemed to coat everything, including the air. He stood on the cracked sidewalk and drew in deep, bracing gulps, but the pressure in his chest didn't ease.

"You all right?" Lucio asked, low enough not to carry.

The pressure twisted tighter. "Why wouldn't I be?"

Lucio shrugged, his words as bland as his expression. "It's a rough scene. Corpses are bad on their own. When they're in that condition..." He shrugged again. "It's enough to unnerve anyone."

"Right." Let him think that—for now. Deacon didn't relish explaining, especially when half his attention was focused on their surroundings. Sometimes, the Kings left behind sentries to make sure their calling card had been found and their message received.

He saw no one, but his skin crawled at the thought that someone could be watching them now, so he picked up his pace. "We need to get back. I'll brief Gideon, but he might want a word with you."

"Sure thing." Lucio paused. "You think it means something, the Kings pulling a job in Sector Three?"

On that count, at least, Deacon could offer him the truth. "I don't know, Lucio. I honestly don't fucking know."

three

More often than not, Ana made the rounds of her dad's old contact network with Ivan. Between her father's impending sainthood and his father's *actual* sainthood, the faithful of Sector One threw open their doors, eager to attract the goodwill of two saints by helping their children.

Reyes opened doors, too, but for a different reason.

"Here," Karen cooed, bustling around the counter with a plate of crusty bread rolls, still steaming from the oven. Flour dotted her weathered cheeks and her gray-streaked red hair, the latter of which marked her old enough to know better when it came to Reyes and his bedroom eyes.

It didn't matter. No one, young or old, seemed able to resist the black sheep prince of the powerful Reyes family.

And he ate it up—in this case, literally. He bit into a roll and closed his eyes in almost erotic bliss as he chewed. "Karen, you're a goddess."

She preened under the compliment before nudging her son forward. "Davin helped with them, you know."

Davin was three years older than Ana and usually spent her visits teasing her mercilessly—unless Ivan scowled and reduced him to tongue-tied terror. But now, facing Reyes, he blushed and stammered like a teenager. "We have more in the back. I can pack up a bag."

"Really?" Reyes lifted one hand to Davin's face, then used sleight of hand to flip one of the newly minted temple coins between his fingers as he pulled back. As Karen laughed, he pressed the coin into Davin's hand. "I'd be grateful."

Davin flushed even redder and rushed into the back. Ana bit back a sigh and shot Reyes a quelling look before turning to Karen. "Any gossip I need to know about going around the market square this week?"

"Pretty quiet. One of the Delgado girls just got engaged." Karen scrunched up her face. "Oh, there is one thing. A new vendor."

"Oh yeah? What kind of vendor?"

"A fortune teller." She shook her head. "Foolishness, if you ask me."

Probably, though Ana had seen Del stare right through a person's soul before. And sometimes she thought maybe Gideon *could* read the future. But she trusted Del and Gideon to use the belief they inspired in others wisely. "Are a lot of people falling for the foolishness?"

Reyes was paying attention now, though the only change in his outward expression was a subtle tightening around his eyes. "And how much are they paying this person?"

Karen tutted. "The girl seems harmless enough, and people are watching. No one will let her take advantage of anyone who can't afford it, not in *this* market." She leaned on the counter, another indulgent smile transforming her face as she gazed up at Reyes. "But you're sweet to care so much."

Ana avoided rolling her eyes. Barely. As Davin bustled back into the front of the shop with a canvas sack, Ana dug up several more temple coins and gave them to Karen. "Let me know if anything changes."

"I will. Go safely."

The bell above the exit rang as Reyes opened the door for Ana. "That was fun."

"I'm sure it was." She retrieved the keys from her pocket and headed for the truck. Leaving with gifts was common, so much so that using her motorcycle to make rounds was inefficient. But dear God, Ivan didn't *chatter* as much as Reyes did. "Let's skip the East Market today. I have a hair appointment next week, and I'll get everything I need then."

"Whatever your heart desires." Reyes swung the bag over his shoulder, then frowned when it crinkled. He rummaged inside it for a moment and came up with a folded note—and a grin. "Looks like I have plans tonight."

Of course he did. Ana clambered into the truck and jammed the keys into the ignition. "Yeah, well, you better enjoy it. The new training sessions with Ashwin start next week, and Deacon expects everyone there."

Reyes stowed the bag in the back seat with a snort. "We wouldn't want to disappoint Daddy, would we?"

"Bite me, Reyes."

"Hey, I get it. I get it *hard*. He's stern but bang-able—that's a deadly combination."

Stern but bangable.

She couldn't consider the words. Couldn't allow them to sink into her skin. Her overwhelming *awareness* of Deacon was already a problem. Irritation and frustration provided a thin layer of armor, but only if she kept Deacon firmly and irrevocably in the not-even-a-little-bit-bangable category.

Reyes kept going. "It's a terrible idea, though."

It sure as hell was for *her*. But most of her tidy, logical list of reasons for staying far away from Deacon didn't apply to Reyes. "It's not like it's forbidden or anything."

"Exactly." He grimaced. "You have a whole fucking sector full of people who think you walk on water. They want to spend time with you—*limited* time. They know you can't stay, and they don't want you to. So you walk away happy—and, more importantly, so do they. No downsides. It's just easier."

Maybe if your idea of *happy* was defined by the time you spent naked with another person. Ana didn't. She knew that Riders weren't supposed to form long-term attachments, of course. It was reckless, considering the fact that the Riders had already willingly put one foot in their graves. But maybe she still couldn't quite believe it.

She blamed her parents for that. They'd been married for years when Gideon formed the Riders with William Jordan at his side. Her father hadn't hesitated, even knowing death could be waiting for him around the next corner. And her mother hadn't complained. It was their duty to the sector, their sacrifice for the greater good. Fiona Jordan had believed with the same passion as her husband, a passion they'd both passed on to their daughter.

In the end, her mother had succumbed to a heart

attack in the safety of her bed, and William had survived fifteen more years of daily danger. There were no guarantees in life. No rhyme or reason to who lived and who died.

Avoiding long-term attachments—avoiding *love*—might be easier. But Ana had yet to convince herself it was better.

And that made Deacon dangerous. The prohibition against long-term entanglements had never extended to the Riders themselves. As long as your feelings didn't get in the way of the job, no one batted an eye. After all, you were both damned anyway—you might as well float in the darkness together.

Stern but bangable.

Goddammit.

Ana waited for Reyes to settle into the passenger seat before shifting the truck into gear. "Whatever, man. Maybe the rest of us don't have your daddy issues. I'm just focused on not dying."

"How *boring.*"

"Well, if you *really* want me to loosen up...your sister's pretty damn cute."

His brows drew together in a stormy frown, the giant hypocrite, but he only snorted. "Good luck with that. She's supposed to be courting Maricela, now that I've failed so spectacularly."

As far as Ana could tell, courtship was the last thing on Nita's mind. In theory, the girls studying under Del were being prepared for marriage to one of the great families of Sector One, but as the eldest daughter of the powerful Reyes family, Nita had been trained in the responsibilities of nobility from the cradle. Now, she was more focused on her work, on perfecting her craft.

Most people in the Sector would kill for a chance to marry the Rios princess. Reyes and Nita were so reluctant, Ana was surprised Maricela hadn't developed a complex about it yet. "Why did you do that, anyway? Fail spectacularly."

"Why didn't you take over your mom's store, or learn your aunt's trade?" He shrugged. "Maricela's a sweet girl, and she's stronger than people think. It wouldn't have been terrible, marrying her. But life should be something better than *not terrible*, don't you think?"

Ana gripped the steering wheel and focused on the road until her brief spike of irritation passed. She *liked* Reyes. She liked Gabe and Hunter, too. She respected the commitment it took to turn your back on a life of privilege, wealth, and luxury, especially when it meant signing your own death warrant.

But *God*, sometimes they could be so oblivious. Sure, life should be better than *not terrible*, but too many people—even here in Sector One—had to settle for *not starving today*.

Sometimes hanging out with princes and princesses was fucking weird.

She turned the truck onto the main road and broke the silence. "I can't cook," she said. "Not worth a damn. My mom always knew I wasn't going to follow in her footsteps. I lived for my dad's visits. This is what I've always wanted to be. What he trained me to be."

"But it still goes against everyone else's expectations." Reyes pinned her with an appraising look. "Yeah, I think you understand better than you let on."

"They're fucking *stupid* expectations." She relented with a half smile. "But marrying people because your parents want more power doesn't sound like a ton of fun, either."

"Then you just answered your own question. Why are you still bothering me?" His eyes narrowed, even as they glinted with humor. "Are you trying to distract me?"

"Hey, you're the one who doesn't shut up. You've already said more today than Ivan has on every run we've ever made put together."

"Hmph." He crossed his arms over his chest with one last look that screamed *I know you're full of shit.*

Silence filled the truck as she drove to their next stop, and Ana could hear her aunt's voice in her head. *Watch what wishes you put out into the world, my girl.* Ivan's silences were icy and empty, with plenty of room for her own thoughts. But Reyes filled the vehicle with his presence, like the barely leashed intensity that seethed behind his eyes was seeping into the air, forcing her to consider his words instead of letting her mind wander.

Stern but bangable.

Fuck.

Reyes got to crack jokes about nailing Deacon. He got to lure the baker's son into a dark corner for filthy sex, or retreat from parties with as many giggling initiates as he could convince to follow him. He got to fuck everything that moved because he would never have to prove himself.

Ana didn't have that luxury. If she even *thought* a sexy thought in Deacon's direction, it would be all over. Every asshole she had beat out to earn her spot in the Riders would use that weakness to salve their bruised ego. They'd tell themselves she'd beaten them on her back in Deacon's bed instead of in the ring, where she'd kicked their motherfucking asses.

It was the one thing her father could never have fully prepared her for. The one thing he couldn't have known, because he'd been there from the beginning. Hell, since before the beginning. He was a Rios family bodyguard before the Riders came to exist, and had stood at Gideon's side as a founding member.

He couldn't have known how it would feel to be hypervisible. To know every move she made was scrutinized by men who couldn't believe she had succeeded. Men who wanted her to fail. That getting in didn't mean victory, just the start of the *real* test. That she wasn't a person anymore, but a trial run. And if she failed...

Stern but bangable.

She wanted to throttle Reyes for opening that door. Deacon was already in her fucking head. She could *not* let him get into her hormones, too.

The firelight cast flickering shadows over Gideon's face as he turned the playing card over in his hands. "So this was in Sector Three."

It took effort—actual physical effort—for Deacon not to flinch. "The fire was to cover up a hit, but that's all we know so far. It could be a coincidence."

"You don't believe in coincidences." Gideon sat back in his chair, rubbing his thumb along the crisp edge. "Such a small token. And so much arrogance behind it."

"Just remember that they earned their arrogance." The calling cards had started as a joke, a throwback to stories about criminals claiming responsibility for their misdeeds with whimsical items left behind at the scene of the crime. But they had turned out to be useful, the kind of marketing money couldn't buy. They inspired respect and fear in equal measure—the Suicide Kings could pull off their jobs so quietly and cleanly that no one would ever know it was them, except that they *let* you know.

Deacon knew all that, and too well. The fucking

things had been his idea to begin with.

Gideon turned the card over again, hiding the king. "Symbols have the power we give them. So now we have to decide if you were meant to see this one."

"The old man hasn't come looking for me yet." The whole thing was a part of his life he'd rather forget, so of course he made it a point to think about it often. Once upon a time, he'd been a part of their mercenary company. He'd killed for money and with little regard for his targets or their crimes or lack of crimes—until the day he'd been sent into Sector One to kill Gideon.

He walked away from the Suicide Kings. He'd like to say that he never looked back, but that would be a lie. He looked back every goddamn day.

But the Kings had never come after him, either to punish him or to drag him home. And where the leader of the Kings was concerned, leaving Deacon alone after his defection was tantamount to implicit approval of his choices. If he'd disapproved, Deacon would be dead. It was as simple as that.

But things changed.

Gideon studied him in silence for another moment before leaning over to pour two drinks. "Six already told Dallas O'Kane about the card. We'll be having a meeting of the sector leaders in Eden as soon as we coordinate our schedules. The Kings showing up here now, while we're still dealing with the aftermath of this war, isn't something we can ignore."

Gideon would never reveal Deacon's past to the other sector leaders—but that wasn't the real problem at hand anyway. "If we go up against the Kings, it can't be blind. I'll have to tell the other Riders."

"Probably." Gideon passed one glass of whiskey to Deacon. "How do you feel about doing that?"

He couldn't stop himself from flashing Gideon a

baleful look as he accepted the glass. "Not great. But leading them out there without all the facts would be worse. I can't put them in danger just to keep them from finding out that I'm a giant fraud."

"Deacon." Gideon's frown matched his stern tone. "I won't hear that word again, so you can drop it from your vocabulary. You're a man with a complicated past, but that doesn't make you a man defined by it. Your character is the sum of your choices, and you've spent twenty years making very noble ones."

"So you tell me. Frequently." But there was no guarantee his Riders would feel the same way.

The hell of it was, Deacon wouldn't even blame them. He'd been around so long that most of them looked at him like he was an extension of Sector One, a piece of the landscape instead of a fallible man. And he liked it that way. Not the admiration or the respect, but the sheer, automatic *trust*.

More than that, it was vital to the way the Riders operated. Whether they were on routine patrol or heading out to confront a problem, they needed to know that they were following the right orders, dealing out justice and mercy where each was required. The moment doubt clouded their minds was the moment one of them might hesitate, and that hesitation could prove deadly.

They would be right to doubt him. They would be right to wonder. And then their blood would be on his hands.

Oh, Gideon wasn't going to like this. Not one bit. But Deacon forced out the words anyway. "I could take a break. Step back for a while, handle this situation on my own."

Gideon's brow furrowed, but his reply was gentle. "No. Whatever this brings us, we handle it together."

"Then let Hunter lead them. He doesn't have the

most experience, but he has the best temperament for leadership."

"Deacon…" Gideon sighed and sipped his whiskey. "Fine. If you want to step back while the Riders process this, I'll allow it. You've earned some space. But you've earned their trust and respect, too, and I think you're underestimating just how much."

All the more reason why he needed to take this step first. Acting as though this revelation shouldn't matter could injure that respect, shatter that trust.

If it mattered to them, it mattered.

"Ashwin already knows." A log in the fireplace spit, causing the fire to flare and jump, and Deacon fixed his gaze on the dancing flames. "Not about the Kings, but about why I came here. That's—" His throat ached, and he coughed to clear it. "That's the part I'm worried about with the others."

"Telling them that you came here to kill me?"

Gideon said it blithely, as if the knowledge didn't bother him in the slightest. "You've had twenty years to get right with it, but I know my Riders. They're not casual about potential threats to you."

"That's right, Deacon. You *do* know them." Gideon sighed softly. "Maybe this is my fault, for letting the secret stand for so long. You know them, but do any of them know you?"

The truth was as simple as it was damning. "No."

"It's lonely, isn't it?" Gideon refilled his drink before holding the bottle out to Deacon. "Let them know you, and not just the bad shit. Because you were sent here to kill me, but you made a different choice. One I happen to think was very wise."

He said it like the joke it was. Like the joke it *had* to be, because if Gideon started taking himself too seriously, the pressure would drive him mad. He reserved all of his seriousness for the importance of his position, as if it existed outside of himself.

Deacon took the bottle. "Tomorrow morning. Do you want to be there?"

"Do you want me to be?"

"I don't know." It would help drive home the fact that there were no more secrets, and everything was out in the open. But it might also be hard for them to ask questions or get pissed off with Gideon standing there as backup. "I think it has to be me. Alone."

"All right." Gideon rose to toss another log onto the fire and stood there, his hand braced on the mantle, his back to Deacon. "I'm going to make sure the other sector leaders let me handle this. I might have to tread on Six's toes a little, but I'll ask Mad to smooth over any tension."

Gideon rarely asked his cousin for favors, though Mad was always glad to oblige. "Thank you."

"And we'll need to consider security precautions." He turned with a wry smile. "I don't want to assign bodyguards to my sisters before it's strictly necessary, but I would like you to coordinate with Johan to make sure the royal guard understands the situation and its potential threats."

"I'll take care of it." Deacon rose. "I should never have asked you to keep this quiet when I first joined up."

"Brooding over past regrets is my job, Deacon." Gideon lifted his glass. "You just look forward."

That dragged a laugh from his raw throat. Gideon's sense of humor was twisted, all right, darker than most people ever would have guessed. "It's not a contest, Rios. Even if it was, there are plenty of regrets to brood about. Enough to go around."

Gideon shook his head, that wry smile still curving

his lips. But his eyes were serious. "That's where you're wrong, Deacon. I get the glory of being one step from God, so I'll be shouldering the regrets, too. Yours, mine. The whole sector's, if that's what it takes."

That was too much for any man to handle—even Gideon. "There's a line between shouldering shit and turning yourself into a martyr. Stay on the right side of it, huh? Your sisters'll kill me if I let you cross it."

"I wouldn't do that to them. Or to you." Gideon waved a hand. "Go get some rest, Deacon. And have a little faith, all right?"

Faith. Deacon pondered the word as he slipped down the hall and out the door, nodding to the guards as he passed. Everything in Sector One was built on that single concept, whether that faith was centered on God or the Rios family legacy or Gideon himself.

But faith was a tricky thing. It was simply trust that was freely given instead of being earned, trust that could withstand the kind of damage that would kill anything else. With faith, devotion didn't just *stop.* True believers kept on believing, even when they shouldn't have.

At the barracks, he bypassed his door and climbed the stairs to the training floor. It was empty, dark, everyone else already tucked away in the sanctuary of their rooms. He left the lights off and stepped up to the heavy punching bag in the corner. There wasn't enough moonlight filtering through the windows to properly wrap his hands, so he left them bare.

This wasn't about training, anyway. This was about penance.

The rough canvas abraded his knuckles with the first punch. He let the pain wash through him, embraced it along with the pressure and harsh heat. Instead of unleashing his self-directed rage in a flurry of blows, he hit the swinging bag carefully. Deliberately.

Once upon a time, Gideon had had faith in him. It was a faith that had spared not only his life, but his conscience. He had a darkness inside him, the capacity to do terrible things. He *had done* terrible things. As a Rider, he had the opportunity to use that darkness for better ends.

But Deacon didn't have Gideon's faith. His life had never allowed for it. From his earliest memories, all he'd ever known was the appropriate fragility of trust. When someone betrayed you, you had to be willing to cut your losses and walk away. It wasn't just under-standable, it was necessary. Anything else would get you killed—or worse.

He would never ask the other Riders for some-thing he couldn't give. Tomorrow, he'd speak to Hunter first. The man had a right to know what was coming before Deacon laid it on him in front of everyone else. And then...

Then they'd all do what they had to do.

four

Ana had always loved the common room in the Riders' barracks. She'd been ten the first time she crossed the threshold—a rare invitation into the Riders' most sacred space, outside the confines of a party.

Still grieving the loss of her mother and struggling to adjust to life on the Rios family estate, Ana had found peace that morning. She'd sat at the table across from her father, surrounded by the golden walls and the colorful murals. They'd disassembled his large collection of guns in silence, precisely placing each component on the table before carefully cleaning them.

Then, as they'd pieced them back together, Ana's father had laid out her choices.

She could go back to the home her mother had shared with Ana's aunts and work in either the bakery or the salon. She could take an apprenticeship in any other trade that interested her, or even enter the Temple as an initiate with a chance at marrying into a noble family.

Or she could stay here—living close to him, if never with him—and shoot for the moon.

Surrounded by the familiar scent of gun oil, the soothing rumble of her father's voice, and the brightly colored renderings of saints, Ana had made her choice.

Fuck the moon. She was aiming for the goddamn stars.

It had taken her sixteen years, but she'd done the impossible. Every time she straddled a bench in the common room or sank onto a couch, she remembered that afternoon. It was a warm glow of encouragement deep in her gut—the memory that William Jordan had believed in his daughter so hard that he'd offered her a future that should have been unattainable.

The glow almost insulated her against the way her body instinctively tensed when Deacon took his place at the front of the room, his silent, brooding presence calling their meeting to order.

"What's the deal, boss?" Reyes nudged Zeke over to make space and dropped to the couch. "You got a lead on that situation in Three?"

"Not exactly." Deacon looked out at them, his gaze touching on each of them in turn. "The mercenary group responsible for the execution is called the Suicide Kings. You know that. What you don't know yet is that I have history with them."

A shiver zipped up Ana's spine.

At first, she didn't know why. Most of the other Riders watched Deacon, unconcerned and relaxed, assuming that whatever history Deacon shared with the mercenary group would be easily explained. But her impossible hyperawareness when it came to their leader had kicked in, and something was *wrong*.

He was too stiff. She'd seen him grumpy and surly and serious and deadly, but for the first time he seemed...

Wary.

On the bench across from her, Ashwin had gone very, very still. Whatever was coming, he knew. So did Hunter, who was standing against the wall, his gaze cast down, his arms tight across his chest.

Deacon's next words were going to shatter the placid peace of her beloved common room. Maybe that was why she wet her lips—as if being the one to force the issue would give her some control over the sudden sinking feeling in her gut. "What kind of history?"

A muscle in his jaw jumped. "I worked with them before I joined the Riders."

Silence.

Her brain started turning over the implications, and Ana shut it down. Survival reflex, maybe—the tension building in the room felt like a brewing fight. Her shoulders tightened, and her heart rate accelerated.

Gabe was the one who broke the silence this time, leaning forward with cold words and eyes that begged for Deacon to refute them. "Are we talking about *the* Suicide Kings? The ones that wiped out the entire Montgomery family so the Colbys could take Sector Seven from them?"

But Deacon didn't refute them, not even close. "I was there. I was part of it."

Gabe's fingers curled into tight fists, and Ana *felt* his heart break. But she didn't understand why until he stood, his entire body trembling. "My aunt was married to the Montgomery heir."

Deacon didn't flinch. "I'm sorry."

"Did you kill her? Do you even *remember*?"

Zeke rose to touch Gabe's arm. "Hey, at least let him finish before you yell at him."

Deacon waved him away. "Gabe has a right to know. Yes, I remember. And no, I didn't kill her." He paused. "But I would have, if she'd been in that study with her husband."

I would have.

The words hit Ana hard, shattering her protective shell. Not the words themselves, but hearing them in that calm, composed voice. She'd heard him say a hundred things the exact same way.

Don't drop your shoulder.

Watch your blind spot.

Check with your father's contacts.

I would have killed your aunt.

The bench clattering jerked Ana's attention around. Zeke had shoved Gabe back into his seat, his fingers biting into the other man's shoulder. "Okay, so you've done some fucked-up shit. So has Ashwin, and we still like him most of the time. So what—?"

"Zeke," Ashwin cut him off quietly. "Deacon isn't done."

Ashwin was hard to read, but Ana had spent a lot of time with him over the past couple months. He knew something else. Something worse. And for the first time in her life she wanted to cover her ears like a child to block out what came next.

But she didn't.

Deacon's expression didn't change, but his eyes darkened. His voice remained steady, but even that was darker somehow. Tense and tight, almost to the point of breaking. "When I initially came here, to Sector One, it was a job for the Kings. My orders were to get close to Gideon Rios, gain his confidence, and then eliminate him."

Shock swept through the room. Even Zeke was stunned into momentary silence, and Ana choked on an inappropriate flutter of laughter at the absurd thought that *finally* they'd found something that could shut him up.

Watching a god tumble off his pedestal could do that.

Bishop muttered a curse. Ivan stared at Deacon with eyes gone glacially cold. Reyes, on the other hand, reverted to his favorite form of communication—sarcasm. "Well, you didn't murder him, obviously."

"Obviously."

Reyes jerked his fingers through his hair, leaving it standing on end. "When did you tell *him* the truth?"

"Gideon has always known." Deacon straightened his shoulders, then nodded once. "You all have a lot to discuss, and more to think about. For the time being, Hunter's in charge. Anything you'd normally bring to me, you take to him."

Then he was gone.

Ivan opened his mouth and snapped it shut again when Ashwin flowed to his feet. "I should leave, too."

"Stay." Hunter shoved off the wall and walked up to the spot Deacon had vacated. "He wants us to talk this out, so we're gonna talk it out. Everything on the table."

Ashwin's gaze sought Gabe's angry one. "For every atrocity he may have committed, I can claim a hundred. If he's not fit to sit with you, neither am I."

"Eh, we've all dabbled in a little crime," Zeke said. "But we *knew* you were a crazy, murderous psycho with potential mind-reading powers. You don't exactly keep that under your hat."

"This isn't a fucking joke," Ivan snapped.

Zeke held up his middle finger. "This is how I

process shit, asshole. We can't all stare at the wall like—"

Hunter cut in. "*Enough.* The question isn't whether we're cool with Deacon's life choices. He's a Rider, and he'll always be a Rider. This is about leadership. Whether you still want to follow him into a fight."

"And what do you think about that?" Reyes demanded.

"Me?" Hunter took a deep breath. "I think, whatever went down, Gideon had his reasons. For making Deacon one of his Riders *and* for putting him in charge. I don't see a reason to second-guess that."

Their voices washed over Ana in a low hum as she withdrew into her self-protective shell. But the *tension* was still there, as if unfocusing her eyes had brought the flow of energy in the room into sharp definition.

Gabe was hurting. So was Ivan, though he'd never admit it. And Ashwin—she'd watched him relax into their family with a tentativeness that bruised her heart some days. Deacon's confession was a grenade tossed into the man's slowly growing sense of acceptance.

And the bastard hadn't even had the guts to stay and help pick up the pieces.

Fuck, he hadn't told them *anything*. Now that her brain had stuttered back to life, the questions tumbled over one another like angry bees trapped in a jar.

Who had hired him? When had he come to Sector One? How long did it take for Gideon to find out, and how had he? Had Deacon actually attempted the assassination? Why had Gideon forgiven him?

Had Ana's father known?

How the hell could the man confess and then *walk away*, as if he didn't owe them the whole fucking story before he tossed them aside like garbage?

"Ana?"

40

She blinked and forced her attention back to the Riders seated around the table. "What?"

Hunter tilted his head. "What do you think?"

I think I've spent the last three months chasing the approval of a murdering hypocrite. Wouldn't that be a revealing answer? Small comfort that she wasn't the only one in the room who had put Deacon up on that pedestal.

She was the girl. She didn't get to be emotional.

"I think..." She curled her hands into fists, but the answer came on a wave of memory. "I think my dad knew Deacon from the beginning. They were never friends or anything, but my father *respected* him. He followed him. He never questioned. So maybe we don't know the whole story yet."

"Maybe the whole story's worse," Reyes muttered.

Hunter shot him an exasperated look, then cracked his neck. "You've been quiet, Lucio."

"Hmm?" Lucio was stroking his beard, his movements almost meditative. "Oh, I had already figured it out. Except for him being hired to kill Gideon. That was the last piece of the puzzle."

Hunter blinked at him. "What does that mean?"

"No one ever chronicled Deacon's rise to the top of the Riders' ranks, because that's where he started. He had to learn his skills somewhere, but he didn't do it here. He wasn't a soldier or a guard, so he had to be a fighter." Lucio's brows drew together. "He reacted badly when we found the Suicide Kings' calling card at the scene of the fire. I don't think Bren and Six noticed, but I did. So I assumed he'd either worked with them, or run up against them in some other way. The hit on Gideon, though, that's...new information."

Zeke let his head fall forward onto the table with a groan. "You could have *told* someone."

"To what end? Besides." Lucio grinned, an expression as darkly amused as it was chilling. "I don't think you want me freely discussing the shit I've figured out about all of you."

Reyes snorted. Then he held up one finger. "I don't want any of you motherfuckers calling *me* crazy ever again."

Zeke lifted his head. "Hey, fuck you. At least Ashwin and Ivan and I have tragic fucking childhoods to make us crazy. You're just a natural overachiever."

Bishop choked on a laugh, which should have cut the tension. But Ana was looking at Gabe, who shuddered as if he'd been shot. It didn't matter that jokes were how Zeke and Reyes dealt with the darkness in the world—Gabe had always viewed it more seriously. More earnestly.

And in a twisted way, Zeke was right. It made *sense* for Zeke to be here. He'd been tossed out of Eden to scrap for survival in the sectors. Ivan and Ana were second-generation Riders—raised to believe in the cause, but born to commoners, like Lucio and Bishop. If any of them hadn't become Riders, chances were good they would have vanished into quiet, meager lives, always wondering if one bad week would leave them hungry or homeless.

But Gabe was like Reyes and Hunter. Born to wealth, born *noble*. With his eldest brother wed into the Rios family, Gabe had stood to inherit the entire family estate upon his father's death. Ana couldn't even wrap her brain around how much money that meant—more than she'd ever see in a hundred lifetimes. Enough to do any damn thing he chose.

Instead he was here. He'd pledged to give his life for the greater good of Sector One. Gabe was a believer, a man who valued peace so much he rarely touched a gun. A man who preferred his kills up close and personal, because he thought distance made it too easy to forget the gravity of taking a life. Who believed you should *feel* every life you took, because if you weren't willing to bear that weight, then you weren't killing for the right reasons.

Ana couldn't imagine a world where Gabe would accept *money* as an acceptable reason.

Hunter must have come to the same conclusion. "We'll all take some time to think it over," he said finally, with a quick, sidelong glance at Gabe. "We owe ourselves that much, and Deacon knows it."

Ivan pushed away from the table, his blue eyes stormy. "Do you still want me to make my rounds in the refugee camp this afternoon?"

"Is there a reason you shouldn't?" Hunter asked coolly.

His tone brooked no argument, and for a moment Ana thought Ivan might challenge him. But Hunter had that *presence*—the result of being born to wealth and raised with power, that invisible, inimitable confidence that only came with a lifetime of being told you were meant to lead.

With his arms crossed over his chest, muscles bulging and jaw fixed, he was a dark, forbidding wall.

And Ivan was smarter than Ana. He didn't throw himself against walls.

With a jerky nod, Ivan pivoted and strode from the room. Gabe shrugged off Zeke's attempt to reach for him and shoved away from the table to stalk toward the back hallway.

"I'll talk to him," Bishop promised, rising to follow. But he stopped long enough to squeeze Ashwin's shoulder. "You're fit to sit with us. Don't doubt it."

Ana missed Ashwin's murmured reply. She was

too busy avoiding Hunter's gaze as she swung her leg over the bench and headed for the door.

She didn't need *time* to think. She needed intel.

And she would damn well get it from the source.

five

The way Deacon saw it, he had two options: he could get raging drunk, or he could do something useful.

The first option held more appeal, but it couldn't lead anyplace *good*, so he ran down the mental list of projects he'd been putting off. Most of them were out because they involved planning and strategy for the Riders, and he gritted his teeth as he reminded himself that he'd *asked* for this. Gideon wouldn't have removed him, and none of the other Riders—no matter how angry or disbelieving or betrayed they felt—would have balked at taking simple orders from him.

Even if they should have.

There was one thing on his list that he could make some headway on, though—a small fishpond beside the path from the temple to the Riders' barracks. He'd mentally slotted it in for the fall, when temperatures were lower and digging in the heat of the day wouldn't be so awful.

What the hell? A little manual labor wouldn't hurt him, and it might be all he was fit for right now. So he grabbed a pickaxe and a shovel from the tool shed behind the barracks and set up the path to the spot he and Delfina had chosen.

He'd just broken ground along the perimeter and reached for the shovel when Ana's voice came from behind him. "So, you dropped a bomb on us, and now you're out here...digging a hole."

God help him. "That's what it looks like." He stabbed the point of the shovel blade into the earth, then stepped on it with all his weight. It sank into the dry earth with a scrape, and he glanced back over his shoulder. "Did you come to tell me off?"

Ana stood with her arms across her chest, her expression fierce. "You'd like that, wouldn't you? Really get your martyr on before you dig your hole and crawl into it."

"It's a pond, not a grave, Ana." He turned to face her, propping his arm on the handle of the shovel. "What do you want?"

Her brown eyes blazed. He'd seen this anger in her before, carefully controlled, but now it was spilling close to the surface. She was gripping her own arms so hard that her knuckles stood out white against her brown skin. "I want the whole story."

"What makes you think you don't have it already?"

"Nobody's born an assassin." Her eyes locked on to his. "You told us all the worst parts, the parts that would hurt us and you. You didn't give us the context."

Maybe that was true, but he couldn't think of a single fact of his circumstances or history that might change things. "I don't know what else to say. But I'll answer any questions you have."

Her grip on her arms relaxed a little, as did her stance. She studied him for a few seconds, and he could see the questions piling up behind her eyes.

The one she finally asked cut straight to the point. "How did Gideon find out?"

"I told him." Deacon tossed the shovel aside. "I'd been here for a few weeks, maybe a month. And I'd seen the difference between the way people spoke in the temples and what they did. Gideon was the only one who was actually serving his people, and I didn't want to kill him. So I came clean."

"And he forgave you?"

Forgiveness was a weak word for it. Insufficient. "I handed him my gun and asked him to make it quick. But he had other plans."

"He usually does." She tilted her head, the tension back in her eyes. "Did my dad know?"

Deacon almost laughed. If Will Jordan had known, he'd have wound up dead, after all—and it wouldn't have been quick. "No. That was Gideon's directive. None of the Riders knew, not until I told Ashwin a few months ago."

"What if that hadn't been Gideon's directive? Would you have told us sooner?"

"I don't know." He wasn't sure he ever would have been able to keep the secret. And if he hadn't, at least in the early years of the Riders, he probably wouldn't be here.

Ana digested that, her thumb tapping idly against her biceps. "Do you regret the people you killed? The ones before."

There was a simple, easy answer—but it wouldn't be the whole truth. Deacon scrubbed his hand over his face. "Some of them. Not all of our jobs had innocent, blameless targets. But I sure as hell regret *how* it all went down. Killing for justice or protection is one thing, but there's no honor in doing it for money."

"No, there's not." Her thumb stilled, and her voice softened. "Do you want us to forgive you?"

If Gideon hadn't forgiven him, he wouldn't be there to debate the finer points of betrayal and acceptance with her. And if the Riders didn't forgive him, his life would change in ways he still couldn't wrap his head around. But he had no right to demand anything from them.

"I left you alone to talk things over because I didn't want to influence any of you," he told her instead. "I wasn't running away. I'm *not*. But forgiveness isn't something you can ask for. You can be sorry to the depths of your fucking soul, but forgiveness has to be *given*."

"Can I—?" She licked her lips. "You don't have to answer this one, but...how did you end up killing people for money? How did you start?"

She didn't give up easily—or at all. "You're sure you want to know? Even if it doesn't make a damn bit of difference?"

No hesitation. "Yes."

"Fine." If it was anyone else, any of the other Riders, he might have still assumed that the question was an automatic one, motivated by reflex instead of true curiosity.

But Ana wasn't any of the other Riders. The only thing greater than her legendary resolve was her self-control. She never did anything without turning it over and over in her mind, examining all the angles— the upsides and the potential landmines. As if every decision, no matter how mundane, could topple everything she'd worked to build.

Maybe she was on to something there.

"Not here," he grumbled finally. He hefted the shovel and pick and headed back down the path. When he reached a fork in it, he veered left—away from the barracks, toward a small shrine half-hidden in the woods. It was nothing more than a couple of benches and a statue dedicated to some obscure saint. Even so, fresh flowers lay at the base of the weathered statue, crowding around charms and other offerings.

He leaned the tools against a nearby tree and gestured to one of the benches. "Sit. It's not what I'd call a short story."

Ana sank onto one of the benches and stretched out her denim-clad legs, crossing them at the ankle. "I've got time."

He sat on the other bench and braced his hands on his knees. The only place to start was at the beginning. "I was born the year the lights went out. The first real memory I have is of my parents just trying to survive."

It had seemed so normal to him. To him, that was life, scrambling every waking hour to make sure you had food, clean water, safety. It had taken him years to grasp the magnitude of what his parents had been thrust into—a desperate fight for survival, and with a newborn, no less.

"We were lucky," he went on. "Things in the cities got bad quick. But we lived out in the country. They already had a garden, some tools that would still work. Chickens. We were lucky."

"Was anyone really, back then?" Her voice was soft. "My dad never was shy about telling me hard truths, but stories from the first few years... He wouldn't tell me those."

Because it didn't matter how lucky you were when the whole goddamn world had fallen apart. Even if you managed to take care of all your basic needs, disaster loomed around every corner. There was always sickness you couldn't treat. Medicine that ran out.

Help that never came.

Giving Ana the horrible details about the illness that had killed his parents just felt *wrong*, like he was trying to curry her compassion, so he glossed over it. "They died when I was young. I tried to make it by myself for a while, but it was too much for me, and I set out for the nearest settlement. I was nine years old."

Ana's fingers tightened around the edge of the bench. "Nine is young to be in the world on your own."

He snorted. "There were kids younger than me living in Sand Harbor already. They'd comb the beaches for shit people had left behind, do odd jobs, beg. Steal, if they had to. But that's what everyone in Sand Harbor does. It's a haven, a place where criminals can meet up and do their business, no questions asked."

If he closed his eyes, he could still feel the gritty, dirty sand beneath his bare feet, hear the birds squawking and men shouting, the music spilling from the taverns and brothels. It was a hard place, and you either adapted quickly or you died.

So Deacon had adapted.

When he opened his eyes again, Ana was watching him, her expression caught between gravity and sympathy. He took a deep breath, ignoring the way her gaze made his skin prickle. "The Kings were the biggest game in town. Their leader was a military vet who believed in three things: training, discipline, and money. He recruited a lot of kids to cook and clean on the Kings' compound."

"And you got recruited?"

"Yeah. I made beds, served meals, maintained weapons." By the time his instruction in *using* those weapons had started, it all seemed...normal. As mundane as helping his mother can vegetables or sharpen axe blades. "It wasn't all murder and mayhem, you know. The day-to-day shit was a lot like being a Rider."

She tilted her head. "They were your family?"

He thought about the men he'd known back then. Fife took the younger kids under his wing and showed them how to survive when things went wrong—because things always went wrong. Glenn had a dog he'd specifically trained to attack, but he'd never take the damn thing with him on jobs because he was afraid he'd get hurt. Nathan and Ned were twins, fiercely loyal to each other above everyone and everything else. The day Nathan fell during a job, Ned had vanished, never to be seen again.

And then there was Seth, another kid from Sand Harbor. He and Deacon ran together on the streets there, were recruited together. Grew up together. Until Gideon, Seth was the closest thing Deacon had ever had to a brother.

None of them were sociopaths eager to spill blood because they craved the violence. That was the old man's one hard-and-fast rule: he wouldn't hire anyone who liked hurting people. He didn't trust them, because that kind of twisted shit was personal, maybe even pathological. You couldn't rely on someone like that to make rational, financially sound decisions.

No, aside from the fact that they killed people for a living, the Kings were mostly just...normal people. Not quite a family, but more than a bunch of strangers. "It's hard to explain. If I try, it's gonna sound like I'm making excuses. And there aren't any."

"Deacon..." She sighed. "No one's going to think you're making excuses. Not for the Kings, and not for yourself. You could have led with all the terrible shit that happened to you, tried to buy a little sympathy. But you didn't."

"Because it's the last thing I want." He rose and retrieved the tools. "I don't lead because you feel sorry for me. I lead because you respect my abilities and my principles. If any of that changed today, then explanations don't matter, and neither does my poor, sad-little-boy history."

She flowed to her feet and planted herself in his path, her body inches from his. "You lead," she said, biting off each word, "because they *worship* you."

He blinked down at her. "Well, Jesus fucking Christ, I hope not."

"Are you *blind*? Everyone trusts you with their lives. They live for your approval. Explanations matter because—because—" Her fingers curled into fists. "God, how do you not *see* it?"

The vehemence of her words made his blood run cold even as pressure squeezed his chest. For the first time, maybe, he understood how Gideon must feel. Being worshipped wasn't a *compliment*. It went straight past flattery or admiration into something almost sinister. You'd have to shoulder an inhuman weight just to try to live up to those kinds of expectations.

And you would always, always fail.

"I do see, Ana." He shouldered the shovel and held the pickaxe by the metal head, letting the handle dangle between his fingers. "That explains a lot. Thank you."

"Deacon—"

He turned away. Instead of following the path that she would also have to use, he slipped into the trees. It might take longer, but he knew the way.

Ana's words had stripped away the last of his hope that the Riders might consider his confession logically and follow their consciences. Because she spoke of *faith*, and he already knew how that worked.

Because true believers kept on believing, even when they shouldn't have.

gideon

Gideon would never admit it out loud, not even with a knife at his throat, but he missed Cerys's meeting table.

For decades, the sector leaders had gathered in Sector Two to bicker and plot and make wary alliances over the polished wooden surface. Shaped like a massive square, it had been the perfect size to allow them to sit two to a side and look each other in the eye without getting within arm's reach.

But its main selling point, in Gideon's estimation, was its location: on the ground floor.

The meetings of the New Council—a grand term Markovic was trying to make stick—took place a dizzying fifty stories up in the air. The floor-to-ceiling glass windows revealed blue sky and the distant mountains, along with a life-ending plummet down to solid concrete.

Gideon recognized the irony of it—a man reputed to hold regular conversations with God being scared of heights. But he'd always been more comfortable with both feet planted firmly on the earth.

The woman next to him, on the other hand, seemed right at home. Jyoti's poise and elegance masked a warm heart that beat against a spine made of steel. Though Gideon had welcomed all of his cousin's lovers into the family, he felt a special kinship to the woman who had taken over Sector Two to protect its citizens in spite of the steep personal cost.

It took a particular sort of reckless masochism to embrace leadership over the place that had broken you. Gideon of all people knew that.

But Jyoti hardly seemed broken now. She leaned back in her leather chair to cross her legs under her brightly patterned silk skirt. One neatly manicured nail tapped softly on the glass table as she listened to Six with an expression of intent interest.

Ah, yes. Listening. Something Gideon had best make a habit of, now that these meetings weren't mostly posturing and sniping.

"...so we figured out what the guy was investigating," Six was saying. Unlike Jyoti, who moved with liquid grace, Six was a ball of tense energy. She leaned forward to brace her elbows on the glass table, brown eyes burning with intensity. "He was investigating a couple of disappearances."

Markovic frowned. "Can you be more specific?"

Six turned to look at the former councilman, and Gideon tried to read the emotion there. The subcurrents between leaders were far more subtle these days—before the war, the old sector leaders had only occasionally hidden their claws, and usually to further some scheme or another. Alliances were rare and brief.

Six seemed respectful, but wary. Maybe that was just lingering mistrust—Markovic was the single remaining member of the corrupt leadership that had misled the city of Eden so badly. He would always be a symbol of that past, though he'd endured torture and emotional turmoil to help the sectors in their rebellion.

Or maybe it was simpler. The New Council was divided along one glaring line—either you were an O'Kane, or you weren't.

"Not really," Six was saying, a slight undertone of frustration in her voice. "It's hard in Three. We have a lot of loners. Sometimes they take off. Sometimes they get stabbed and their bodies are dumped. It's too soon to be sure what's going on. It *could* be nothing..."

Hector, the man who'd been running Sector Five since the end of the war, shook his head. "He must have been on to something hot if someone had him murdered for it."

"How much do the Suicide Kings cost?" Jyoti asked Six. "Did Bren know?"

"Cruz did," Dallas rumbled from the head of the table. The king of Sector Four had arrived late, but the others had left that symbolic chair open for him—by instinct or design, Gideon wasn't sure. But with half of the New Council composed of O'Kanes, Dallas was undoubtedly the most powerful man in the room—and out of it.

He glanced at the tablet in front of him. "Cruz says the leader doesn't open his door for less than fifty thousand credits, and that's for the one-man jobs. Something like that coup they pulled in Sector Seven back in the day would put you closer to a million."

Derek Ford, another one of Dallas's people—though currently in charge of the manufacturing hub of Sector Eight—snorted. "Not many people have that kind of money, not to waste on maybes. So...what do we think? Human trafficking? We've all seen it before."

"But the usual destinations aren't an issue anymore," Jyoti countered. "We shut down the communes and illegal farms that wouldn't agree to the new worker-protection rules."

"And I came down hard on the stakeholders I caught trying to reinstitute any kind of unwilling labor," Alya said. The newly minted leader of Sector Six wasn't an official O'Kane, but her son was one of Dallas's men, and she addressed him when she continued. "But we'll need to do something about Seven, sooner or later. I know Ford's trying to keep an eye on the wind farms, but that's a *lot* of empty space. A lot of potential for mischief."

"You're not wrong," Dallas said, tapping his fingers on the table. "But I don't think Seven's the problem here. The demand just isn't there. Those farmers don't have the money to fund an operation as profitable as this one would have to be."

"So the usual destinations, as you call them, are out." Markovic surveyed everyone at the table, one by one. "Time for us to look for new ones."

"And to look closer to home," Dallas added. "Make sure people aren't disappearing from our own backyards, too. We have more movement than ever now that the borders are down between the sectors and Eden. If you wanted to snatch some folk without anyone noticing right away, there's never been a better time."

Jyoti swiveled her chair. "Gideon? You're quiet."

"I've been thinking about the Suicide Kings." He leaned forward, rested his elbows on the table, and steepled his fingers. Casual, meditative—and giving the subtle impression of being moments from dropping into prayer. He'd taunted the more God-hating sector leaders with the gesture for so many years that it came naturally now.

And he'd thought about how to phrase this. "I'd like to take point on anything involving the mercenary group. Not only are my Riders best equipped to handle something like this, but I also have...certain unique resources at my disposal."

One of Dallas's eyebrows swept up. "Ashwin?"

Gideon gave his most beatific smile and shrugged gracefully. "I've been blessed with an embarrassment of riches."

That earned him an eye roll from the king of Sector Four, which meant he'd done his job well. "Fine," Dallas grumbled. "Any objections?"

His gaze swept the table, and everyone shook their heads. No surprise—Hector and Markovic were the only people seated at the table who weren't bound to Dallas O'Kane by oaths or family.

Gideon had to admire the neatness of the coup Dallas had pulled off. All the privileges of influencing every decision made in their new world—and he still got to go home to his own sector, secure that his people would shoulder their share of the burdens of leadership.

It wasn't something Gideon could have managed. The loyalty he received in Sector One was too tied up in faith and belief to be anything but blind. Most people simply obeyed him without question. Even the ones like Deacon, the ones who questioned, still trusted Gideon more than their own instincts.

O'Kane's people believed in him, no doubt about it. Their loyalty was beyond reservation. But they followed Dallas with their eyes open, and when he set them free to build their own empires, they did just that. Autonomous, but still deferential.

A tidy coup, indeed.

The conversation moved on, and Gideon retreated again and let the voices flow over him. The negotiation over trade and the details of manufacturing held little interest to him. Sector One had been all but self-sufficient for decades. Of course, new opportunities had opened along with the borders between sectors, but the scramble to take advantage of them might distract the noble families of One and give him some breathing room.

One way or another, the Riders would have to deal with the threat the Suicide Kings posed. And they'd have to do it *without* losing Deacon, or anyone else. Gideon would sacrifice a lot for the greater good. But perched as he was at the top of the world, in the capitol building thirty of his men had paid for in blood...

He had to admit he was tired of watching his Riders die for a peace they never got to enjoy.

SIX

Ana spent an afternoon and evening being frustrated with Deacon. When he skipped the training session she'd arranged with Ashwin, the confusing tangle of emotions churning in her middle boiled into hot anger. But when he didn't appear the next day—not for breakfast, not during their afternoon debriefing, not even for dinner—her anger twisted with infuriating shards of sympathy and performed some sort of sinister magic.

By the time Ana was sprawled on top of her brightly colored quilt, still clad in her sweatpants and sports bra, guilt had wiggled its way deep into her heart and planted hooks that left her bleeding.

She knew what she'd put on Deacon. She knew it like no one else but Gideon *could* know. It was the truth that drove her out of bed before dawn and settled in her bones as a soft ache when she'd trained too hard. It was the weight that kept her up some nights, staring at the stucco ceiling by the light of a single flickering candle, her restless mind refighting sparring matches she'd lost.

Being worshipped was a double-edged sword.

She still remembered the first time it had happened to her. Every detail of the moment was carved into memory. Ivan's gray T-shirt with the rip along the hem. The faint smell of paint from her newly detailed motorcycle. The vague throb of the fresh ink on her shoulder, and the way the breeze tickled over the bare skin of her arms—she'd worn a tank top that day deliberately, proudly.

Showing off her Rider tattoo.

The little girl had been nine or ten. Brown skin a few shades lighter than Ana's, with silky black hair as curly as Ana's own. She'd shaken free of her mother's hand and bolted across the parking lot as Ana kicked down the stand on her bike, her big eyes going impossibly wide.

"Girls can be Riders?"

With that sweet, innocent question, Ana's life had changed forever.

She'd loved it, that first time. And the second, and the third. Even the tenth time still made her heart leap. But after three short months, she'd been swallowed whole by the hopes of dozens upon dozens of little girls—

And she hadn't seen it coming.

She *should* have. The other Riders always attracted excited young boys and swaggering teens. Kids didn't understand the more serious implications of a Rider's duties. They didn't understand death. They just saw heroes, larger than life and celebrated by the sector—and they wanted to be heroes, too.

The boys had never doubted they could achieve that goal. But the girls... The intensity of their newborn excitement clung to Ana like invisible threads wrapping her tighter and tighter. Their dreams weighed ten thousand pounds.

Ana had to carry them alone.

No wonder she'd lashed out at Deacon. Even when he scraped her nerves raw, he'd always been a solid, unshakable foundation. The hero of heroes, uncompromising and unchanging. The wall she threw herself against in order to toughen up. She needed him to be something more than human so she could believe it was possible. Because a human couldn't hold up under the pressure Ana felt every time a little girl's eyes lit up at the sight of her. A human would falter. Fall. Eventually, it had to happen.

Deacon's fall had wounded a dozen people. Ana's would break the hearts of thousands.

Exhaling roughly, she swung her feet over the side of the bed and sat up. The wooden floor was cool beneath her bare feet, but not so chilly that she had to find her boots. She padded to the door and slipped into the darkened hallway and down the stairs.

The kitchen was abandoned, as usual. Sometimes Gabe or Bishop claimed it to concoct elaborate meals, but most of the time the Riders just ate whatever food someone brought over from the temple, where initiates practiced their cooking skills with varying success. The fridge was stacked with leftovers—tonight's lasagna, last night's fried fish, and a bowl of fresh strawberries that must have come from the greenhouse.

Ana snagged one of the remaining bottles of the hard cider Nita's cousin brewed and twisted off the cap. She drained half of it in three long gulps, savoring the sweet and tart apple flavor as she made her way back up the stairs. She paused at the top, shadowed in the dim hallway, and strained to hear past the quiet hum of silence.

Thwack. Pause. *Thwack.* Pause. *Thwack.*

It was soft but unmistakable, a sound she knew as well as her own heartbeat. The sound of a frustration-fueled fist slamming into the heavy bag.

Instead of turning left toward her bedroom, Ana swung right and followed the sound to the workout room.

The harsh electric lights illuminated the space, leaving nothing in shadow. In the corner, Deacon—clad only in his jeans—was pounding his bare fists into the bag. The muscles of his back tensed and bunched with every solid swing. The power in each punch sent the canvas bag rocking wildly.

The rough fabric had to be scraping his knuckles raw. She tried to focus on that, and not on the hypnotic flex of strong muscle under smooth skin, like a work of art that was somehow both exquisite and functional.

"What do you want?"

He hadn't turned to look at her, but Ana supposed that made what she had to do easier. After another bracing sip of her cider, she exhaled. "I came to apologize. I'm sorry for snapping at you the other day."

He stopped pummeling the bag and caught it in both hands as it rebounded. He stood there, silent, his shoulders shaking.

When he turned around, the bastard was *laughing.* "All you do is snap at me, so you're gonna have to tell me which time you mean."

Her cheeks heated. Guilt withdrew—mostly. "Because you're an asshole. But I still shouldn't have said that shit. About people worshipping you. That's our baggage, not yours."

"Maybe." He frowned and flexed his fingers absently. "Or maybe you were right."

"It's not about being right." She drained her cider and stepped through the door to set the empty bottle on a bench. "I know people worship you. And I know how much being worshipped sucks sometimes. So...I'm sorry."

"Yeah." Deacon turned and swept up a towel from the floor near him. "Did you want this?" he asked, jerking his head toward the bag.

She weighed the restlessness inside her against the placid bulk of the bag. "Honestly, I'd rather swing at something that hits back."

One of his eyebrows swept up in an arch.

A single bottle of cider wasn't enough to get her drunk. It wasn't even enough to get her tipsy. But she could feel the bubbles in her blood, and the tattered shreds of her self-control weren't enough to keep her quiet.

She arched her own eyebrow in turn and pulled one arm across her chest in a slow stretch. "C'mon, that bag can't be giving you a satisfying fight."

"The bag can hurt me more than I can hurt it." His expression was full-on challenge now, confident and self-assured. "Can you say the same?"

A few days ago, the answer would have been *no*. As the leader of the Riders, Deacon had held her fate in his hands, cradled next to the dreams of a thousand little girls and her chance of living up to them. A few days ago, he'd been a god.

Today, he was human. A flesh-and-blood man.

Ana stretched her other arm and grinned. "Why don't we find out?"

He swiped the towel over his face and lifted one

huge shoulder in a shrug. "Why not?"

It didn't take long for Ana to warm up. Her limbs felt loose and ready, her mind blissfully focused. She made sure her hair was secure in its bun on top of her head as she strode to stand across from him on the thin floor mats.

Then she rolled her neck, poised on the balls of her feet...and waited.

Seconds ticked by. She felt them, just as she always did, but the chattering doubt didn't fill her head. Ana would stand here all night if she had to, waiting for him to move.

She didn't have to.

Her first clue was a tensing in his chest. Subtle, followed by the tiniest shift in his heel. That was all the warning she got before he flew at her, his massive body barreling straight for her midsection.

Muscle memory kicked in. Ashwin had charged her a thousand times now, and she knew how to get the fuck out of the way. She flowed out of Deacon's path and ducked under his arm. The back of his knee was a beautiful, tempting target, but as soon as she lifted her foot to take him down, he twisted with impossible speed, and Ana had to pivot desperately to avoid being grappled to the floor.

She danced out of the way and immediately regretted it. Deacon's reach exceeded hers, and getting inside his guard without being hit was going to be hard. With any other man his size, she could taunt him into taking massive swings to wear himself down while she ducked and dodged.

There were two problems with that. First, Deacon was *fast*. She couldn't count on evading him, and one or two solid hits from him would hurt.

Secondly, trying to wear Deacon down was a

mistake. The man could go all night.

All night.

No, fuck him. She wouldn't allow the bastard back into her head. Pushing the thought away, Ana circled, testing him with feints he ignored.

Fine, she'd give him something real to react to. What was the worst thing that could happen? She'd end up on her back?

She'd be there anyway if she didn't *move*.

She followed the next feint with a real swing, coming in fast and hard at his side. If she miscalculated, she'd leave herself totally exposed. But Deacon moved to protect himself and Ana shifted directions rapidly, crashing into his body and catching him off balance. She ignored the heat of his skin under her hand as she hooked her heel behind his and jerked, pushing back at the same time.

Too late to disengage. He went down and she followed, pinning one arm to his side with her knee. She lunged to catch his other wrist and slap it down against the mat next to his head, leaving him trapped on his back with her straddling his stomach.

The giddy thrill of success filled her. For a few seconds, that was all she could feel. Deacon was on his back, and she was on top of him, and she'd *fucking won*, and she wanted to laugh at how light she felt, how *clear* her head was. No nagging voices, no thousand pounds of other people's dreams. Just victory.

And a prickle under her skin that built as she flexed her fingers and felt Deacon's steady pulse beneath them.

Deacon was on his back.

And she was *on top of him*.

As if a dam had shattered, observations flooded her no-longer-clear head.

Her face was two inches from Deacon's, and he was staring up at her with brown eyes edged with gold that she'd never seen up close before. His dark hair was short and spiky from the sweat of exertion. Mussed. He looked mussed. The beard and mustache she'd never really paid attention to framed lips she suddenly couldn't stop looking at—that forbidding mouth that, this close, looked almost yielding.

The parts of him she was sitting on weren't yielding. His abs tensed under her ass, and Reyes's words came back to her, mockingly accurate.

Stern but bangable.

God help her, if she'd settled a few inches lower...

His hips arched. Just a little. Maybe as involuntarily as the way her fingers tightened around his wrist. Her other hand splayed on the mat. The air between them crackled.

She *had* to stop staring at his mouth.

His lips parted, and he sucked in a sharp breath that tugged at her in places she was trying to forget existed. Then, a heartbeat later, the world tipped over in a disorienting blur.

Ana landed on her back, the unimaginable heat and hardness of his body pressed to hers.

The fact that she was only wearing a sports bra hadn't seemed important a few minutes ago. That was before his skin came in contact with hers. The coarse hair on his abdomen tickled her stomach, and the thin cotton of her bra wasn't nearly enough protection. Her nipples contracted into stiff points that would have humiliated her if Deacon's body hadn't been in the process of betraying him far more apparently.

His dick was hard. The slightest shift of her hips made him tighten his fingers around her wrists, and he opened his mouth. "Ana—"

He'd never said her name in this tone before, low and tense. Soft, which was ridiculous, because nothing about him should be soft. She dragged her legs up his sides and wrapped them around his hips. It settled him more firmly in the cradle of hers, his erection grinding against her pussy to spark a heat she refused to consider.

He shuddered, his breath catching in his throat, and in that moment of inattention she pushed off the mat, surged upward, and rolled them again.

His back hit the floor, but his fingers stayed locked around her wrists, stretching her body above him. Her hips aligned over his, her sweatpants and cotton underwear feeble protection from the grinding pressure of his cock straining against the fly of his jeans.

Deacon wasn't stern anymore, just bangable, and holy fucking *hell*, she wanted to do it. Throw caution and preparation and the weight of everyone else's dreams aside and just tear open his jeans and *ride him* until she'd fucked every thought out of her head. Hard, sweaty, *relentless*, because if she knew anything about Deacon, it was that the man had stamina.

He could fuck her until she fell into bed, too tired to stare at the ceiling and fret, until she was weak-limbed and sated for the first time in *years*. And it would be so, so good...

Until he stepped back into his leadership role, and Ana was stuck being the only girl *and* the one who'd fucked the boss.

She could taste the curve of his lip under her tongue already, so she broke his grip on her wrists and flung herself away, rolling to her back on the mats with a groan. "Fuck."

"Well." He didn't move, except for the harsh rise and fall of his chest as he panted. "I did not see that coming."

It was ridiculous to feel the sting of that. It wasn't like she'd wanted Deacon to think of her sexually— all she'd ever wanted was for him to think of her as a soldier.

But he didn't have to sound so *shocked.* "You're not the first guy to get a boner when I kick his ass. You won't be the last."

The look he flashed her was half surliness, half consternation.

That made her feel better, so she poked harder. "What, you're not even the first Rider to do it. Reyes gets hot and bothered every time I put him on the ground. Of course, I think Reyes gets a hard-on any time Ashwin knocks him over, too. Or any time he encounters a stiff breeze."

"That's Reyes," he rumbled. "Not me."

Her body was still buzzing with arousal. It was a mistake to touch him at all, even just to nudge his leg with her toes. "Welcome to being human. You can go back to being worshipped any time, you know."

"Can I, though?" Deacon grunted as he folded one arm behind his head. "How are the others?"

Ana arched to snag a towel from the nearby bench and swiped it over her forehead. "Gabe's still kinda messed up. And Ashwin's unsettled. I think he's waiting for the others to decide he's done too much bad shit and has to be kicked out. Bishop and Zeke have been spending a lot of time with him."

He grunted again.

"But the one I'm worried about is Ivan." Ana rolled onto her side and propped her head up on her hand. It was weirdly intimate, talking to him like this. If she squinted, she could imagine they were sprawled out in bed—

No. She wouldn't squint. "Ivan," she repeated. "You know his upbringing was...harsh."

"I think you mean *fucked the hell up*." Deacon sighed and slowly sat up, every muscle working in careful, controlled concert. "I'll talk to him."

In a lot of ways, Ivan's childhood was an ugly mirror of her own. He was only four years old when his father died thwarting an assassination attempt on the Prophet's daughter. Ana had grown up in the care of a flesh-and-blood Rider who urged her to excel. Ivan had been stuck with a father who decorated the wall of saints in every temple in Sector One, a sacrificial ideal his mother hounded him to emulate with every waking breath.

And that was *before* his grandfather and uncles had committed treason.

"He might not be able to hear you," Ana warned, staring at Deacon's back. It was a nice back. Broad at the top, where his shoulders sloped into strong arms, and narrow at the waist. Ink peeked around where his ravens had spilled from his arm onto his back, as if Del was running out of room to catalog all the lives he'd taken.

"He'll hear me," Deacon countered. "He may not believe what I have to say, but he'll listen."

"True enough." She couldn't stop staring at those little black birds. If she counted them, how many would there be? "Deacon?"

"Yeah?"

She started to reach out, but curled her fingers toward her palm and forced her hand to the mat. "Your ravens. Do you have them for the kills you made before?"

He half-turned toward her. "No. No, those kills are mine to remember."

With his face in profile, *stern* was back. Still bang-able though, dammit. Even with his brows drawn down and his voice serious and heavy, speaking as though he didn't need tattoos because the blood he'd spilled as a mercenary weighed as heavily on him as all the little girls' hopes and dreams did on her.

No, remembering was never the problem. It was finding enough space to forget long enough to draw in a full breath. She wondered if Deacon ever had.

Ana tossed the towel aside and rolled to her knees. "We're cool, you know. In case you need to hear it. Whatever bad shit you did, you've risked your life and bled for twenty years to make up for it."

He rose and held out his hand to help her up. "I never doubted it. You wouldn't punish me for something that was always true just because you're aware of it now. You're too...practical for that."

She didn't feel practical. Gripping his hand tingled, and the air close to him felt too warm. Her hyper-awareness of him had lost its uncomfortable edge. What had once been sandpaper across her nerves had turned to silk.

Shit was going to get really, really awkward if that didn't go away.

Ana released his hand and retrieved her empty bottle. "You should get some sleep. And show up for a meal tomorrow, or something. Don't shut us all out."

"I had a very solid plan to wait three days."

"Very practical." She paused in the doorway to glance back at him. "Three days is a long time to be alone, Deacon."

He snorted out another laugh. "Is it, princess?"

Ana had never been a princess. Even though Gideon had gladly brought her to the compound after her mother's death, it hadn't been into his household.

Isabela had been married already, and Maricela had been little more than a baby. Ana had played with the children of gardeners and servants. She'd snuck into the kitchen to charm cooks, had evaded the tutors to run wild with the sons of the royal guard.

She'd grown up sliding back and forth between worlds, a commoner whose father had one foot in sainthood.

But she'd *never* been alone.

Something far more insidious than desire slid through her, a quiet, dangerous emotion that blunted the sting of his teasing and softened her voice. "Yes," she said, fighting a swift and ugly battle against the tenderness rising inside her. "Yes, it is."

His eyes met hers, and for a moment, it was like looking into a mirror. The same feeling that wound its way through her was reflected in his eyes, deep and endless—

Then it was over. He blinked, shook his head, and turned away. "Thanks for the brawl."

"Any time."

She left before she could do anything stupid, popping back down to the kitchen only long enough to rinse out her bottle and drop it into the recycling bin. Then, like a coward, she checked the hallway before bolting back to her room.

When she sprawled out on her bed this time, the quilt felt cool under her skin. She was still running too hot, restless and irritated, balanced on that sharp edge where arousal could come roaring back. If she closed her eyes, inched her hand down her body...

She tried to visualize the last person she'd had sex with. It was back before she'd become a Rider—hell, before the war, even. The training schedule her father had set once she hit her teens hadn't left a lot of time for socialization, and he'd only grown more militantly insistent as the sectors seethed toward rebellion. Kora had been checking Ana's contraceptive implant at regular intervals, but it wasn't getting a lot of use.

There was that pretty blond orchard supervisor. Ana had bumped into him at last year's midsummer festival and spent an enjoyable afternoon proving haylofts were less romantic than they sounded but still perfectly serviceable. But when she closed her eyes and attempted to call up his features, Deacon's face intruded. Hard and brooding, with those dark eyes and stupidly kissable lips—

Fuck. *Fuck.*

If he were still alive, her father would kill her. Maybe he'd kill Deacon, too, for good measure. To come this far and achieve this much only to be betrayed by *hormones*, by the aggravating need to rescue Deacon from his loneliness...

Ana rolled over and buried her face in her pillow, muffling a frustrated groan. Then, giving in to the inevitable, she rolled back out of bed and gathered up her towel and robe.

She'd take a bath. And if she couldn't summon that damn orchard supervisor's face from memory, she'd fucking well track him down. Or find a suitable substitute, whatever was necessary to get her head back in the game. Anything to satisfy the itch beneath her skin before it got so pressing that she did something she couldn't take back.

Deacon got to put down the burden of being worshipped. But Ana had a long, long way to go.

seven

People tended to assume that everyone in Sector One eschewed technology as much as the Prophet had. And it was a fair assumption, though it wasn't entirely correct. Such things were only forbidden by the religious teachings of the temple if they made you less *mindful*—of yourself, other people, your surroundings.

Deacon enjoyed watching videos in his downtime and listening to music while he worked out. He appreciated lights and heat and refrigeration, and whenever Zeke cobbled together a new handheld device or computer, he made sure to at least look at it, just in case. But he always made sure he knew how to survive without any of it.

Sometimes it slowed him down, but that was the entire fucking point. Rushing led to mistakes.

Now, for instance, he and Ivan were working on

framing a cottage for one of the royal guards and his wife. It was a task Deacon usually despised. He was fond of construction in general—the sheer labor of it exhausted him, in the very best ways—but he loathed framing. It was persnickety and precise, the kind of task he might have been tempted to hurry through, if he'd had the tools to do so.

So he passed over the drivers and nail guns in favor of a simple, old-fashioned hammer. The *mindful* choice, because the bones of a house had to be exactly right or the whole thing would be crooked. Walls would crack and windows would leak, all because Deacon hated framing so much that he half-assed the job.

Beside him, Ivan worked in careful, focused silence. Deacon knew he didn't like the job any more than he did, but for different reasons. Ivan didn't like any tasks that pulled him away from what he considered his primary duty—protecting the royal family. Which would have made him an excellent royal guard, but was a hell of a fixation for a Rider.

One of them had to break the silence, and Deacon knew it would be him. Because Ana had lain on the training room floor, her head propped on her arm, and all but asked him to in her soft, rasping voice.

He missed the next nail.

He cleared his throat. "Do you have anything to ask me?"

Ivan froze with the hammer hovering over his shoulder. After a few tense seconds, he followed through with his swing, pounding the nail deeper into the wood. "How did you get close enough to Gideon for any of this to happen to begin with? After the shit with Mad and Adriana, they should have had the royal family protected."

A deceptively simple question with a shit ton of

complicated answers. *Things were in chaos. Their attention was focused elsewhere. You're underestimating how good I was at infiltration.*

It was in the Prophet's best interest to allow me to complete the job he hired me for.

No, that last one wasn't his secret to tell. Besides, none of that came close to the deepest truth of all. "You know Gideon now, but he was a different person back then. Young and cocky, out to single-handedly rebuild the sector. He wasn't about to let them keep him under lock and key. Made my job easier."

"I met him back then. Once." Ivan hit the nail again. "I was about eight, and he was seventeen or eighteen. He came to take me and my mother to a new apartment he'd secured for us."

Deacon had heard the story. Ivan's mother had been shunned because of her family's involvement with the insurrection that had led to Adriana's kidnapping and eventual death. It didn't matter that she was devout, that she would have stepped in front of a bullet herself to save the lowest member of the royal family. She was tainted by association of blood.

After that, she struggled to raise her young son alone. For nearly two years, she managed. She worked for people who sometimes wouldn't pay her, because they knew she wouldn't report them. She sold off bits and pieces of her family's past, heirlooms that should have been handed down to Ivan.

They were practically on the street by the time Gideon found out and immediately interceded on their behalf. The only injustice that mattered to him was the one before him—a woman and her son, abandoned and surviving on nothing.

No wonder Ivan was so fanatically devoted to him.

"Then you already know the real reason," Deacon

told him simply. "Gideon will protect everyone but himself."

"Sometimes Gideon gives us more credit than we've earned. More than we deserve." A final swing pounded the nail home, and Ivan finally turned to look at Deacon. "While we spend the rest of our lives trying to live up to the person he sees when he looks at us."

"Some people, maybe."

"You don't?"

Maybe it seemed backwards from the outside. If anyone deserved to spend every day trying to live up to an ideal of grace, it was Deacon. "Gideon isn't delusional. He knows who I am. That has to be enough."

A frown creased Ivan's brow as he turned back to the frame. "Does it feel like enough?"

"What it feels like doesn't matter." Deacon abandoned his hammer and fetched two beers from the ice bucket beside the lumber pile. He opened both and offered one to Ivan. "If you spend your life only being satisfied when you're perfect, you'll be worse than disappointed. You'll be nuts."

Ivan sipped his beer and shot Deacon a knowing look. "Maybe it's too late for me to be anything else. I assume Ana told you to talk to me."

"Of course she did." The sun was high in the sky already, and sitting down in the dappled shadows cast by the half-framed house felt good. "But don't make the mistake of thinking I wouldn't have done it anyway."

Ivan nodded. "I know. You're a good leader. And if you meant to do the Rios family harm, you've had a thousand opportunities."

"But?"

"No *but*." Ivan sank to the ground next to him and tilted his head back against the house. "Being perfect's not the point. We're all damned anyway, Deacon. All that matters is the good we do before we go down. I've been thinking about how skilled you are with tactics. You know how the bad guys think. If you weren't here, maybe more of us would be dead, along with all the people we've saved."

On occasion, Deacon had wondered if that was Gideon's very practical, very human rationale for asking him to join up. He still wasn't sure it wasn't. "Better the devil you know than the devil you don't," he murmured.

Ivan twirled the bottle between his fingers. "That's just it, isn't it? Gideon looked into your eyes and saw something worth saving. He looked into Ashwin's eyes and saw the same thing. If I start doubting him, where does that leave me? I don't care if we're all devils. Gideon knows us. That's enough."

An image of Ana's earnest face and pleading eyes formed in Deacon's head, and he shook it away. "And the others?"

"Gabe's gonna be a problem." Ivan glanced sidelong at Deacon. "Not for you. He'll work his way around to making things right with you. But you know how he'll have to do that."

By killing as many of the Suicide Kings as he could get his hands on. "If this goes the way I think it will, we'll all have plenty of chances to fight the Kings, whether we want to or not."

"So you think they're coming for you?"

He still wasn't sure they'd seen him investigating in Three. Posting sentries after a kill was standard operating procedure, but they might have been long gone by the time he and Lucio showed up. Hell, they might not have *needed* to see him, because they'd known where he was the whole goddamn time.

That was the thing, wasn't it? He had no idea. "I

think...it feels like something's about to happen. The way the air gets heavy before a storm."

Ivan nodded. "Then we should be ready."

"We're Riders." Deacon finished his beer and set the bottle aside. "We're always ready."

Ivan twirled his bottle again, watching the glass catch and refract the light. "I'll fight beside you. I don't care why you're good. I just care about doing our job."

"Why?" he found himself asking. At Ivan's puzzled look, he shook his head. "Not why will you fight with me. I'm grateful for that. But why is *this* your job? Why be a Rider? We both know your heart is in guarding the Rios family."

Ivan set his bottle aside and rose. He gripped the edge of the house's frame and stared into its open recesses, as if seeing into the hazy future when it would be finished and filled with a cozy little family. "Back in my father's day, there wasn't much difference. The civil wars were so bloody that the Rios family was in constant danger. A week couldn't pass without someone trying to kill one of them."

"I know," Deacon reminded him. "I was there." Hell, he'd *been* one of those people.

"Yeah." Ivan glanced at him. "I guess that's the point. All of the other Riders who were there are dead now. But we're building houses for the royal guard and their families. They're having kids and grandkids. Sometimes they still have to take lives, but not as often, and they can serve long enough to wipe their souls clean. Maybe that's because the Riders stop trouble now before it can reach the royal family."

The explanation might have appeased someone else. But Ivan's words echoed in Deacon's mind—*we're all damned anyway*—and he knew the truth. The house and its happy ending were foreign to Ivan. He'd never settle for being a Rios guard these days because too few of them had to make that ultimate sacrifice, so he would live his doomed life as a Rider instead.

"You don't have to die to serve the royal family. *Shouldn't* have to, in a perfect world." Deacon hesitated. "It's not too late. I'm sure Gideon would transfer you—"

Ivan gave him a slashing look before turning back to the house. "I'm a Rider. I have too many ravens to be anything else. I'll serve the Rios family until my last breath."

Deacon studied Ivan's arm, where those ravens surrounded the Riders' tattoo. There were a few dozen— an accounting of maybe forty deaths etched onto his skin. The civil war between the sectors and Eden had left a heavy mark on him, just as it had on others.

Gideon could forgive that blood debt with a single word. For a time, Deacon had wondered, somewhere in the recesses of his mind, why he didn't do it. Surely his people didn't deserve to be damned to hell for necessary evils. Slowly, he'd figured out the truth—Ivan wasn't an anomaly. He was the rule rather than an exception. He felt he deserved this damnation, and nothing and no one would dissuade him.

Not even Gideon Rios.

Certainly not Deacon.

Sighing, he rose from his shadowed spot. "You'll have to indulge me in hoping that last breath is far in the future, Ivan. We need you."

"I'm in no rush to die," Ivan replied, picking up his hammer again. "Tell Ana not to worry about me so much. Maybe she'll actually listen to you."

Ana would listen to him, but sometimes he imagined it was only so that she would know where and how to take him down, like the way you carefully studied an opponent's moves before a fight. "I don't tell Ana what to do. I know better."

Ivan quirked an eyebrow. "You've never had any problem telling the rest of us what to do."

"That's different. That's business."

"Oh."

A single syllable, but loaded with such innuendo that Deacon punched him on the shoulder. "Handing out orders is business. Telling someone how to feel—or what to worry about—isn't."

"If you say so." Ivan scooped up a handful of nails. "I never had a sister, but Ana's been close. I know she worries about me, you all do. You think I've got a death wish." Ivan placed a nail and swung the hammer, raising his voice to be audible over its steady *thump*. "I'm not eager for death, I'm just not scared of it. But she is. Ana's scared shitless that she's going to fall before she fixes the world. So maybe you can't tell her not to worry, but someone needs to. I know she seems tough, but no one can carry the load she's set for herself forever."

Deacon had no idea Ivan could bring himself to say so many words at once without taking a break to grunt and glare. "She's not the only one who worries about you, and you're not the only one who worries about her. But all of the Riders are headstrong, and it's not always easy to change your minds."

Ivan merely snorted as he placed another nail, as if he'd used up all his words. Hell, he probably had, so Deacon lapsed into silence as well. It was a companionable sort of quiet, broken only by the sounds of hammers and murmured instructions. Neither of them was any happier with the job at hand, but now they could do it comfortably, without the specter of unanswered questions looming between them, dark and damning.

eight

Ana still had a mouthful of bobby pins and her hair half-secured into a topknot when Hunter arrived with a look in his eyes that sent excitement soaring through her.

The intel had come in that morning—a whisper passed through one of her dad's old contacts—but it came from a trader who plied his wares on either side of the border between Sectors One and Two, and she'd already known what Hunter was going to say when she brought it to him.

Before they could deploy into another sector, they needed Gideon's approval.

Judging by the anticipation in his eyes, approval had been secured. Ana shoved the last pin into her hair hard enough to scrape her scalp and forced herself to take one slow, steadying breath.

"We got word of something going down in Two tonight," he announced.

Lucio rose from his chair by the window. "Is it related to the possible trafficking?"

"Think so. Gideon wants us to handle it." He paused, his gaze lighting on each of them in turn as he looked around. "Get ready for a fight."

The excitement inside her crackled through the room, but Ana couldn't stop her gaze from swinging to Deacon. He'd joined them in the common room that morning, sitting at that window table with Lucio to clean a couple of handguns.

Right now, he was watching Hunter carefully, listening to his instructions. He could have been any other Rider, waiting for the signal to grab his gear and move out.

But he wasn't, and it felt *wrong*. Ana swung her leg over the bench at Hunter's gesture and joined the Riders heading for the armory. The big room dominated the side of the barracks that bordered their gravel parking lot, boasting enough lockers to store the gear of four times their number.

Ana had never been in the room when it was full. When the war with Eden had come, the Riders had paid in blood. Thirty men died during the final siege of the war, enough to break through Eden's army and give the O'Kanes a chance to take down the corrupt man who'd seized control of the city.

Ana's father had been one of those Riders.

She stopped in front of the locker that had been his and pulled it open. Her gear was inside—light, custom-fitted body armor Gideon had gifted her, along with her favorite weapons. But she'd left some of her father's things there—a golden saint's medallion hanging from a hook, as well as a palm-sized postcard of

Santa Adriana, the Rios princess who had attended Ana's birth and become her namesake.

But Ana's favorite discovery had been the pictures.

The larger one was of her parents together, her mother wearing a brightly patterned summer dress that stretched over her pregnant belly. William stood behind her, his fingers laced with hers, their joined hands resting over the bulge. Ana could see herself in him sometimes—in the stubborn set of his chin, in the dark brows drawn severely over serious eyes. But she had her mother's full lips and narrow nose and thick tumble of curly brown hair.

The second picture was just Ana. She couldn't remember it being taken, but she must have been only five or six. Her hair was drawn up into pigtail poufs, and she wore a wide smile missing two teeth. With skinned knees and scabbed elbows, she perched in the branches of a tree she recognized well—one of the big willows in the park behind the central temple.

Riders weren't supposed to have families. Ana didn't know when or how the tradition had started—though she suspected that Gideon's guilt at potentially creating an army of grieving widows and partially orphaned children was to blame. For whatever reason, her father had been the exception. Had been *allowed* to be the exception.

After him, some of the Riders had formed long-term partnerships with one another. But even that came with complications—and impossible choices. Belief and loyalty were one thing, but to charge into a fight knowing you might have to sacrifice your lover for the greater good...

Terrible idea. She needed the reminder as she shouldered the rest of her gear and slammed her locker shut. Deacon's presence was a tangible force to her right, as if he gave off some sort of heat only she could feel.

He wasn't even in charge, and she was still hyper-aware of him. Apparently, straddling a hot guy's raging hard-on wasn't the best way to deescalate tension.

Who could have fucking known?

"We're riding together." Reyes tossed her a set of keys, then jerked his head toward Ivan and Zeke. "I tried to grab Gabe, but I think Hunter wants to make him ride with Deacon. Shifty fucker."

Someone else giving orders to Deacon still seemed bizarre. But a final glance at him showed only a stern, blank expression as he loaded his pistols. Ana shook off her unease and slipped the knife she'd inherited from her father into the sheath strapped to her thigh. "Grab some extra ammo on your way out the door," she told Reyes. "I have a feeling shit could get ugly."

Shit didn't *get* ugly. It started out that way.

The intel led them to a staging area a few miles over the border into Two. Before Eden had bombed the sector, Two had been responsible for the vast majority of trade between the sectors and other cities that had survived the Flares.

The remnants of that industry showed in the hundreds of massive metal shipping containers abandoned in disorganized rows. Scavengers had already picked over the place thoroughly, so thoroughly that the huge crane once used to transfer the containers to barges and trucks had been stripped down to an ugly, awkward skeleton.

Broken glass and scraps of metal littered the cracked asphalt. Grass poked up between the cracks, and vines had twisted their way over the chain-link fence to creep toward the closest structures. It felt long abandoned, like they'd stumbled across some remnant of the pre-Flare world instead of a place that had been a busy hive of activity only one short year ago.

It gave Ana the creeps.

It also seemed like a great place to set a trap.

Hunter knew it, too. Ana could tell by the way he studied the terrain in front of them, the tiniest frown furrowing his brow. She also knew it wouldn't deter him—more often than not, the Riders strode into traps, dared them to snap shut, and punched their way out.

No matter how carefully they planned, enemies always underestimated the Riders. People who cared about living couldn't anticipate the fury inherent in martyrs who didn't fear death.

"All right," Hunter said. "Lucio, get up high with your rifle, someplace with a good overall vantage point. Everyone else, pair off and pick a quadrant." He used two fingers held aloft to indicate the four cardinal directions. "Let's clear this place out."

Ana joined Ashwin, her head blissfully clear. Adrenaline had finally kicked in, banishing the last hint of nerves as she pulled her sidearm and checked the safety. Anticipation simmered in her blood now, a delicate tingle beneath her skin, a burning need to test herself. To match wits and skills against an opponent and come out on top.

To crush her enemies.

In the quiet times between battles, Ana could rationalize the blood she was about to spill as heroic and righteous. But in this moment, with her heart pounding and every sense alive...

The truth was simpler, starker. Ana was a Rider because she was *good* at it. Because she *liked* being good at it.

She let Ashwin take the lead as they slipped inside the fence and put their backs against the first container. A glance to her left showed Deacon disappearing down an opposite row with Gabe, but she wrenched her gaze away before worry could pierce her cool focus.

Deacon was a big boy who could take care of himself. She would *not* worry.

She wouldn't.

A touch on her arm dragged her attention back to Ashwin. He gestured to the edge of the first container. "We'll do this one row at a time. Cover me."

Ana trailed him to the corner, carefully stepping over rusted metal and broken crates. When they reached the edge of the mammoth shipping container, Ashwin held up a flat palm, then folded in his thumb and pinkie. *Three.*

Then he folded down one finger, and Ana nodded. On *one*, she lifted her weapon.

Ashwin swung around the corner. She followed, gun up, her gaze jumping to his blind spots as he moved forward. As soon as they cleared the row, Ashwin edged forward to the next corner and repeated the countdown.

It made for slow, treacherous progress. It would have been too easy to have the shipping containers laid out in a neat, orderly fashion. Sometimes they found one sitting perpendicular to another pair, creating dead ends that Ana tried to fix on her mental map of the place.

Near the middle of their quadrant, Ashwin stopped abruptly and held up his hand. Ana stilled immediately, straining to hear whatever Ashwin had sensed.

She heard it a second before Ashwin whirled around. The container behind them was open, the door completely off its hinges and leaning precariously against one corner. From within came the soft, echoing rasp of boots on hollow steel.

Someone was crouched on top of it, tracking their movements.

Ashwin reached for one of the endless pockets on his cargo pants and pulled out a grenade. "Get ready," he murmured softly. "Once this goes off, I'll make you a ramp to get up there."

At Ana's nod of understanding, he slipped the pin free, and Ana braced for his throw.

And waited.

A second ticked by. Two. How long had it taken the last time he'd thrown one of these? A few seconds at most? In spite of her overwhelming trust in him, her nerves started to assert themselves. "Ashw—"

He launched the grenade onto the container and dragged the steel door over them. The grenade exploded at the top of its flight arc, and Ana hunched next to Ashwin as deadly shrapnel rained down on their make-shift shield.

The moment it stopped, Ashwin heaved the door aside with a grunt. It flipped against the opposite side of the container with a deafening crash before settling at a manageable angle.

The sound was still echoing when Ana raced up the makeshift ramp and launched herself onto the container. Her boots hit and nearly skidded in a pool of blood. She used the momentum to drop to a crouch, her gun pointed forward, and tried to get her bearings.

The man who'd been stalking them lay face down, bleeding out from a dozen wounds. His shredded leather jacket was soaked with blood, but not enough to obscure the patch on the back—a crowned skull thrusting a blade through its own head.

Suicide King.

She caught movement out of the corner of her eye

and whirled in time to see two more figures pop up several rows down. She fired, sinking a bullet into the first man's shoulder. He spun at the impact, but the second man was already aiming at Ana—

The side of his face caved in. Blood splattered as he toppled backwards off his perch, and Ana gave mental thanks to Hunter's foresight—and Lucio's excellent aim—as she took a second shot and dropped her original target.

The clatter of boots behind her alerted her to Ashwin's arrival, and she realized that only seconds had passed since the grenade. Each moment stretched out impossibly, giving her all the time in the world to scan the terrain.

Ana saw no one else—Lucio had taken care of that. She pivoted, surveying empty rooftops and the spaces between them.

Two rows to the north, something darted across a narrow break between containers. "Ashwin—"

"I saw it." Two running steps, and Ashwin launched himself into the air, sailing across the empty space to land nimbly on the next container over. Secure in that calm, quiet place in her head, Ana measured the distance, backed up to the far edge of the container, and ran.

Open space yawned beneath her, and her stomach dropped. Her flight wasn't nearly as graceful as Ashwin's, and neither was her landing. But she compensated the way she'd learned from a hundred rough landings, rolling forward to disperse the shock of impact.

Leaping containers was fast, but it sure as fuck wasn't quiet. A shout of warning rose ahead of them as Ashwin sailed across the next gap. Ana listened to the thud when he landed, and an idea seized her. "Ashwin!"

He glanced back, and she pointed to herself and

then the ground and twirled her finger in the air. Ashwin nodded and watched as she lowered herself over the edge of her container and dropped.

The sound of her boots hitting the asphalt was cloaked by the noise of Ashwin firing his first shot.

Shouts rose all around her, and running footsteps echoed eerily from multiple directions. Ana slipped behind a partially open door and followed one set approaching rapidly from the east. The person paused just on the other side of the door, and she knew instantly what he was doing—trying to get a good angle on Ashwin, who made a visible, tempting target.

Moving as quietly as possible, Ana holstered her gun and slid her knife from its sheath. Her boots crunched on gravel as she swung around the door, alerting her target. He spun, his mouth opening, and Ana was out of time.

It wasn't clean. Her knife slashed across his throat deep enough to reach bone, silencing his scream before he could give it voice.

She kept moving. Two steps put her back against the container wall. She listened for a shout of warning, but the next sound she heard was the light thud of Ashwin's feet as he ran the length of the roof above her and launched himself onto the next one.

The noise drew another attacker. Ana plastered herself into the shadows as he darted by, so intent on staying out of Ashwin's line of sight that he didn't even notice the dead body in the alley to his left.

He went down a lot cleaner. Ana got a grip on his hair and jerked the knife across his throat from behind. A spatter of shots rang out ahead of her as he slumped to the ground. Ana wiped her knife on his pants and thrust it back into its sheath before reaching for the gun next to his outstretched hand.

A bullet dug into the pavement beside it, and Ana jerked upright, slamming her back against the shipping container. Her hand went automatically for her pistol as a voice said, "Uh-uh. Don't move."

She eased her hand away from her hip and into the air as she turned to face her attacker. The man was at least six feet tall, with muscles that could give Hunter a run for his money. The gun in his hand was steadily trained on Ana, and his gaze drifted up and down her body—but not in a remotely lascivious manner.

Too bad. The pervs were easy to deal with. Their dicks made them stupid, and Ana heartily enjoyed applying the heel of her boot to the source of the problem. But the look this guy was giving her was something far less disgusting and far more dangerous—curious assessment mixed with fascination.

His roving gaze stopped in the smart places. Her muscles. Her weapons. He catalogued them the same way she studied him, picking out strengths and envisioning weaknesses. Ana wanted to put him down simply to end the threat he represented, but this bastard wanted to smash her down. Make her small. Put her in her place. Convince her she never should have left it.

Not as stupid as the pervs. But she could work with it.

"So." The man strode closer, stopping only a few paces away. "You're the one who got Axel."

Ana raised both eyebrows. "Which one's Axel?"

"Smart mouth." He glanced past her to the corpse on the ground, and though his brow furrowed with mild displeasure, there was nothing of the vengeful rage Ana would have felt if their positions were reversed.

He looked back at Ana, his eyes still amused. Still curious. With his gun trained on her forehead, he raised his voice. "I've got the girl. You can come down here nice and friendly-like, or I can put a bullet between her eyes. And that'd be a waste. She seems fun."

Ana nearly laughed. A smart man would have pulled the trigger and taken his chances with Ashwin. Faced with a physically intimidating foe like Hunter or Reyes, Ana didn't doubt he would have.

But she was the girl. So she was hostage-bait.

God bless men and their rampaging, incapacitating egos.

Boots slapped on the pavement behind her. Something made the man's eyes widen, and in the next moment he lunged for Ana. His arm wrapped around her throat tight enough to choke as he hauled her back against his chest like a human shield.

The gun barrel dug into her temple as she stared at Ashwin, who filled the mouth of the alley, his gun trained toward them. His eyes caught hers for a split second, and her brain kicked into gear as he nodded slightly and then spread his hands, pointing his pistol at the sky.

He'd spooked the guy on purpose, to let Ana get inside his guard. They'd spent weeks training on this scenario, but her muscles still burned with the effort it took not to let instinct take over until Ashwin nodded a second time.

She flowed into the defense like they were back in the Riders' barracks. Her left hand slapped down on the arm around her throat. Her right caught the muzzle of the gun and shoved it behind her head. Her attacker's height worked against him as she spun under his arm, twisting his hand with her until his wrist bent at a torturous angle and the gun was pointed back at him.

One hard strike opened his fingers. She caught his weapon with one hand and slammed him in the chest with the other, startling him into stumbling back.

A guy like him would have aimed for the knee. A guy like him would have gloated. Ana raised her arms and shot him in the head three times with his own weapon.

She didn't bother to watch him fall. She ejected the magazine, cleared the chamber, and tossed his gun aside, then turned to face Ashwin. His normally blank expression broke into something *almost* like a smile—close enough for Ana to feel an answering grin curving her lips.

"Perfect form," was all he said, but coming from Ashwin it was the greatest of compliments. Her adrenaline surged again, stronger than before, and she knew she should be afraid. That she should be somber and serious like Gabe, not high on the thrill of being *better* than these assholes.

Maybe she wasn't as righteous as she liked to think.

And maybe, after a lifetime of being challenged and doubted, it felt fucking good to win.

More footsteps raced toward them, drawn by the sound of gunfire. Ashwin reloaded his sidearm and glanced at her with one eyebrow arched. "You ready?"

Her gun slid into her hand like an old friend. Her mind was clear.

It was trite as hell. If Reyes had been there, he would have given her shit for the next year. But as she met Ashwin's gaze, the words tumbled out, and they'd never felt truer. "I was born ready."

gabe

For Gabe, nothing felt right. Nothing had for days, not waking or sleeping, not keeping to himself in solitary thought or being surrounded by other Riders, not even engaging in the meditative dance of sword practice.

Nothing felt right until the moment Deacon confirmed the identity of their attackers, and Gabe drove a knife into the heart of the first Suicide King and felt the man's blood slick his fingers in a hot river of righteous vengeance.

Gabe had never savored a kill before. He'd savored his skills, perhaps. His efficiency. The training that ended lives as neatly and painlessly as possible, because his goal had always been to stop his target from hurting anyone else.

But as the first Suicide King bled out under his

hands, Gabe thought of his aunt, who had cradled him on her lap and read him stories. The aunt who'd kissed them goodbye with tears in her eyes as his grandfather sent her to forge an alliance in another sector, one meant to bring them precious livestock and feed that would give the family's textile business an edge over the Reyes ranch.

He could barely remember her face, he'd been so young. But he could remember his mother's grief-stricken tears, the hysterical demands for vengeance that had fallen on devout, unwilling ears. The noble families of Sector One did not take lives. They didn't take revenge. Trading one of their daughters to an outsider in one of the brutal, godless sectors had been a desperate gamble, and it had paid off in humiliating failure.

Gabe's aunt had disappeared from family discussions, written off as if she had never existed—at least until Deacon's quiet confession resurrected the pain and the terrible injustice in Gabe's imagination. It taunted and tortured him with no appropriate outlet until today, when he'd finally come face-to-face with an acceptable target.

But now even that fleeting feeling of *rightness* was slipping away. The mercenary's heart stopped, so Gabe shoved himself to his feet and went to find someone else to kill.

The fight around him was chaos, with too many hired men he didn't have time to deal with. A blur of movement caught his eye—a man in a leather vest with the Suicide Kings' emblem emblazoned across the back. The stylized king from a deck of cards holding a knife through his own head—only on the vest, the face was a skull and the knife dripped blood.

Appropriate. Gabe's knife was dripping blood, too.

But not enough. Not nearly enough.

He launched after the retreating figure, flying around the corner of one of the massive shipping containers. He was almost to the end of the row when a black hole opened next to him and an arm shot out.

There wasn't time to dodge. Strong fingers caught his arm and jerked. He stumbled, pitching into the darkness of the container and ramming into the opposite side hard enough to stun him.

Metal screeched. He twisted in time to watch the door slam shut, every bit of light seared into a painful afterimage as total darkness fell.

A boot scraped over metal. He heard an indrawn breath and lunged, crashing into the person who'd trapped him and pinning them back against the wall with the weight of his body.

"Relax, man." A low but decidedly feminine voice echoed in the darkness. "Jesus fuck."

Gabe tensed and tried to remember if the Kings counted any women amongst their ranks. The body pressed against his was long and slender—taller than Ana, less muscular. But when he shifted his weight to check her for weapons, he encountered curves—full breasts and hips that flared under his hand as it ran down her body.

Nice curves, but not nice enough to distract him from the guns. So many fucking guns—a large-caliber revolver on her hip, a semiautomatic tucked into a holster strapped around her thigh, and another at the small of her back. She probably had another in an ankle holster, but when he slid his hand down her leg, she slapped it.

"I'm heavily armed," she bit out. "And you're welcome, by the way."

"For what?"

"For saving your life, that's what. They almost got me with that trap, too."

He still held his knife in his opposite hand, but he eased back—mostly so he wouldn't stab her by mistake if she moved. "Who *are* you?"

Her hair brushed his arm and snagged on his shirt as she edged past him. "I'm Laurel. I work with Six."

Gabe turned to follow the sound of her voice, his mind sifting through his memories of the war. He could remember Six and her squad of female fighters. Several of them had rivaled the Riders when it came to hand-to-hand combat, and a few snipers—

The memory caught. "You're the sharpshooter."

"A little overly simplistic, but I'll take it." She lapsed into expectant silence.

Waiting for his name, no doubt. With adrenaline still pounding through him, answering was reckless. She could be lying. She could be with the Kings. She could be *anyone* in the dark.

An arrogance he rarely felt rose inside him, decades of pride in his heritage and the family name. "I'm Gabriel Montero." *And if you turn out to be one of the Kings, I'll kill you.*

"Sounds fancy."

He'd never had his lineage so blithely dismissed before. Some people hated the Monteros. Some envied them. Some aspired to join them.

No one was...*bored* by them.

Perturbed in ways he didn't want to admit, Gabe felt for the edge of the doorway and froze when his fingers collided with her shoulder again. "What are you doing in Sector Two, Laurel? This isn't Six's territory."

"It's not Rider territory, either." Something metallic clicked, then rasped, and the flame from a small lighter blazed in the darkness. "Looks like we both fell for the same bad intel."

The flame danced as her words stirred the air, casting long shadows on the walls of the shipping container. He could see her face now, gilded by fire and clear enough for him to recognize. She was the silent warrior at Six's side during the final battles of the war, memorable for her piercing eyes and the bright pink streaks of hair framing her face.

She looked irritated now. And as her words penetrated the lingering bloodlust, he understood why. "Bad intel? This was a trap?"

Her expression changed, her brows drawing together over suddenly concerned eyes. "Did you take a whack to the head or something? Of course it's a fucking trap."

His pride stung, and he glared at her for a moment before dropping his gaze to the knife in his hand. Blood still clung to its edge, and if he didn't wipe it away soon, it would dry there. He dragged up the hem of his T-shirt to clean the blade, his brain finally starting to work. "A trap with a wide net, if we were both caught up in it."

"Truth." She rubbed the back of her neck. "Wish I knew what they were after."

Gabe had a strong suspicion. His churning emotions had been so focused on the pain he felt at Deacon's revelations that he'd stopped thinking. A deadly mistake.

Deacon had done terrible things, things that might make it hard for Gabe to ever look at him the same way again. But if he was forced to be honest, none of those things had betrayed Gideon or the Riders. Deacon had committed his sins before knowing what alternatives existed, and when the choice to follow a different path had been presented to him, he'd taken it.

The only person Deacon had ever truly betrayed was the one who'd sent him to kill Gideon.

nine

Deacon's first three kills went down easy. The fourth drew blood with a move he recognized in his bones.

The memory buzzed in his head, stronger than the searing pain of the shallow slash across his abdomen. *Keep your knife hand low, see, and tuck the blade behind your arm. And when the bastard comes at you, you wait. Wait until you think he's gonna end you for sure. Then, last second, you jerk that blade up. You'll be cleaning the bastard's guts off your shoes, kid.*

Damn near thirty years, and he could still hear the words, hoarse and firm. Three decades, and Deacon remembered the old man's lesson when it counted—in the center of a chaotic jumble of shouts and screams and blood.

As the fourth man slumped to the ground with a

blade buried in his heart, Deacon confronted the truth. Some of these were hired guns, little more than thugs picked off the street with the promise of a few hundred credits, but the man at his feet was well trained and well equipped.

He was a King.

And Gabe, God damn his sudden impulsivity, had run off into the fray, with no one to watch his back.

Deacon turned. All of his people were still on their feet, and he bit back the urge to warn them. They didn't need it. They'd fight well, no matter who they faced.

Instead, he motioned to Hunter, who answered him with a quick nod that turned into a spine-chilling shout as he knocked an attacker away from Reyes's back.

Deacon slipped down a shadowed alley near where he'd last seen Gabe. Christ, if he ran off in a blind rage and got himself killed because of *Deacon*—

No.

Up ahead, the shadows lightened into an open space—an empty lot between two buildings. Deacon readied his pistol, crept up to the clearing—

The unmistakable sensation of a gun barrel poking him in the back of the head drew him up short. "Drop it."

Before he had a chance, another black-clad shadow melted forward to pull the gun from his hand. Deacon glared at him, but he didn't know his face. Just the casual, unconcerned look that burned in the man's eyes.

Fuck, he'd walked straight into this one.

"Better get the rest of his weapons." Seth's voice rasped out of the darkness, deeper than Deacon remembered. Harder. "I'd hate to take a knife in the face before we finish our conversation."

Then he stepped out into the light, clad in leather and beat-up denim, and Deacon studied him as two other men patted him down for weapons. Seth's hair and beard were a little silver now, his face lined by the years. He'd lived hard, and Deacon didn't mind telling him so. "You look like shit."

A bitter smile twisted Seth's lips. "And you look soft. Running into traps, now, are you?"

"I couldn't miss seeing you. Wasn't an option." Deacon shook his head. "What do you want?"

"Oh, just to spend some time with an old friend." Seth gripped the knife at his side, rubbing his thumb slowly over the hilt. "Been looking for you for a while, now."

"Bullshit. It's no big secret where I've been."

"That's where you're wrong. If the old man knew, he held that real close." Seth's blue eyes were like chips of ice. "He always had a soft spot for you, even after you knifed him in the back."

Something about the way he said it prickled over Deacon's skin. "Had?"

"Too bad you missed the funeral. We did it up real nice for him. Sent him off into Lake Tahoe in a burning boat like a goddamn Viking."

Why did it hurt to hear? The old man would have been at least seventy by now, old by anyone's reckoning. Ancient for a merc. "I'm sorry, Seth."

"Don't you fucking dare." With a swift jerk, Seth unsheathed his knife and flipped it in his hand, holding the edge up to catch the light. "I'm glad you weren't there. He deserved better than to be soiled by the blood of an ungrateful traitor. And we would have had to kill you fast."

"I couldn't stay. Doesn't mean I wanted the old man dead."

"Don't pretend you give a shit." He flipped the knife again, catching it by the blade and balancing it on his fingers as if preparing to throw it. Then he grinned. "Or maybe you do. We could use you, you know. I'm sure you know all sorts of useful shit about the sectors. What do you say, Deacon? Wanna come home? Everything forgiven, no hard feelings?"

He was alone, unarmed, surrounded by half a dozen men who could put a bullet in his skull at any moment—if they even had to. He and Seth had trained together. A flick of his wrist, and Deacon could be dead before he hit the ground.

It didn't change his answer. Maybe it should have, but there was one thing Deacon had always prized, even above his own survival. Honesty. "I can't, and you wouldn't want me. I'm not that person anymore."

Seth barked out a laugh. "Oh, I know exactly who you are. You've always been too good for the rest of us. Maybe the old man never saw it, but I did. You were happy to live large on the Kings' reputation, but you never would get your hands dirty with the ugly shit it took to earn it, would you?"

"You're right." There were some lines he would never cross—not for the Kings, and not for the Riders. Not for anyone or anything. "See? You don't want me back. So where does that leave us?"

"Someplace beautiful." Seth pulled his wrist back and laughed when Deacon tensed. Instead of letting the knife fly, he flipped it again, gripped the handle, and shoved it back into its sheath. "You don't think I'm going to let you off this easy, do you? Not when you still don't regret a goddamn thing?"

"*Seth*—"

"But you will, Deacon." Seth bared his teeth in a chilling, terrifying grin. "By the time we're done with you, you're gonna regret it all."

There were only a few things worse than death, but Seth's glare promised that he would bring every single one to bear on Deacon before it was all over. The possibilities shattered out before him like shards of a mirror, wicked and sharp. Before he had time to ponder them, one of the men to his left stepped forward, his rifle raised.

But the blow came from behind, quick and hard, and Deacon tumbled into darkness.

ten

Kora usually had a light touch, so Deacon knew he was at least moderately fucked when she gently prodded the back of his scalp and he had to grit his teeth to hold back a savage curse.

"It's not good," she said finally. "I want a scan, and you'll have to be under observation for at least twenty-four hours."

"I'll take the scan, but no observation," he shot back, ignoring Ashwin's furrowed brow and telltale frown.

Kora's eyes gleamed. She squinted at him and tilted her head. "Twelve hours of observation."

"One."

"Six."

"Three."

Ashwin's frown deepened. "She said six."

"Three's fine." Kora smiled at him, then patted Deacon's cheek. "He only really needs two."

Deacon grumbled. "You're sneaky, Kora."

"Best way to deal with you." She picked up her tablet and headed for the door. "I'll get things ready. Watch him, please."

Ashwin inclined his head in agreement, his gaze following Kora until she disappeared into the hallway. Then he turned back to Deacon. "You shouldn't argue with her. You were in bad shape when we found you."

A rifle butt to the skull would do that. "Head wounds always look worse than they are. They bleed like motherfuckers."

Ashwin stared at him.

If Deacon didn't know better, he'd think the man was offended that he would dare to try to tell *him* about head wounds. "Right."

"You were in bad shape," Ashwin repeated. There was an edge there, and he studied Deacon in curious silence before adding, "But you were alive."

Deacon would have kicked his ass if he hadn't at least wondered why. "Death is easy. The Kings have bigger plans for me."

"That seems inefficient."

He laughed, and immediately regretted it when his head throbbed like a bitch. "I don't think efficiency is Seth's main goal. He sacrificed money and men on a ruse to draw me out. And now he wants to make me hurt."

"Revenge?" At Deacon's terse nod, Ashwin crossed his arms over his chest and leaned back against the wall. "How personal is this?"

"Will he get bored or distracted and drop it, you mean?"

"Not everyone's cut out for the commitment that

revenge requires. The longer you let it drag on, the more you expose yourself. The more you risk." Ashwin tapped his fingers on his elbow. "Not killing you outright was a big one. How many more will they take?"

The terrifying answer had been etched into Seth's murderous scowl. "As many as it takes." Deacon rubbed a hand over the back of his neck and winced when he bumped the sore spot on his head. "Every single day is risk for the Kings. They're not scared of it. But this is worse, Ashwin. Seth and I grew up together, joined the Kings together. He doesn't know jack shit about my life now, but he knows *me*."

"So he'll be able to ascertain how best to hurt you." Ashwin tapped his fingers again. "When you were with the Kings, were there jobs you would and wouldn't accept? Things you wouldn't do?"

It was Deacon's turn to glare.

Ashwin made an impatient gesture. "I'm not interested in your ethics. I'm interested in any perceived weaknesses you telegraphed through your willingness or refusal to execute certain targets. Those are the things that could hurt you the most. Those and your... personal attachments."

"I don't have personal attachments." Everyone knew that. His only loyalty was to Gideon, his only concern the Rios family. Nothing beyond that could touch him—ask any Rider, and they'd tell you exactly that.

But it was a lie.

His first thoughts when he was swimming up out of unconsciousness hadn't been of Gideon or Isabela or any of the Riders—except for one. His stomach had clenched in a sick sort of dread that refused to abate until he opened his eyes and saw Ana. Her face was drawn, one shirt sleeve was torn and bloodied, but she was on her feet, cursing with an animated fury that had eased the worst of his—

Fear. There was no other word for it, nothing else to capture the crawling terror that maybe Seth had somehow *known*—and hadn't waited to exact his vengeance.

Ashwin watched him, something close to sympathy in his dark eyes. "I thought the same thing. Until I didn't."

Everyone had things that would hurt them. For some, it was a small, precise number. For others, it was an expansive list, one that could be—and often was—weaponized easily and frequently.

But there were deeper things, weaknesses that went straight to the heart and soul of a person, like permanent bruises. Places where one swift blow could break you into so many pieces that putting them back together wasn't just impossible, it was unthinkable.

Ashwin proved it a moment later, when Zeke entered the room and held the door open. "Hey, I'm gonna handle Deacon's scans. Kora had to sit down for a few minutes. She got a little dizzy."

Ashwin pushed off the wall in one swift, graceful movement and somehow made it halfway to the door in two steps. "Where is she?"

"Down the hall in that sitting room with the couches. I got her—" But Ashwin was already gone, brushing past Zeke as his final word fell into the empty air. "—settled."

Deacon snorted. "You didn't actually expect to get that whole sentence out, did you?"

"Hey, I talk fast." Zeke let the door swing shut and moved to Deacon's side. "How's the head? Are *you* dizzy? Because I'll carry your ass down the hall if I have to."

"I'm fine. How's everyone else?"

"Mostly good. Ana and Reyes have scratches.

Ivan's got a black eye." Zeke snorted. "Gabe missed half the damn fight because one of Six's foxy femme fatales hauled him into a shipping container to keep him from running into a trap."

Well, that made one of them. "Too bad she didn't bring a friend."

"Yeah, you stuck your foot in it good, boss." Zeke picked up one of the tablets Kora used to store medical data and grinned. "So, let's get these scans rolling. And then I get to stick to your ass for the next three hours. Excited?"

"That depends." Kora refused to be intimidated, and Ashwin would always have her back. But maybe Zeke could be swayed. "You do the scans, then let me go, and I promise I'll have someone check in on me."

"Uh, and when Ashwin murders me for making Kora sad?" Zeke's fingers slid over the surface of the tablet, but when Deacon's gaze didn't waver, he sighed. "Fine, but I'm going to hide until three hours is up. And if Kora asks, I was with you."

"Deal." If Kora really was feeling ill, Deacon would bet every weapon in the Riders' arsenal that Ashwin would make her rest, hovering over her the whole time. The last thing on his mind would be the state of Deacon's brain. "It'll be fine, Zeke. Trust me."

eleven

Ana's arm itched.

She ignored it, working carefully around the bandage wrapped around her biceps as she rubbed body butter into her skin. The scent was sweeter than she preferred, some sugary mix of vanilla and cinnamon, but if she closed her eyes, it was almost like being on the bakery side of her aunts' shop.

Maybe that was why Naomi had chosen it. Her elder aunt's quest to lure Ana back to a less dangerous life hadn't abated when Ana was initiated into the Riders. It had just gotten more...

Passive-aggressive.

Subtle.

The itching on her arm was her own damn fault. She should have demanded that Reyes slap a few butterfly bandages on the shallow knife wound and turn her loose to endure the throbbing ache as a reminder not to drop her guard. But regeneration tech took a lot longer...and had given her an excuse to linger in the infirmary while Zeke ran scans of Deacon's brain.

Leaving hadn't been an option. Not when her heart hadn't been beating right from the moment they found him, sprawled unconscious in an alley, his hair so dark they didn't notice the blood at the back of his head until Ana's hands came away smeared with it.

She'd scrubbed them raw and rubbed enough lotion into her fingers that she'd smell like cinnamon for a week, and she still couldn't get the *feel* of it off her.

Her fingers drifted back toward her freshly healed skin, and she wrapped her fingers around her arm to stop herself from scratching. Seeing Deacon had brought her crashing back to earth, hard. She still felt hungover. Hollowed out, aware that her fingers covered unmarked skin that would soon sport six new ravens.

Taking a life should hurt more. But that hollow feeling wasn't guilt—not at the easy way she'd killed, anyway. Every man who had fallen beneath her knife or dropped at one of her bullets was a man who would never kill again. She didn't regret stopping them.

That was the source of this uncomfortable guilt— her sheer lack of remorse. It had blazed in full strength last time, sorrow for what had been necessary clashing with the immeasurable weight of the deaths she'd caused.

This time, whenever she tried to feel bad, she remembered Deacon's blood on her hands.

If he hadn't opened his eyes again, she might have driven out to the Kings' compound and figured out a way to blow them off the fucking map.

A single rap at her door interrupted her mid-shudder, and she embraced the distraction. "Come in."

The door cracked open, and Deacon peered inside. "I need to talk to you."

Relief at seeing him up and moving crashed over her, swift and unwelcome. Being relieved was fine—she was *always* worried about her fellow Riders. But this felt raw, revealing. Deeply personal.

Smashing it back down, she twisted the lid onto her glass jar and tilted her head toward the spare bed in her room. "Have a seat."

He didn't even argue, the surest sign that something really was wrong. "Thanks." He dropped heavily to the bed, with little trace of his usual easy grace. "The op tonight was a ruse to draw me out. I guess you've all figured that out by now."

"We talked about it," she acknowledged, which was a mild description of the curse-laden conversation that had ensued as Ana burned the treads off the tires in her haste to get an unconscious Deacon back to Sector One. "I should have double-checked the intel before I passed it on. I knew we were dealing with worse than the usual petty sector criminals."

He shook his head. "It was inevitable."

Wariness prickled up her spine, far different from her typical awareness of him. She twisted to swing her legs over the side of the bed, planted her feet on the floor so she was facing him, and for a silent moment she just...looked at him.

Deacon was *tired.*

His dark eyes were shadowed. His beard wasn't as neatly trimmed as usual, lending him a rougher, rawer edge. His body was a riot of conflicting messages—tense muscles but slumped shoulders, as if he was gearing up for a fight he'd already forfeited.

"Nothing is inevitable." She leaned forward to rest her elbows on her legs. "We just need to work together, now that we know what we're facing."

"Working together isn't always the best option."

"Why not?"

He faced her squarely, some of the tension melting out of him. "Killing me would have been too easy. They want to make me suffer instead."

It was an impulse Ana couldn't fathom. Suffering was the enemy, and its alleviation the goal. Sometimes that meant ending a life, but there was no honor or glory in inflicting pain. She could feel satisfied with her skills, sure. Relief that she'd done her job well. Even the guilty pleasure of winning.

Hell, she *wanted* to kill the Kings, to burn their world to the ground. But if she got her chance, she'd be damned if she would waste an opportunity to end their ability to do harm simply to prolong their agony.

That kind of sadism wasn't just cruel. It was fucking stupid tactics.

"Fuck them." She pushed off the bed so she wouldn't have to look up at him, but he was so close that she still had to tilt her head back. "Fuck them and anyone like them. If that's what their goal is, I'll happily kill the shit out of them."

"You don't understand. You wouldn't understand." He turned away, toward the window, bracing his arms on the sill as he stared unseeing through the glass. "These aren't strangers. I've known their leader for thirty goddamn years, Ana. We grew up together, joined the Kings together. He knows—" Deacon bit off the words.

"What?" she asked softly. "What does he know?"

For a long time, he didn't move. Didn't speak. Then he asked softly, "If you wanted to hurt Reyes, how would you do it? Zeke? Ashwin? And don't say you don't know, because it's a lie."

She wanted to argue. To say she couldn't imagine *wanting* to hurt anyone. But that was a truth wrapped in a technicality—the only people she wanted to hurt were the ones already doing too much damage to ignore. That might feel righteous, but it didn't leave her hands clean.

And she knew what the Kings would do, because her father had raised her idealistic, but he hadn't raised her stupid. To fight evil, you had to understand evil. You had to know how bitterness and hate and rage twisted inside people, how darkness always sought to obliterate the brightest thing it could find.

If you wanted to hurt Reyes, you gave him a victim he couldn't save. The straightest path to Ashwin would always be through Kora. And Zeke... Zeke would deny it until the sun set in the east, but his guilt over Jaden's death was a quietly bleeding wound, and until Jaden's sister was settled somewhere safe, it would never heal.

She knew how to hurt them because she *knew* them.

It cut deep to realize she couldn't say the same about Deacon. She knew how to irritate him. How to get under his skin, to make him snap and snarl and, on rare occasions, even smile. But if she had to cut the heart out of him...

Ana wouldn't know where to start. The leader of the Suicide Kings did.

"So..." she said finally. "He knows you."

"Not the same as he used to." He looked at her with an expression she couldn't begin to decipher—until he reached out and smoothed the hair at her temple. "But it won't take him long to figure it out."

Her skin prickled under his fingertips, but it was his words that slammed into her, and for a heartbeat she couldn't breathe under the force of them.

Deacon was staring at her like the path to his heart led through her.

She wet her lips. "Deacon—"

"I can't stay," he whispered. "Once Seth figures it out, it'll be too late. You'll be a target."

Anger pricked at her, battling the seductive spell cast by his softly stroking fingers. "Don't," she said, twisting away from his touch as her voice cracked. It was every fear she'd ever had about Deacon doubting her, refracted through affection to turn her into his weakness. "Don't do this to me. Don't *blame* this on me."

"There's only one person responsible for this shit, and it's him." He heaved a sigh. "But that doesn't change reality. I have to go to Kings' Canyon."

She had already braced herself for some patronizing speech about pulling her from active duty for her own protection, so this abrupt turn stunned her. "You *what?*"

"Rejoining is out of the question, but I have to face this head-on." Determination squared his shoulders. "He thinks I betrayed him, so he wants to punish me. I'll let him. It'll keep him away from Sector One."

"You'll—" She bit off the words, fisting her hands to stop herself from shoving him. "So that's your big plan? Walk over there and let him kill you slowly?"

The bastard had the gall to *smile.* "It's what a Rider would do, isn't it?"

"It's what a martyr would do," she snapped. "And only an idiot Rider becomes one of those before it's necessary. I'm not going to let you do it because—because—" Her frustration boiled over, and she thumped one fist against his chest. "It's *hormones*, Deacon. Your dick got hard once, and now you think you have to protect me. You don't. No one does."

"I'm not asking you for anything, Ana. I just thought—"

"What? That I'd shrug and wave goodbye?" This time she did push him, spreading her fingers wide on his chest and pinning him back against the windowsill. "Stop giving up on us, Deacon. Let us fight for you."

"I'm not giving up." She hadn't wrapped her hair yet, and he slid his fingers into the loosely bound strands, tugging them lightly. "Why is the worst thing about me always the first one you think of?"

Because she had to. Because he had always been the single greatest danger to her ambitions, the one man whose disappointment could shatter her. He was the one who decided where she got to fight and how she got to prove herself—but victory was only proof if everyone knew Deacon hadn't gone easy on her.

She couldn't afford his affection, couldn't afford to feel it in return. She had to hate him, at least a little, just to keep putting one foot in front of the other without going mad from the pressure.

But even that wasn't the full reason. Maybe Ana needed to hate him, but Deacon had made it easy. So easy. She curled her fingers into his shirt, gripping the cotton until the soft weave of the fabric abraded her skin. "The worst is all you ever let any of us see."

"Fair enough." He stared down at her, searching her face. "What would you do? Tell the truth."

He was asking seriously, as if he not only cared what she thought but valued her insight. Nervousness should have seized her, but her thoughts fell into the well-ordered soldiers her father had been training since she was old enough to understand the word *tactics*.

"First, I'd make sure the most vulnerable people were protected. The ones who can't defend themselves. Maricela. Isabela's children. Del and her initiates.

Kora." She paused. "Ashwin would have to guard Kora. He wouldn't have the capacity to do anything else, not while she was in danger. But the royal guard could take care of the rest."

"Gideon alerted them the moment Lucio and I came back from the fire in Three."

Logical. It didn't surprise her they were on the same page about that—though he wasn't going to like the next part nearly as much. "Then I'd set a trap. Use bait they wouldn't be able to resist. Someone they'd underestimate." She didn't flinch away from his gaze. "Someone you cared about who could take care of herself."

A muscle in his jaw jumped. "And what if that's what Seth wants me to do? I can hear the son of a bitch now—*work smarter, Deacon, not harder.*"

Ana tightened her grip in his shirt until her nails dug into his chest. "Then he'll be real surprised when I put a bullet between his eyes."

He covered her hand with his. "I'm not the one you'd have to convince. Gideon isn't real fond of using people as bait."

It was the truth and a lie, because Gideon loved his Riders, but he never hesitated to accept their sacrifices when it served the greater good. But the lie wasn't why the warmth of Deacon's hands over hers provoked delicious heat. It wasn't why the air between them crackled with the sort of electricity that heralded a wild storm.

Ana went up on her toes, until her lips were so close to his that his gaze dropped to her mouth. Until they were so close a kiss was inevitable.

"I don't have to convince you," she whispered. "You're not my boss anymore, Deacon. And you can't stop me."

"I'm not ordering you not to do it, Ana." He closed the distance between them until his next words moved his lips against hers, a whisper and a kiss. "I'm asking you not to. Please."

Please.

It might be the first time she'd ever heard him utter the word. Deacon didn't ask. He didn't plead. When it came to work, Deacon issued commands. And when they were off duty...

God. Had Deacon *ever* been off duty?

Her lips parted on the start of his name, but at the slight brush of friction, her body staged an unanticipated mutiny. She couldn't remember tearing free of his hands, but she must have, because her fingers were suddenly at the back of his neck as she tilted her head and licked his lower lip.

She slid her hands higher, shivering at the tickle of short hair against her palm—and froze when she remembered his wounds. "Shit," she gasped, pulling back. "Deacon, your head. Is it—?"

He stilled her words with his tongue gliding over her lips. Ana shuddered, a reaction totally out of proportion to the teasing caress, and finally understood the allure of chasing something you weren't supposed to have.

Fucking Deacon was a terrible idea, and knowing that turned every forbidden touch into something explosive.

She gripped his shirt again, tugging at it, trying to haul it up his chest. He caught both of her hands this time, but instead of pulling them away, he began to move. He stepped closer, driving her back toward the wall. When her back hit it, he urged her hands up, over her head, and stared down at her, his face shadowed.

Then *he* reached for *her* shirt, drawing the

wash-worn cotton up her body. The slow drag of fabric was torturous, the caress too light, too glancing. Too *teasing*. She wanted more—fast, rough, *hard*.

But Deacon had always been implacable, and now he was implacably bent on slowly dismantling her sanity.

He discarded her shirt and pressed her to the wall. The rough stucco gently scraped her skin, contrasting dizzily with the soft brush of his shirt against her breasts. She sucked in a breath and reached for him again—

But he was already stripping his shirt over his head. By the time it fell, his hands were on his belt, and she was free to slide her fingers up the chest she'd spent so many hours watching during sparring matches. She scratched her nails over his shoulders and down his arms, one thumb tracing over the ravens that spiraled down toward his wrist.

Who gave a fuck if this was a terrible idea? They were both damned anyway.

Her hand reached his, and she dragged her nails across his abdomen as the click of his belt giving way filled the room. His muscles jumped under her touch, his breath hissing out, and the power of it made her giddy. After all these years, being the one inside *his* head felt like the sweetest revenge.

So she inched her fingers into his pants and curled them around his cock.

Deacon bit off a curse and smacked his forehead against the wall.

It put his face next to hers. She turned into him, shivering as his beard abraded her cheek, and let her words drift over his ear as she stroked him with her thumb. "How do you wanna do this? Naked in the bed? Half-naked against the wall?" Her thumb reached the tip of his cock and circled the crown. "Or we could just jerk my pants out of the way and do it over my desk."

"Too fast." His voice had dropped to something silkier than a growl, but harsher than a purr. Something uniquely *Deacon*, and it melted her bones. He waited—breathing hard, one eyebrow arched—until she gave in to the silent demand and eased her hand from his pants.

He stepped back, not quite out of reach. The muscles in his chest and arms—even his *abs*—flexed as he looked at her, a slow perusal that started and then also stopped at her face.

His hand drifted over her hip, his thumb barely nudging the waistband of her pants. "Take them off."

She was wearing loose cotton, comfortable for lounging. As soon as she edged the waistband past the curve of her hips, her pants slid down her legs to pool on the floor. She stepped out of them, only to find Deacon in her space again, his body angled so that her instinctive step back took her closer to the bed.

He pressed the advantage, stalking towards her, his eyes glinting. "How long has it been, Ana?"

Too long. Way too long, judging by the erratic pounding of her heart. It had been difficult to summon to memory the details of her last tryst while lying in bed by herself, but it was fucking *impossible* with Deacon prowling toward her like he was ready to ruin her world.

The backs of her thighs bumped against the edge of the mattress, but she held her ground, turning the question back around on him. "How long has it been for you?"

"I can't remember." The corner of his mouth kicked up in a wicked smile. "Looking at you does that to me."

"Good." His jeans were still hanging open. She

grabbed them and hauled him closer, until his cock ground against her stomach and his chest was right there, irresistibly tempting. She brushed a kiss to his collarbone and traced it to his shoulder, where she closed her teeth in a challenging nip.

"You won't distract me." His hands closed on her hips, tight enough for his fingers to dig into her flesh. "Not this time."

"Distract you from what?"

"My plans." His fingers skated up her sides, a light-as-air touch that she might well have imagined. Then his nails scraped her shoulder blades, raising goose bumps on her flesh.

It went on like that, careful caresses alternating with hard, deliberate grasps that felt almost like reminders—he wasn't a gentle man, he was *Deacon*. Rough. Dangerous.

Delicious.

When his fingertips circled her nipples, she sucked in a breath. When they grazed the tops of her thighs, she shuddered. And when they slipped beneath the cotton fabric of her panties to grip her ass, lifting her off the floor and drawing her toward the solid heat of his body, she wrapped her legs around his hips and caught his mouth in a desperate kiss.

His tongue danced over her lips as his chest vibrated with a rumbling groan. "If you want it quick and hard, I'll give it to you. Or…"

Quick and hard sounded just about right. She was hot enough for it, already so turned on he'd have no trouble driving into her. But as his fingers dug into her ass, grinding her against his cock, a tiny voice rose from the deepest, most carefully guarded place inside her.

This might be your only chance to have him.

If she was going to be bad, she might as well get

the full experience. Maybe if they fucked slow and long and deep enough, she could fuck all this dangerous curiosity out of her system.

"Or," she moaned against his mouth. "I choose *or*."

The world tilted as he laid her back on the bed. "Good girl."

Smug bastard. He felt too good for her to push him away, so she dug her nails into his back instead, raking them down in sharp warning. "Don't get used to it."

"Wouldn't dream of it." The hair on his chest chafed her nipples as he settled over her, one strong, denim-clad leg slipping between her thighs. The pressure was exquisite, sparking just enough friction against her clit for a shudder to tear through her on a bolt of pleasure.

Ana released his back and reached above her to grip her quilt, arching her body up to his. It tilted her head back against the covers, and he took advantage of the opening as swiftly as he ever had during a sparring match. Those soft, incredible lips coasted up her throat, gentle and warm, as he traced the line of her jaw with kisses and dragged his tongue over her pulse.

She'd always known Deacon was patient, but now he was *relentless*. She melted into the mattress as he explored her, ranging down to the upper curve of her breast and then back up to her ear. His beard scratched, his lips glided, his tongue licked with a suggestive rhythm that had her rocking mindlessly against his thigh.

And when she was strung out on the sweetness of it, he returned to her throat and bit her so hard she arched off the bed, her hands digging into his shoulders as the startling pain liquefied into hot, needy aftershocks. "Fucking *hell*, Deacon."

"Not sorry," he rasped. He moved again, sliding

lower to settle on his knees between her thighs. "These are nice."

His finger brushed her underwear, where the thinnest ribbon of lace lined the waistband. Not the hand-tatted stuff that decorated Maricela's more elaborate gowns, but even machine-manufactured lace from Sector Eight was a frivolity for anyone who hadn't grown up noble. "I got them the first day I went into the market as a Rider."

"They suit you." He peeled the lace down. "But they have to go."

She lifted her hips to help him, but as the cotton dragged past her toes and vanished over the side of the bed, she felt the first stab of vulnerability. There was naked, and then there was *exposed*—and sprawled back on her bed with Deacon kneeling between her thighs, his gaze hot as it drifted over her body...

Arousal and nervous anticipation tangled together until she couldn't find the line that separated them, and she turned that nervous energy into action by cupping her breasts as she locked gazes with Deacon.

"Impatient." A low groan rolled out of him as he stretched out on the bed beside her. His skin blazed hot against hers, and his cock pressed into her hip. She started to reach for him, but as soon as her hand left her breast, Deacon's mouth replaced it, redefining *blazing* and *hot* as his tongue lingered on her nipple.

Then he tightened his lips and sucked, and Ana's priorities narrowed to getting his hands or her hands or *something* between her legs before the empty pulsing ache shredded what was left of her sanity.

As if he'd anticipated the need, his fingers were already sliding down her body. He hummed around her nipple, the sound anything but soothing. It vibrated through her, deepening the ache. And when his hand finally, *finally* reached her pussy, he touched her lightly, the rough pads of his fingertips barely grazing her outer lips, forcing her to chase the caress.

He was maddening. He was a goddamn tease.

And she was going to be damned if his control outlasted hers.

She tried to still her hips, not to whimper as his touch returned, so soft, so careful. She knew his strategy now—recognized it, even, from the countless times she'd faced off against him in the ring. Endless patience erupting into decisive action, a shock that left his opponent staggering.

The spot where he'd bitten her still throbbed hotly. Knowing the next sneak attack was coming should have made it easier. Instead, anticipation twisted, her body trembled, and every flex of his arm had her tensed for a rough, direct touch right where she needed it most.

Instead, his teeth closed on the painfully tight peak of her nipple.

A startled moan escaped her, and her senses reeled. Pleasure brightened into pain, then subsided into pleasure once more. She dug her fingers into his arm just to have something to cling to. But when the shock faded, she followed his arm down to where his fingers cupped her—still so gentle—and pushed hopelessly at his hand.

As if anyone could move Deacon before he damn well wanted to move.

A moment later, his hand flexed, and he drank in her gasp with his lips on hers. "Show me."

The heel of his hand pressed down against her clit, *finally*. She moaned and gave him what he wanted, guiding his touch until he was rocking in the quick, rough rhythm she needed when she was already this turned on. Pleasure roared over her, driving her toward a dizzying orgasm, and she flung her arm aside and wallowed in the confidence of his touch and the intentness of his focus.

Being the recipient of Deacon's undivided attention was like drinking the finest O'Kane liquor straight from the bottle—hot, intoxicating, and likely to leave her hung over in the morning.

And worth it. As the first orgasm broke over her, she turned her face to his cheek to muffle her helpless moan. It burned through her like wildfire, fierce and unrelenting, and she found herself clutching his arm again, unsure if she wanted to still his touch or beg for more.

"So wet." His low whisper tickled her ear. "So ready." He opened her, delving deeper in another teasing quest that ended with the heady thrust of two fingers entering her. They were strong and thick and it *had* been a while, long enough for her to feel the stretch as she arched her hips into his hand.

Her body rallied, as if she hadn't just ground her way to release against his damn hand. Maybe she could blame the illicit thrill of the forbidden, the way every touch felt like something she'd stolen, something she was never supposed to have.

It had to be that. Because if this was just what Deacon did to her...

Shuddering, she sank her nails into his arm until she knew he'd have little marks tomorrow and bit the lobe of his ear. "Do you want me to come around your fingers?"

His hand jerked, driving his fingers into her deeper. Harder. "I want you to come all over me, princess."

"Then stop holding back." She pulled away so she could meet his eyes—his dark, dangerous eyes—and dragged them all the way down into debauchery. "Show me why you're the fucking boss."

His eyes flashed, but all he did was lick his lower lip. "It's not that easy to push me, Ana." Then his fingers moved deliberately inside her, just as slowly as before, but with a determined purpose that curled her toes.

She knew what he was trying to do, but she wasn't prepared for him to get there so *fast*. Her hips jolted off the bed as his fingers brushed her G-spot, and her whole body spasmed when he returned, centering his touch on the place that built tense pressure so quickly she tried to squirm away.

But his leg rested heavily over one of hers, and wiggling just opened her to him even more. She panted, her fingers clenching helplessly on the rumpled quilt, and told herself not to whimper. Not to plead.

Not to *beg*.

"That's right." His free hand slid into her hair, anchoring her. "It's there, all you have to do is take it."

It was too much. *Too much*, especially when he shifted his thumb to nudge her sensitized clit with every strong thrust. This wouldn't be a swift orgasm that burned through her fast and clean. The cliff he was driving her toward ended with a swift drop into an endless chasm. It would be messy and raw and vulnerable, three things she usually hated.

Three things that were *turning her the fuck on* right now.

So she closed her eyes and took it—every rock of his fingers, his low, filthy murmurs, the clever, knowing touch of his thumb as it sparked bright lights behind her eyes with each rough caress. She took the heat of his skin on hers and the tickle of his breath and the way he groaned as her body began to tense and clench around his fingers.

She took the sharp tug against her scalp as his fist tightened in her hair, as well as the tingles that started deep inside her, a warning that she was close, so close, so yearningly, desperately close—

And when frustrated heat finally bloomed into fierce, overwhelming relief, she took the pleasure. She took it greedily, riding his fingers, so blissed out on the feeling that she wasn't even self-conscious about the depth of her orgasm and the slick sound of his fingers fucking into her.

Deacon's open mouth traveled over her—her shoulders, throat, cheeks, breasts—trailing groans across sensitized skin. But as his fingers stilled, he pulled away to tower over her, his weight braced on one rigid arm.

Her brain was still buzzing on the high, but her body knew what to do. Muscle memory kicked in, and she surged up and rolled him onto his back, coming over him with her knees sinking into the bed on either side of his hips and the unyielding length of his cock snug against her still-fluttering pussy.

Ana braced both hands against his chest and struggled to catch her breath. "You are a filthy fucker, you know that?"

He didn't answer, just lifted her hips in an iron grip and drove into her.

The shock of it knocked the air back out of her lungs. Her pleasure-drunk senses reeled, unable to reason past *big* and *hard* and *full*. Her fingers curled, nails pricking his chest, and she had to lock her elbows to stay upright when he dragged her back down, sinking even deeper.

"Fuck—" It was all she could get out. God, the stretch of him inside her was exquisite. It didn't matter that she was slick from two orgasms. The friction of the slightest shift of her hips scraped across sensitive nerves, and she was starting to wonder if going for the full Deacon experience had been smart.

"Take it," he murmured again, soft words full of explicit, undeniable command. "Ride me."

Take it. Funny how such simple words could sound so filthy—and how they could contain shades of meaning. She'd taken his fingers passively, wallowing in all the pleasure he had to offer. But for all his steely-fingered grip and domineering gaze, there was nothing passive in the way she rolled her hips to glide up his cock and slam back down.

She *took* him. Claimed him. Dug her fingers deeper into his chest, not caring if she left behind marks, and used the strength she'd cultivated for violence toward a much more enjoyable pursuit—finding the perfect angle so that his cock dragged over every place inside her that was hungry for touch.

She took every damn inch of his cock, and took her pleasure with it. And with her eyes, she dared him to meet her thrusts, dared him to take back the power she seized every time she clenched her pussy around him and drove a groan from his throat.

His hands trembled as they slid up her body to cup her breasts. He squeezed them too roughly, a delicious slip in his unending self-control. She shuddered and threw her head back, thrusting her breasts into his hands and moaning when he pinched her nipples.

She had come too hard to rebound into another orgasm. But riding him still felt good, and the noises he made and the way his body tensed beneath her felt better. But the roughness of his touch, the crack in his rigid demeanor—*that* twisted her up again.

Shameless now, she caught one of his hands and dragged it down her body. She felt the first brush of his thumb all the way to her toes, and her rhythm faltered as she realized how close she was. So close the blood roared in her ears, so close his name fell from her lips—a tortured moan, and then a plea, and then a chant as he lifted his hips to meet each thrust, slamming into her roughly enough to send her hurtling over the edge.

He flipped her over onto her back, grinding her into the mattress as he fucked her through the pleasure, through the violent waves of it crashing over her. He rode her orgasm to his own, every muscle shaking as he went rigid, threw his head back—

And for a moment, he was utterly naked.

Ana struggled through the haze, scrambling to fix his expression in her memory. Deacon, unguarded. His lips parted, his eyes closed, his face contorted with pleasure so raw it looked like pain.

Then he slumped on top of her, his face buried in the hollow of her neck, his ragged breaths hot on her damp skin.

The tenderness she thought she'd banished roared up again, and she knew it was mostly whatever chemical cocktail took over your brain when you'd been well and truly fucked. But she still wrapped her arms and legs around him, holding him close enough to feel the rapid thump of his heart against her breast.

With one last groan, Deacon rolled away and blinked up at the ceiling. "I'm still wearing my boots."

"And your pants." Her muscles had liquefied, but somehow she managed to roll onto her side and prop her head up on her hand—the same positions they'd found themselves in on the mats the other night.

Except this time she didn't have to squint—they *were* in her bed and it *was* impossibly intimate.

She reached up and brushed her fingers through

his spiky hair. At the temples, the tiniest smattering of silver dusted the dark strands, like stars in a night sky. She smoothed her thumb over them and ignored the funny flip in her stomach. "Want me to take them off?"

"I shouldn't stay," he rasped. "Training ceremony's tomorrow. You need your rest."

"I'm not the one who got hit in the head," she retorted, though she dropped her hand to his chest. "But you're right. You probably shouldn't stay, either way. If people see you coming out of my room in the morning..."

"They'll talk," he agreed, then turned his head to meet her gaze. "It bothers you."

She shrugged and rolled to her back so she wouldn't have to look into his too-understanding eyes. "It wouldn't bother me if no one would make a big deal out of it. But people watch me. They watch to see if I really deserve to be here, or if you let me in for...other reasons."

He snorted. "I didn't let you in. I don't choose the Riders, I only comm—" He bit off the words. "I don't choose the Riders."

"But Gideon listens to you." She nudged him with her elbow. "And you'll command the Riders again."

"I don't know that, and neither do you."

"I know it." Ana rolled upright, found her discarded underwear tossed across her desk, and pulled them on. "You need to stop hiding from everyone else. I know you think you're giving them space, but I know what it feels like from this side, too." She glanced back at him. "It feels like you don't trust us."

"Ana," he chided softly.

"Hey, I get it now." She arched an eyebrow. "But that's because you *talk* to me."

"I'll handle it." He stretched slowly, then buttoned his pants and swung his legs over the side of her bed. "I told you I would, and I intend to."

"Good." Her shirt was in a puddle on the floor. Ana swept it up and hauled it over her head, wincing when her hands encountered the disheveled tangle of curls on the top of her head.

Just the memory of Deacon's fingers tugging through the strands, destroying the sloppy bun, brought the tingles back, and she banished them with an irritated shake of her head as she retrieved Deacon's shirt. But when she turned, she was struck by the image of him perched on the edge of her bed, shirtless and mussed and more relaxed than she'd seen him in...

Ever. She'd *never* seen Deacon relaxed.

The urge to crawl into his lap and kiss him until *relaxed* turned into *hungry* again nearly overwhelmed her. So much for fucking him out of her system. He was lodged under her skin more deeply than ever, which wasn't a surprise. She'd known going into this that it was stupid, just like she'd known every time she talked back to him that the smarter path was silence.

She always knew what she *should* do around Deacon. But she could never seem to do it.

Irritated with herself, she tossed the shirt at him—mostly to avoid getting close enough to touch him. "You should eat with us tomorrow morning, too."

A wide grin curved his lips as he caught his shirt. "Yes, ma'am."

Oh, *God*. Now he was being charming. Relaxed Deacon was bad enough. But charming, teasing, sweet Deacon?

It was like she had put her foot down on what she thought was solid ground only to discover ice. Slippery, treacherous ice that could crack under her weight at any moment. She struggled to summon a scowl, but the dancing warmth in his usually chilly eyes had her stomach doing backflips. "Oh, get out of here. You're old and you need your sleep."

His low laugh rocked her, but not as strongly as his hands on her shoulders. He spun her around and kissed her—nothing as simple or straightforward as a *good night* or a *thank you* or even a *who are you calling old?* It was pure promise, that kiss, slow and hot and sure, and Ana stopped caring if she plunged through the ice—the deep, dark depths of whatever lay beneath it could claim her as long as Deacon kept kissing her.

He finally pulled away, his eyes twinkling. "See you in the morning."

Then he was gone.

Ana shut the door behind him and leaned against it, her body a riot of conflicting emotions. Lazy satisfaction, bone-deep weariness—along with the tiniest hint of freshly stirred arousal.

They had fucked so hard she'd feel it tomorrow, which wasn't ideal considering the circumstances. She'd have to spar in front of the Rios family, with Deacon watching, and every twinge would remind her just how hot it was to climb on and ride him.

Groaning, she thumped her head against the door once. Another stray curl escaped her scrunchie and slipped into her eyes, and she blew out an exasperated breath.

Maybe it was good that the training ceremony was tomorrow. The ritual could serve as a much-needed reminder of just how high the stakes were. All those little girls, and all their dreams.

If that couldn't anchor her to solid ground, nothing could.

maricela

There were times that hearkened back to Maricela's childhood so strongly that it almost hurt. She clung to that pain, because it made the memories real. Some people preferred memories like pearls—precious, rare, smooth to the touch. Maricela had her share of those, but what she treasured most were the *im*perfect ones. The ones you knew had to be true because they were too complicated to be fantasies.

The ceremonial training days in the palace courtyard evoked that nostalgia more easily than anything else. They had begun in the days of the Prophet's rule, when his children had trained alongside the volunteer guard. As he had gained more power, the purpose had slowly shifted, evolving into a demonstration of the guards' skills, a show for the Prophet's benefit.

By the time Maricela had come along, the guards

had abandoned the ceremony entirely. Gideon had picked it up for his Riders as a way for them to display their talents to the family they'd sworn to protect— and, in return, receive their sincerest gratitude.

As a child, she'd spent those days in rapt fascination, sitting between her mother and her sister Isabela, watching blades flash and trick shots split arrows as Gideon commanded his men. It was half battle and half exhibition, all of the excitement of war with none of the danger.

The ceremony had taught her the value of spectacle. And then it taught her about death.

His name was Radek. He wasn't one of the first Riders, or the most well-known. He was never sainted, and there were no monuments dedicated to him, just a single, smiling portrait on the wall in the Riders' inner sanctum. But Maricela still remembered him, his laugh and his flashing eyes and his broad, easy grin.

Mostly, she remembered settling down on a blanket one warm spring day, ice pop in hand, to watch the training—only to realize that she hadn't seen Radek in months. But when she asked her mother about it, all she would say was, "He's no longer with us, Mari."

Not the clearest answer to give a child. But the day Maricela figured out what it meant was the day she finally understood the Riders—even with his death portrait already outlined on the temple wall, Radek had smiled, laughed, fought. *Lived.*

Every day as if it was his last, because it very well might be. And, eventually, it was.

The training ceremony looked different now. A casual gathering more than anything, because there weren't enough Riders left to fall into anything resembling a formation. The war had taken its toll on every sector, and in One, the price had been exacted on the

Riders.

"Maricela." Her sister swatted her lightly on the thigh with the fan she held in one hand. "You haven't listened to a word I've said, have you?"

"Mmm, no." A blithe admission that most wouldn't have dared to make. "I was watching Lucio go through his kata. Is that judo or aikido? I think I'd like to learn."

Isabela heaved a put-upon sigh, and Maricela hid a smile behind her own fan. Her oldest sister was the religious leader of their sector, the most powerful woman among them. But to Maricela, she would always simply be *Bela*, the person who had taught her how to braid her own hair and covered for her when she broke their mother's favorite vase.

She could be a little self-important sometimes. And since so few people in the sector were at liberty to poke and tease Isabela Rios, Maricela considered the job hers, by right and responsibility.

Unfortunately, no amount of teasing could distract Isabela when she was on a mission. "I *said*," she repeated archly, "that I had lunch with Estela Reyes yesterday. And she was very eager to open negotiations for a betrothal between you and Nita."

Maricela should have expected it, honestly. Ever since Reyes had joined the Riders instead of marrying her, his appalled parents had been *very eager* to find an acceptable alternative that would still ally their family with the Rios clan.

But *Nita*? Maricela dismissed the idea with a swish of her fan. "She's one of my best friends, and completely uninterested in marrying me. You may as well forget it."

"Maricela…" This time, Isabela's sigh was long-suffering. "Sweetheart, in our position, marriage isn't always about interest. Especially not your first marriage. A convenient arrangement could allow Nita substantial freedom, and give you both plenty of time to yourselves before anyone begins to wonder about children."

Kora was *so* lucky she'd already settled down with Ashwin, so she didn't have to listen to these lectures. "Children? Really?"

"Plenty of time," Isabela repeated. "You're still young. But I was only nineteen when I chose my first husband."

"Well, it's not like you did that out of some keen sense of duty. You married John because you were desperately in love with him."

"I loved John," her sister conceded. "But not as much then as I do now. Love blossoms in a relationship. Leo came to us through a pragmatic arrangement with his family, and I love him just as much." She reached out. "You're so fond of Nita, Mari—I wish you'd at least *consider* it."

"I don't doubt how much you love your husbands and wives, Isabela." No one with eyes could. "But I'm not ready to settle down yet. I've never even had a proper lover, for Christ's sake."

That silenced Isabela for a moment. She frowned slightly while absently fanning herself. The resulting breeze stirring her long, loose brown hair. "Well," she said finally. "If that's an obstacle, perhaps you should remedy it."

Maricela laughed.

Isabela swatted her again. "I'm serious. Obviously, certain precautions must be taken to ensure your safety, but any of the royal guard can be trusted." A flick of Isabela's wrist waved the fan toward the men currently demonstrating their skills with swords. "Or the Riders. You could do far worse in a first lover. And with the Riders, there's no danger of...complicated attachments."

She *did* sound serious. Maricela's cheeks flamed. "Every single one of the Riders looks at me and sees a little sister. There's no way one of them would climb into my bed."

"Don't be silly."

"Reyes couldn't bring himself to do it, and he'll fuck anything that moves."

"*Maricela.*" Isabela cast her eyes heavenward. "If you'd given that boy any encouragement at all, he would have done his duty, and we wouldn't be in this situation."

When Maricela opened her mouth, Isabela held up a finger. "Listen to me. This is a volatile time. You know that the noble families have always maneuvered for position and influence amongst themselves, but with new trade opportunities springing up since the end of the war, it's more important than ever that we ensure all of their interests are aligned with ours. We need a tie to the Reyes family. Soon."

"Then maybe Gideon should marry Nita." Maricela barely managed to keep a straight face. Isabela would swallow her own tongue before she tried to pressure him into something like that.

Shockingly, Isabela just shrugged. "Don't think I haven't tried to convince him, but he's being...obstinate about her age. He says he's not interested in a wife whose christening he attended."

"So you're stuck with nothing but stubborn siblings." Maricela reached past her sister to retrieve a beer from the ice bucket on the bench beside her. "Sucks to be you."

"You're impossible." But there was a fondness to her tone, and she smoothed a few strands of Maricela's hair back into place. "Fine, I'll play politics with Estela Reyes. But *you* should think about finding yourself a lover. A patient, generous one. You know, Gabe has quite a reputation with the initiates."

"Oh, I know." The only difference between Gabe and Reyes was that Gabe was more discreet. But the initiates still talked, and Maricela had spent more than one evening being regaled by blushing tales of Gabe's prowess.

But she couldn't take a lover who would be related to any of her potential future spouses—it didn't bother everyone, but it would bother her—so that left out all the Riders from noble families. Maricela screwed off the cap of her beer and took a long drink as she perused the courtyard.

Lucio had abandoned his forms and was examining a gleaming rifle that Bishop had just commissioned from the gunsmith. Either of them would be a fine choice, except that Lucio had never shown the slightest bit of sexual interest in *anyone* that she could remember. And Bishop liked to ruffle her hair sometimes, like she was still ten years old.

Ana was sparring with Hunter near one of the fountains, and Deacon was deep in conversation with Reyes. Ana and Deacon had potential, but they'd spent the entire morning so far sneaking secret glances at one another, and the message couldn't have been plainer if they'd shouted it from the roof of the palace—if she wanted Ana or Deacon as a lover, she'd have to take Ana *and* Deacon.

She was *not* ready for that.

Zeke was in the middle of the courtyard, with most of Isabela's children literally climbing him like a piece of play equipment. He growled and roared as they clung to his arms, laughing and screaming with glee, only to be flipped upside-down a moment later.

Isabela adored Zeke, and she would approve wholeheartedly of her baby sister forming a temporary attachment to him. But there was something deceptive about Zeke—he seemed nice and easy and simple on the surface, but beneath that...

He'd been running at a fever pitch for months, and just looking at him exhausted Maricela.

The thud of a knife driving into wood caught her attention. Ivan was practicing his throws off in a corner of the courtyard, away from everyone else. He wore his usual severe expression, but that did nothing to diminish his appeal. If anything, it only made her want to clear his stormy frown with a smile, perhaps even a laugh. If she was lucky.

Maricela moved without thinking, muttering an apology to Isabela as she snagged a second beer from the bucket.

He glanced up at her approach. The final knife left his fingers without him looking, yet somehow still sank into the target near its painted center. Ivan drove his fingers through his short blond hair to smooth it down before turning to nod at her. "Maricela."

He was wearing a blue-gray shirt that made his eyes look ridiculously bright. But she was burning up in light colors and no sleeves, so he had to be sweltering. "It's hot," she breathed, then immediately fought a wince. "I brought you a beer."

"Thank you." He accepted the frosty bottle from her hand and held it to the strong column of his neck.

Her throat went dry. She would have rolled her eyes if he'd been trying to make her think filthy thoughts, but somehow the fact that it didn't even *occur* to him, it just *happened*—

She swallowed a whimper. "Do you have a date

yet? To the midsummer festival, I mean."

One of his eyebrows rose marginally. "A date?"

"Someone to go with," she elaborated. "You talk, laugh, have fun. Go home together afterwards."

With his brow still furrowed, he opened his beer and took a sip. "I don't date, Maricela."

There was a tiny chip of wood caught in a fold of his shirt near his broad shoulder. She reached out and brushed it free as an excuse to touch him. "Could I persuade you to make an exception?"

"Are you asking for an escort?"

Anyone else, and she would have giggled at the absurdity of the situation. To hear her sister talk, Maricela only had to snap her fingers or wave her hand, and potential lovers would come running.

In reality, not so much.

But, somehow, she didn't want to laugh. In fact, part of her positively wanted to cry. So she smiled and nodded. "Right, an escort. I couldn't think of the word. Would you be so kind?"

"Of course." He took a step towards her, looming into her space, so close she could smell the sharp pine scent of his aftershave. For a moment, she thought he might have understood her intentions, after all, but when he leaned down to her ear, his whisper was purely practical. "With the heightened security risk, you should always have a Rider or one of the royal guard with you. It's important."

"My hero." She meant it as a tease, the kind he had probably come to expect from her, but it came out sounding solemn.

His blue, blue eyes were equally serious as he inclined his head, and it was more than agreement. It was almost a bow. "My princess."

Princess. He offered her his arm. She took it, and

let him lead her toward the refreshments table without argument.

At the end of the day, there were worse things to be.

twelve

Ana was dropping her guard too early.

She and Hunter had been sparring for nearly an hour, and Deacon had been watching in between nods and murmured conversational encouragement to Reyes. He'd promised Ana he would talk to the rest of the Riders, but all Reyes seemed to be interested in chatting about was Davin, the baker's son, and how imaginative he could be when properly, carnally motivated.

There were some things Deacon simply didn't need to know.

So he watched Ana instead. She ducked swings that would have certainly taken her down, only to immediately leave herself open for more by dropping her blocks at the last moment. Hunter couldn't match her for speed, but if he managed to land a blow, she'd be left reeling.

But the fight was taking its toll on him, and slowly Deacon realized that was her intention—keep him committed to those heavy, draining swings by luring him in with the hazy promise of a solid blow, then dance out of the way at the very last millisecond. Wear him down and wait him out.

He was so proud he didn't know whether to laugh or cry.

"So then he gets all nervous, right? And I'm thinking he's about to suggest some sincerely kinky shit, but all he does is ask me if I've ever been to that brothel near the border with Eight, the Pink Pearl. I swear, Deacon, it was so goddamn cute. You wouldn't believe—"

"Reyes," he barked.

"Yeah, boss?"

Deacon pinched the bridge of his nose between his thumb and forefinger. "Will you please just tell me what I need to do to make things right between us? What sort of penance do I have to pay?"

Reyes pressed his lips together, then burst out laughing. "This *is* your fucking penance. I was wondering how long you'd last. Zeke owes me fifty credits."

Deacon glowered at him. "Reyes—"

He was already backing away, well out of arm's reach. "Don't worry, I'll finish the story some other time. You should go have a drink." He was still chuckling when he ducked around a hedge and out of sight.

"Want me to kick his ass?"

Bishop was standing behind him, holding two beers between the fingers of one hand. Deacon shook his head as he reached for one of them. "And miss the chance to do it myself? Never."

Bishop snorted and twisted the top off his beer. "I wish you would. He gets unmanageable if someone doesn't smack him down once in a while. And I don't think Ashwin's trying very hard. Those two like fighting way too much."

"Eh, let 'em have their fun." He eyed Bishop over the rim of his bottle. "What's up?"

"Figured we should talk. You know, about those things you wanted me to think on."

"Right." It was impossible to know just from looking at him how Bishop was dealing with the revelations about Deacon's past. He'd seen the man jump into gory, screaming fights with a stony expression that looked more like boredom than bloodlust. "What's the verdict?"

Bishop turned to where Isabela sat, surrounded by her spouses now, with a dozen children clambering over their parents, demanding immediate attention. His gaze took in the sweetly domestic scene, still utterly unmoved. "Not all of us who were born here belong here, you know. I came into this world...angry. The harder my family tried to press me into a peaceful, obedient little box, the more that rage grew. They couldn't understand why I was dark and morbid and twisted. They told me I was broken, made me think I was evil."

"You, evil?" He was a hard man, no one would argue with that. But Bishop would step in front of a bullet before he would use his power to harm an innocent. "That's bullshit."

"Maybe. But when all you know is peace and love, there's not a lot of room in your world for people who see shadows." Bishop gestured with his bottle, pointing to Ana and Hunter and then Gabe. "Some of them? They were born for this place. They see the hope in someone when it's barely more than a flicker. They'll nurse it into a blaze to light up the world. We need them to keep us honest. But they need us, too. Because the rest of the world isn't Sector One. There are plenty of shadows out there."

Once upon a time, there were shadows in One, as well. Gideon had nearly broken himself trying to stamp them out, and for the first time, Deacon realized that he'd been a *part of that*. Bishop could stand here and marvel at how pure and clean this place was, because those battles had already been fought and won.

Now they just needed to *keep* Sector One that way.

He drew in a deep breath. "So you understand, then."

"Well enough." Bishop held up his beer. "I don't care what you've done. I care that you're here, bleeding every day to make shit better. I'll follow you as long as you keep doing that."

It meant a lot, because Bishop wasn't just reassuring him or trying to make him feel better. He was telling the flat, unvarnished truth. "Thanks."

"You're welcome." Bishop drained half his beer and nodded. "I promised Lucio I'd fight him next."

"He thinks too much," Deacon advised. "Don't be afraid to use that against him."

"I never am." He gave Deacon a rare grin and strode off to where Lucio had just finished a bout with Gabe by knocking him into the dirt.

Ana and Hunter had finished sparring, as well. They stood by the station where the acolytes were serving snacks and drinks, downing water and laughing like beating the shit out of each other was the most fun either of them had had in forever. Deacon watched as Ana draped a towel around her neck and used the ends to wipe her face.

"She kicked his ass," Zeke said from behind him, his tone light and cheerful. "Maybe you shoulda made *her* boss, boss."

"It's about temperament." Deacon turned to face him and almost—*almost*—cracked a smile at the dozens of tiny footprints smudging Zeke's clothes. "Hunter can make decisions when he needs to, and then stand behind them. That's the most important thing."

"I dunno, Ana's pretty stone cold when she wants to be." Zeke tilted his head and studied Deacon. He had that look in his eyes, the one that meant no one was going to like what came out of his mouth next. "Councilman Chadwick."

"What about him?"

Zeke waved his hand in a *go on* gesture. "I have an actual fucking Suicide King—well, former King—standing in front of me. Obviously, I'm going to ask about the biggest conspiracy theory Eden's ever had."

This was one assassination Deacon had no trouble owning up to. "The Kings pulled the hit on Chadwick," he confirmed. "Paid for by one of his fellow councilmen, if I'm not mistaken. I wasn't part of the planning on it, but I heard it went off without a hitch."

"*That* was without a hitch?" Zeke snorted. "He walked into the most expensive restaurant in Eden and shot the bastard in front of three dozen witnesses. Then he just...stood there, waiting to get arrested."

"Of course he did. He wasn't a very good marksman, so he had to be close to take the shot. There was one thing he was really good at, though."

Zeke's eyebrows went up. "The disappearing act?"

Deacon finished his beer. "Never saw a cell that could hold the guy. The old man called him Houdini."

"Goddammit," Zeke breathed, eyes wide with delight and honest glee. "Abel was *right*. Eden told everyone they'd executed him, but a crime like that? They would have given him the firing squad in the town square at high noon as a warning to the rest of us. Abel swore he hacked the records and found out the guy vanished."

"Yep. He erased a human stain from existence and made a shit ton of money doing it. Those were the jobs no one minded doing—the ones you might have taken for free." He shrugged and held out both hands. "Okay, here it is. Free shot, just this once. If you're curious about any other Council assassinations, ask away."

Zeke's eyes went even wider. "Wait, there were *more?*"

There were always more. "The best hits don't look like hits. They look like heart attacks, strokes, accidents. Drug overdoses. No one asking questions means no loose ends."

"Jesus. How often did those assholes kill each other?"

"How many active Council members died?"

"Fuck." Zeke slid his hand through his spiky blond hair, his eyes barely focused. Deacon could see the wheels turning, and he knew Zeke was already antsy to get back to his tablet and start pulling up death records.

But when he spoke again, it was with uncharacteristic seriousness. "Chadwick killed my parents, you know."

It was the absolute fucking last thing Deacon expected to hear. "He what?"

"Killed my parents." Zeke's gaze snapped back to Deacon's. "They were part of a resistance cell working to destabilize the Council. My mom was a hacker. My dad did black-market shit. They got snatched up when I was thirteen. I didn't know why for years, but the first time I breached the Council mainframe, that's what I was looking for. The name on the order. It was Chadwick. They were marked as killed while resisting arrest."

Holy shit. "Then I'm especially glad he's dead. But the Kings didn't kill him because he deserved it, Zeke. They killed him because the price was right. Don't forget that."

"I know." Zeke shrugged and looked away. "Trust me, when I went digging for information on jobs the Kings have pulled, I found a whole lot of ugly. You did some fucked-up shit, boss. But a lot of people in this world have been doing fucked-up shit for years. At least you know it."

Always, even when precious few other people knew or remembered or gave a shit. "Want to hug it out?"

"Think it'll make everyone else jealous?"

"Of course it will. I mean, you've seen me."

Zeke recoiled in dramatically overdone shock. "Deacon, I think you just made a joke. Are you feeling okay?"

Deacon punched him on the arm. "Get lost before I make another one."

"Perish the thought." Zeke put two fingers to his forehead in a cheerful salute. "Boss."

Ana had moved on to the cluster of blankets and benches where Isabela sat with her family. She was talking animatedly with two of the older girls, who were mimicking punches and grabs while she patiently corrected their form.

A moment later, her shoulders stiffened slightly. She didn't look over at him, but he knew she felt the weight of his gaze.

Soon.

Movement at the corner of his eye drew his gaze. Gideon was seated on a bench at the edge of the court-yard, a bucket of beer at his feet. He raised one eyebrow and crooked a finger in summons.

He had a beer open and on offer as soon as Deacon sank down beside him. "You've been making good use of the afternoon."

So he'd been watching. "Someone told me that my plan to give the men three days of space before I approached them again wasn't such a great idea, after all."

"I'm glad you listened. I know you meant well..." Gideon smiled gently. "This will change how they think and feel about you. How they see you. But that's not always bad, is it?"

Embracing change wasn't something that came easily to him. "It is what it is."

"I suppose that's true." Gideon returned his gaze to the festivities spread out before them. "The royal guard has stepped up patrols and is prepared for trouble. Ashwin even identified a few points of vulnerability he noticed during his initial surveillance of the sector. We should be in good shape."

"What about the midsummer festival?" It wasn't particularly dangerous, no more than business as usual at the marketplace, but he had to ask.

"It will go forward as usual."

"Sir?"

"We can't let life in Sector One grind to a halt every time someone wants to kill us, Deacon." Gideon's smile was wry. "Maybe we've all been living too soft for too long. Before war with Eden, we got used to weeks and months going by without any real danger at all. But even during the worst of our civil wars in the past, we got up every day and we laughed and we loved and we lived. We're going to do it now, too."

The best of what Sector One had to offer, just like Bishop had said. "Understood. I'll help Hunter coordinate with the guard."

"Good. The people need this celebration. We were still grieving and struggling through winter and spring. But I think we're ready to look forward now." Gideon clapped a hand to Deacon's shoulder. "And I like the shape of the future we're building."

The answer came as easy as breathing this time, easier than he ever thought it would. "So do I."

thirteen

As much as Ana usually valued the peaceful quiet of the Riders' common room, she also loved the parties.

The doors had been thrown open to the rapidly cooling night. Music throbbed from the unobtrusive speakers Zeke had installed in strategic corners. Dimmed lights left plenty of shadowed alcoves for stealing kisses—or more, if you dared—and the crackle of the hearth and dozens of candles cast romantic shadows and filled the air with spice and the clean, earthy smell of burning wood.

Grace was a new addition to the parties. Ana had gotten to know her as the sister of a fellow Rider—a sister Jaden had brought around more than some people thought was wise. The siblings from Sector Seven hadn't been raised to understand the emotional distance necessary between a Rider and the loved ones who one day would, inevitably, be left alone to mourn.

Sadness still shadowed Grace's eyes, even two months after her brother's death, and her reddish-blonde hair was pulled back in a messy ponytail. Its color, combined with her hazel eyes and the shape of her chin, reminded Ana forcefully of Jaden. Like Nita, she'd abandoned the robes common to Del's students. Instead, she wore khaki shorts and a flowing blouse as she curled up on the couch closest to the hearth, a sketchpad balanced on her bare legs.

Ana sank into the spot next to her with a smile. "Hey, what are you working on?"

Grace started, then covered the paper with her hand. "Nothing, it's—" She stopped, smiled, and sighed. "Sorry. Maricela asked me to make her something."

"Like a dress or something?"

"For special occasions." She moved her hand and tilted the pad toward Ana.

The sketch was still rough, with the figure's arms and legs fading away and an oval representing the head. But the dress was a masterwork—long flowing skirts split up past the knee and flaring out, as if caught in a wind. No sleeves. A neckline that plunged in a deep vee.

It gave the impression of somehow being tremendously formal and utterly sweet at the same time—like Maricela. "It looks perfect."

"Thank you." Grace lowered her voice. "I know she's just trying to help me out by giving me something to do, but I'm going to do it well."

Ana scanned the room again, but Maricela hadn't appeared yet. Deacon had—he was over in the corner with Zeke, nodding every so often at the torrent of words. But his gaze was on Ana, like it had been damn near all afternoon, and her skin prickled.

deacon

Forcing her gaze back to Grace, she told herself to ignore the tingle at the base of her neck. "How are you settling in at the temple? You've been there a couple of weeks now, right?"

"It's different," she confessed. "I'm not used to being around so many people all the time."

"And they're not exactly quiet, are they?" Ana enjoyed dropping in for an evening of socialization, but she also valued her ability to leave. "If you ever need hints about all the places you can hide on this compound, I'm your girl."

"I might take you up on that." Grace twirled her pencil idly between her fingers. "Deacon is staring at you."

Deacon needed to be more subtle. Ana was saved from trying to come up with an excuse for *why* by Nita's abrupt arrival in a swirl of multicolored skirts. She beamed at Grace and dropped a kiss to Ana's cheek before claiming the spare spot on the couch.

Then she leaned in closer to Ana. "Why's Deacon staring at you?"

Ana dug her nails into her palm and promised herself she would murder Deacon. Slowly. "Beats me. Why'd that new guardsman trail in here behind you like a puppy?"

Nita dismissed him with a wave of her hand that set her dozens of gold bracelets clattering. "He has a crush. He'll get over it, especially once he realizes the head cook's daughter's been watching him like he's the only man in the world." Nita glanced at Grace. "You have to watch out for the baby guardsmen. Protecting temple initiates is very romantic. I bet half a dozen of them are in love with you by autumn."

Grace looked so alarmed at the idea that Ana elbowed Nita and patted Grace's arm. "Don't listen to

159

her. Nita's an overachiever in that regard. I think she read too many pre-Flare tales about ladies of the court and their adoring knights."

And for all her fondness for playing in the mud, Nita still carried herself with an inborn grace that drew attention. Added to the tailored bodices that hugged her generous curves, her flawless golden skin, huge brown eyes, and full, sultry lips, it was probably a miracle *more* guardsmen didn't follow her around, begging to get their asses kicked by her overprotective brother.

Nita knew it. She winked at Ana with a laugh. "Those were my very favorite stories," she agreed. "There are worse things than innocent adoration."

The words were cheerful, but Ana knew Nita. Sure enough, the girl's gaze snuck to the right, fixing on Hunter for one brief, heart-wrenching moment.

Sympathy tightened Ana's chest. If the prohibition against Riders forming attachments was strong, the idea of a noble heiress like Nita tying herself to a man with a doomed future was inconceivable. It didn't matter that Hunter came from a noble family himself— the ink on his arm condemned him.

Nita's family would drag her back home by her hair and lock her in the cellar until she regained her senses if they even *thought* she was considering it. And Hunter knew it. He was too responsible to allow an attachment that would only lead to her heartbreak. If he ever found out about Nita's crush, he'd do everything in his power to discourage it.

Maybe Ana was too hard on the children of the great families. In a sector built on the glory of following your heart, they were the only ones forbidden to love as they pleased. Money made up for a lot, but some boxes were too small to survive inside.

Nita caught Ana watching her and replaced her

happy mask. "Maybe you should go find out what Deacon wants. He looks pretty intent."

Ana glanced at him again. *Intent* was a weak word to describe his expression—it held all the heat and filthy promise of their last kiss, and it prompted her to squeeze her thighs together, as if that could relieve the sudden ache.

Trusting that Nita would see Grace through this first party, Ana rose. "I think I'll do that."

Deacon watched her as she started across the room, the corner of his mouth ticking up in a tiny smile. Ana judged the distance between them—and then veered hard left. When she reached the shadowed doorway, she glanced back over her shoulder, daring Deacon to follow her with one searing look.

She was nearly to the armory when his fingers brushed the bare part of her lower back beneath her shirt. She whirled and tangled her hand in his shirt, dragging him with her as she took another step back. "You have got to stop that."

"Stop what?" He spread his hand wide across the small of her back. "Touching you?"

"Stop *watching* me." Another step had her back to the armory door, Deacon's body pressing hers against the wood. She groped for the doorknob with her free hand. "You've been doing it all fucking day."

He shrugged one shoulder. "I like looking at you." He reached past her and twisted the knob.

The door swung open, and Ana nearly lost her balance. Deacon's hand tightened at the small of her back, steadying her. She tugged at his shirt and swung them into the dark room. When she caught the door with her boot and kicked it shut, the only illumination was faint moonlight streaming through the high, narrow windows.

It was enough. She gave Deacon's chest a shove, and was rewarded with the metallic clatter of his back knocking into a row of lockers. "And what are you thinking about while you're watching me?"

"Different things. How strong you are. How you don't let anything stand in your way." Instead of straightening, he leaned against the lockers and raised one eyebrow. "What you look like when you come."

Heat worked its way through her limbs and settled low in her body. "Well, that's not fair." His belt buckle was cool under her fingers as she rubbed her thumb over it, then slipped the leather free. "You got to see that a bunch of times. I only got to see you come once."

"And you're aiming to even the score."

She didn't know what she was aiming for. Sense had abandoned her. She hadn't thought this through, hadn't considered the angles. There were a hundred ways she could end up regretting this, and by tomorrow she'd have a list.

Tonight, she had the soft kiss of leather under her skin as she opened his belt. She had the giddy beat of her heart, the thrill of doing something so, so reckless. Damn near everyone who mattered in the world was a few dozen paces away...

And she was sliding to her knees in front of Deacon as her fingers worked the button on his jeans.

His eyes glinted as he braced one hand on the door, his arm flexing. "Everyone's right outside."

"*Now* you care?"

"Fuck, no." He rubbed his thumb over her cheek. "But you do. At first I thought it scared you, because you want to keep this secret. But it's turning you on, isn't it?"

"Maybe." She turned to catch his thumb between

her teeth as his zipper rasped in the shadows. His calloused thumb was rough against her tongue, and she stared up at his moonlit face and met his shadowed eyes as she sucked hard.

He hissed in a breath, then scraped the pad of his thumb over her bottom teeth as he pulled it from her mouth. "Come on, Ana. You're strong, remember? You don't need to hide from the truth."

Everyone hid from some truths. Ana had faced plenty of hers head-on, but this one had sharp edges and felt alarmingly self-destructive. Maybe she'd finally found her own inner darkness, the one trait all Riders shared in one form or another. The naked willingness to throw themselves into whatever danger they could find.

And when they couldn't find enough of it, they created their own.

Ana curled her fingers under the edge of his underwear and pulled it slowly down. His cock was already hard and thick when she wrapped her fingers around it. His groan shot through her like an electric shock, and she *was* self-destructive, because even knowing they risked being overheard, all she wanted was to coax more of those sounds from him.

So she dragged her tongue up his shaft and closed her lips around the crown.

His fingers sank into her hair. "You left it down."

She licked her way around the head before pulling back to feather a breath over him. "You'll just mess it up if I don't."

"Is that—" Another flick of her tongue cut off the words. "Is that why?"

Ana answered by enveloping him with her mouth again, taking him as deep as she could. His fingers clenched in her hair until her scalp tingled, and the shivers continued down her spine. But it was still careful—too controlled, too deliberate.

So she set about unraveling his legendary composure.

He hissed in another breath when she teased her lips back up and shuddered when she sucked gently on the head. She cataloged his reactions, tormenting him with her hands and lips, licking from base to tip and finally gripping him in one hand as she slid her mouth down to meet her fingers.

But it wasn't until a sudden tightening of his fist provoked another wave of heat and a deep shudder that her teeth accidentally grazed his shaft.

"*Fuck*." His head fell forward. His eyes squeezed shut, and he wrapped his hand around hers, urging her fingers into a stronger grip.

There it was, the key to his self-control—the loss of her own. Ana moved her mouth back up his shaft, fast and messy, letting her teeth graze him again. With her lips brushing the head, she glanced up to meet his shadowed eyes. "Take it."

He groaned her name and cupped her face, stroking both thumbs over her lower lip as he tilted her head back a little. "Your mouth? Is fucking deadly, woman."

A drunk, giddy warmth filled her. Like the time Maricela had convinced her to drink a bottle of champagne—like the bubbles were beneath her skin and in her blood. "You like it that—"

He urged her mouth open, held her head steady, then thrust forward between her lips, and it was hotter than it had any right to be.

There was something different in his loss of control tonight—a heady mixture of rough and tender. His fingers locked her head in place as his cock filled her mouth, overwhelming her with the salty, bitter taste and the stretch of her lips as he pushed deeper, to the very edge of her comfort zone. But his thumbs swept in soft, encouraging strokes, and when he pulled back and thrust again, he knew just how deep she could take him.

Sweet and hard. Messy and careful. Perfect. She sucked when he let her and moaned around him and didn't care if it was sloppy and raw, because he was groaning with every stroke, low, guttural noises torn out of him as if against his will.

His hands closed on her shoulders *hard*, just shy of pain, and he dragged her up his body until they were face-to-face. He licked his lower lip, his burning gaze focused on her mouth. "I should have taken you to my bed."

He spun her around, lifting her as he switched their positions. The bank of lockers was cool against the skin bared by her shirt, but his fingers were hot on the button of her pants as he worked them open.

"Beds are overrated," Ana gasped out, bracing her hands on the lockers on either side of her as his fingers plunged into her underwear. He circled her clit lightly, a torment when she was so turned on his fingers slipped against her.

Growling, she slammed a fist into his shoulder. "Stop teasing."

Deacon nuzzled her cheek, then caught her earlobe between his teeth and bit down just as his fingertips pressed hard on her clit. Pleasure jolted through her, bringing her hips up off the locker. She wrapped one arm around his neck and clung to him as the next rough stroke of his fingers did something funny to her knees.

But nothing could stop the moan. It came from somewhere deep inside her, and she struggled to hold it in, struggled to stay quiet. She dug her teeth into both lips and pressed them to his cheek, muffling the noise as it spilled out in a broken whimper.

She sucked in a breath before he could circle his fingers again. "Don't let me scream."

"Uh-huh." He caught her mouth in a bruising kiss.

Her world became Deacon. The air she dragged into her lungs tasted like him. The moans that escaped disappeared into his kiss. His body held her upright as his fingers tried to destroy the ground beneath her feet.

He'd paid attention last night. He'd memorized the speed and pressure and rhythm she'd showed him, and he used it without mercy. He didn't even bother working his fingers inside her, and she would have killed him if he'd paused long enough to try, because her heart was already in her throat and she went up on her toes, straining, *reaching*—

His teeth closed on the tip of her tongue in a teasing scrape, a tiny shock, and she tensed. When his tongue swept over hers, suggestive, matching the tempo of his fingers on her clit, she shuddered and gave in.

It was the brightest orgasm she'd ever felt, blazing all the hotter when her head thumped back against metal, driving home the reminder of where they were. Every time she stepped into the armory she'd remember the way this *felt*—crushed up against a locker, coming in helpless waves as his fingers drew out the ecstasy and his mouth muffled her cries.

Pleasure careened toward hypersensitivity, and she whimpered and twitched her hips away. "Enough," she gasped, turning her face just enough to pant the word. "I can't—I need a second—"

"Shh." Deacon eased his hand free, balancing her weight between his body and the lockers as he touched her face. "Ana..."

She panted and turned her face into his hand, still shivering at the tiny aftershocks. But when she forced her eyes open, Deacon was watching her like she was the most precious, beautiful thing he'd ever seen, and she knew with sudden certainty that *this* was what she'd remember every time she reached for her locker.

Deacon, stroking her cheek, staring at her like she'd invented sunrise.

The quiet moment shattered with a rough knock on the door, and Reyes called out through it. "Sorry, boss. Gideon needs us."

Ice flooded her veins. Not because of Reyes's words—though Gideon interrupting a party had to be bad—but because Reyes had knocked. No one knocked on the armory door—on *any* public door—unless they knew that something private was happening on the other side.

Deacon lowered her until she stood firmly on the floor and steadied her before stepping back. She watched him through a numb haze as he calmly fixed his pants, as if his impressive erection hadn't been grinding into her hip a few seconds ago.

Reyes knew. Hell, everyone probably knew. She could walk back through the events that had led her here and clearly identify every reckless choice she'd made. Every adrenaline-filled dare. Every intoxicating flirtation with danger.

She hadn't just played with fire. She'd watched the flames die down and had reignited them again and again, because something inside her rebelled at anyone saying *no, you can't do that*—even if *she* was the person saying it.

Ana had taunted the flames. Now she'd find out how much of her house was going to burn down.

"Hey." Deacon straightened her shirt, then

buttoned her pants. "You're here because you deserve to be. You worked your ass off. This doesn't change that."

She blinked and forced herself to focus on his face. "You can't know that. No one can know that."

Another knock rattled the door, and Deacon sighed as he reached for it. He stopped with his hand on the knob, then pinned her with a questioning look. "You crawled my ass for assuming no one would want me around after they found out about my past. You trusted them with that. Why not with this?"

The words landed hard, but there was no time to *think* about them. Summoning up every lesson she'd ever learned about compartmentalization, she rolled her fear and uncertainty and doubt into the tightest ball she could manage and shoved it aside. Not perfect—and not healthy—but it would do for the night.

Her hair was a mess. She ran her fingers through it, straightening the curls until they at least looked like a purposeful chaotic tumble. Then she squared her shoulders and jerked her head in a nod to Deacon.

By the time he pulled open the door, she was a Rider. The only thing she'd ever wanted to be.

fourteen

It wasn't strange for Gideon to call the Riders together without notice when shit was going down. He had interrupted parties, projects, mealtimes. Hell, Deacon had only abandoned the habit of sleeping in his boots sometime in the past few years.

But he never, *ever* brought his baby sister with him, and that killed Deacon's lingering arousal faster than anything.

Maricela stood behind Gideon, her face pale and drawn. She'd twisted her hands in her skirt until it looked like the fabric might rip, and she kept her gaze cast down toward the floor.

Gideon, on the other hand, was furious.

The placid, benevolent leader of Sector One was gone, replaced by the steely-eyed man who'd formed the Riders through sheer grit and will, the man who had ridden out with them to deal his own share of necessary death.

He crossed his arms over his chest, every muscle rigid, and waited until Ana slipped into an empty seat around the huge strategy table. Then he stepped aside. Deacon saw the effort it took him to unclench his jaw and soften his voice as he reached out a hand to his sister. "Maricela, tell them what happened."

She blanched even paler. "I—I was visiting one of the temples. To bless the evening prayers."

It was a common enough occurrence, though she usually attended in the mornings. "Which temple?" Deacon asked.

"East. I didn't plan to stop in, but I was coming back from a dinner visit, and I had time..." She trailed off, nervously licked her lips, and glanced at Ivan. "I had guards with me."

"It's okay, sweetheart." Gideon put his arm around her shoulder and pulled her into a half hug. "Just tell them what happened, and we'll get you back to the house."

"I didn't find it until I was nearly home. I was looking through the prayer requests." She slipped one trembling hand into her pocket and pulled out a playing card. "This was tucked inside one of them."

Deacon's blood turned to ice.

As if he couldn't stand the thought of her touching it any longer, Gideon plucked it from her fingers and tossed it onto the table. It slid across the polished surface, stopping in the middle with the suicide king facing up. "They put it right into her goddamn hand."

And the guards had let them, because there was no overt threat, no attempts at violence—just someone masquerading as a faithful follower, pressing a card into Maricela's hand along with all the other written prayers and gratefully bestowed trinkets. A devious psychological taunt with a crystal-clear message: *look how easy it would have been.*

No wonder Maricela looked like she'd seen a ghost. It was a peculiar feeling, obliviously staring down death only to realize later just how close you had come to it.

Deacon picked up the card. He felt about a hundred years old as he turned it over in his hand. "The guards aren't equipped to deal with cat-and-mouse mind games."

"No, they're not." Gideon's eyes were still impossibly hard. "Which is why I want a Rider assigned to each of my sisters full-time until we've resolved this. And I want to resolve it soon."

There was one Rider dedicated to serving the Rios family above all else, and Deacon turned to him now. "Ivan, will you escort Maricela back to the palace? Stay with her until further notice." The guards would protect her from most threats, and he would take care of the rest.

Ivan rose and silently circled the table. When he reached Maricela and Gideon, he held out his arm, and she clung to it like only he could keep her from drowning. They walked out, and Deacon tilted his head toward Gideon. "Will Isabela tolerate a personal guard?"

"Not gracefully. But when I remind her that her ten children and four beloved spouses make for tempting hostages, she'll capitulate."

"Then I want Bishop with them."

Bishop nodded. "I know the head of Isabela's household guard. I can work with him."

"Good," Gideon said shortly. "Debrief with Deacon before you go, but I'd like you there tonight. As for Kora—"

"Kora's pregnant," Ashwin said abruptly. In the

silence that followed, his gaze sought and found Gideon's, and there was something wild and dangerous there. "Kora stays with me."

Gideon stared back at him, so stunned that this was obviously news to him. Deacon took a step closer to Ashwin, then another, until he could lay one hand on the man's shoulder. "I wouldn't have considered anything else. You're the only person I trust with her safety."

A little of the tension in him faded, but then he rose. "I should go find her."

"Not yet." Gideon held up a hand. "I'll sit with her until you're done here. But I need you to help Zeke figure out how we can get up-to-date intelligence on the Suicide Kings' headquarters. We're going to take the fight to them and end it."

He pinned them all with one last imperious look, then swept out of the barracks.

Shit. Deacon turned to Hunter. "I should have let you handle—"

The man shook his head, a tiny smile kicking up the corner of his mouth. "You got this. Right, guys?"

"Damn straight," Zeke agreed, and the others murmured agreement. Even Gabe gave a sharp nod without quite meeting Deacon's eyes.

"Okay, then. Ashwin, get Zeke going on the drone so you can get back to Kora. If he needs anything from you, he'll come to the palace."

"Got it." Zeke bounced out of his chair. "We'll probably need two or three days, minimum, if we want to do this without getting Ashwin's fancy drone shot out of the sky. So factor that into your planning."

Deacon caught his arm. "The important thing is to get it right." Zeke and Ashwin headed down the hall, and Deacon turned to Lucio. "You have your favorite rifle scoped and ready for long-range shots?"

Lucio lifted one eyebrow. "Always."

"Then use this time to brush up on your fundamentals. And what the hell?" He flipped the playing card across the room, where Lucio snatched it out of the air. "You may as well use that for target practice."

Reyes shifted his weight from one foot to the other and back again, the restless dance of someone ready to fight. "What about the rest of us?"

Ana was watching Deacon. Tense, wary—and maybe a little suspicious. As if she was remembering his offer to walk into the den of the Kings alone.

That wasn't an option, not anymore.

"Stay paired up, if you can," Deacon told them all. "And you heard Zeke. We have a few days—a week, tops. Use it."

Most of them heard the dismissal. Gabe rose and followed Reyes and Hunter toward the door. Lucio trailed after them, flipping the Kings' calling card between his fingers. Then it was just him and Ana, staring at each other across the expanse of the smooth wooden table.

"Tell me you're not going to do anything stupid," Ana said finally. "Promise me."

The same restless energy and anticipation that would have had him as riled up as Reyes any other time was absent. He felt numb. Exhausted. "Not in the next five minutes."

She watched him for a few silent moments, her huge brown eyes unreadable. Then she pushed slowly to her feet and circled the table. Her hand sought his, and their fingers twined. "Come on."

She led him down the hallway and up the stairs, bypassing his room in favor of hers. With the door closed firmly behind them, she urged him to sit on the bed, then knelt at his feet.

She deserved the words. "I'm not running off to Kings' Canyon by myself. It's too late for that."

"Good." She tugged at the laces on one boot, working the knot free with patient fingers. "If you did, I'd have to follow you."

"That's not funny, Ana." Especially since he knew she wasn't joking.

She got the laces loose and dragged his boot free. "You're just going to have to face reality. Loyalty to fellow Riders isn't conditional." She stripped off his sock and started in on the other boot. "They took you back. They'd follow you into hell."

For once, the statement wasn't hypothetical, meant to capture a sentiment more than an explicit plan. "Think about what you just said," he told her quietly. "Tomorrow, I'm going to show Maricela a picture of the leader of the Kings. And I already know she'll remember Seth's face, because he was the one who came here. He smiled at her, handed her that card, and asked her for a blessing. That's the kind of man he is. That's the kind of place we're going—hell."

"They've been there before. It's what we signed up for." She jerked his second boot and sock off and braced both hands on his knees, staring up at him. "Deacon, even if you'd never met Seth in your life, we might still be facing off against him. But without any of your knowledge, any of your insight."

And without Seth's very personal vendetta. "Ana—"

She tightened her fingers on his legs. "Do you know what kind of man Seth is? A stupid one. If it had been me, I would have put three bullets in you in that alley and called it a day. I've never had the luxury of being *emotional*. But that's all he is. Taking risk after stupid risk just to fuck with your head. He'll give us an opening, because he can't stop himself."

An opening to take him down, sure, but one that could cost them dearly. But he was in no mood to argue. "It's been a long fucking day."

"I know." She rose and hit the switch on the lamp next to her bed. Then she nudged him gently on the shoulder. "Move over."

"I can go back to my place, you know."

"Shut up." Ana urged him onto his back and vanished into the darkness. He heard the soft whisper of fabric over skin and the rattle of a desk drawer.

Then the bed dipped next to him, and she pulled him into her arms, his head resting on her shoulder. Her fingers traced softly through his hair, fingernails scraping gently against his scalp. "It's going to be okay, Deacon."

He relaxed into her touch, letting her soothe away the tension. He needed it, needed *her*, but it was too much to ask for, this gentle acceptance—especially when he didn't have the energy to return it.

"He came after Gideon's baby sister," Deacon whispered. "What if leaving was the right thing to do, and I missed my chance?"

"You can't take it all on yourself." Her fingers drifted through his hair. "You don't even know if offering yourself would have stopped any of it. Maybe he'd have locked you away somewhere and kept on trying to kill us all, just to hurt you more."

"I guess we'll find out." The scent of her shampoo and soap wreathed him, along with something uniquely Ana. He breathed it all in as they stretched out on the bed, this time with Ana's head on his shoulder.

Her hand settled over his heart. "Together," she murmured. "We'll find out together."

It seemed like ages ago that he'd been proudly watching her spar with Hunter. Was it really only that morning? The prospect of the coming days stretched out before him like a gauntlet he had no choice but to run.

It would be one thing if they mounted up and headed out to the canyon immediately. But they desperately needed that intel—Gideon was right about that. In the meantime, they could increase patrols, train, and prepare their equipment, but they mostly just had to *wait*, and nothing was more exhausting than that.

Still, a part of him was glad, because it meant that, no matter what went down with the Kings, at least he'd have a few more days with Ana.

fifteen

The soft glow of dawn had barely kissed Ana's window when her tablet chirped an insistent reminder to get up. Moving carefully, she reached out to silence it before turning under the arm Deacon had flung across her.

He'd slept through the sound, a sign of just how weary he was—or how safe he felt curled in her bed. His arm tightened reflexively, tugging her closer, and she couldn't help but smile as she stroked the hair at his temple.

Vulnerable Deacon. Every day truly was an opportunity for miracles.

It had been a long time since Ana had enjoyed the luxury of showing vulnerability. When she was fifteen, she lost her temper when the son of a guard suddenly decided that Ana, with her growing curves, was a *girl*-girl now, and no longer a fit sparring partner.

Ana had kicked his ass, of course. And when she was kneeling on his back, her fist in his hair, rubbing his stupid face in the dirt, her father had arrived on the scene. He'd plucked her off her opponent, marched her to the stables, and unceremoniously dumped her into the water trough.

Stunned by the betrayal as much as the shock of cold water, Ana had dripped and shivered in silence as her father laid out the hard truths of her future life in stark, uncompromising terms.

People who wanted to challenge the status quo didn't get to have temper tantrums. They had to be smarter, and calmer, and faster, and *better*. Beyond reproach, beyond critique. As perfect as a human being could be, because you could whine about fair and unfair all you wanted, but at the end of the day, you did the extra work or you failed.

With humiliation burning in her gut and water dripping down her back, Ana had made a tactical error. She'd channeled all the fifteen-year-old petulance she possessed to snap, "What would *you* know about it?"

William Jordan had never been a soft man, but the hardest parts of him had never been directed at Ana before. Not until that afternoon, when he'd crouched down to put himself on eye level and delivered a blistering lecture that remained carved into her mind.

You don't know how good you have it, girl. You don't know how lucky you are to have been born into a sector where the color of your skin will never hold you back. Your grandparents and every ancestor who came before them had to fight every day for the life you take for granted. And some people in other sectors are still fighting.

She'd been too young to fully understand what he

meant then, even as she'd sheepishly taken his lessons to heart. She'd learned to leash her temper, control her emotions. To focus on smoothing away any rough edges that someone could point to and say—*see, she's not good enough. She doesn't deserve this.*

When she grew old enough to accompany her father into other sectors, she saw the truth of his words. Some people still dealt with prejudice and hate over the stupidest of things—how they looked, how they dressed. Who they loved. If her father had been right about this, he must have been right about everything.

The lessons learned in childhood always seemed so simple. Right and wrong. Good and evil. She traced a finger over Deacon's brow and had to acknowledge that he was both. Capable of horrible deeds as well as heroic ones. A man who had done so much harm, but also so much *good.*

Maybe her father had been wrong, even when he was right. She'd had to learn self-control in order to earn her spot. She'd had to prove herself in a way the men never had, fair or not. But she was *here* now. A Rider, until the day she died.

And she was creating the reality of what a female Rider was. Any bright-eyed little girl who followed behind her would have to live in the box she had built, survive in the narrow, claustrophobic space she'd carved out for herself inside all this control and perfection.

Was this the dream she was making for them? A life without love? Without passion? A life where she was terrified to be seen touching the man who made her heart race, all because some bitter asshole who had no power over her fate might decide she wasn't worthy?

Gideon's was the only opinion that mattered, and Gideon believed in her. The assholes would just have to stew in their own misery for a while. Ana was tired of giving a shit about what they thought.

Deacon wrinkled his nose without opening his eyes. "It's too early."

"I know, but I have an appointment." She smoothed her finger down the strong bridge of that nose, lingering on the bump where it hadn't healed right after some long-ago fight.

He opened his eyes wide, then smothered a yawn with the back of his hand. "What kind of appointment?"

"I'm going to visit my aunts." Ana touched her fingers to the silk scarf she'd wrapped around her hair in the darkness last night. "Aunt Naomi's going to braid my hair. And Aunt Olivia will send me home with more donuts than Zeke needs."

He sat up and stretched. "Let me grab a shower and I'll come with you."

Last night, he'd let himself be vulnerable. And still, she hesitated. There was letting the other Riders see this *thing* happening between them, and then there was taking it outside the compound walls. Her aunts would circle and interrogate, and every person who came through the bakery or salon would see them together and gleefully carry the story to all their closest friends.

Which meant the gossip could hit the sector borders by nightfall.

"Are you sure you want to?" she asked to buy herself a little time. "I know you don't want us going out on our own, but I'll probably be there until lunch."

He swung his legs over the edge of the bed and studied her for a moment. "Is it a problem?"

Fuck the assholes. Fuck the bitter, hateful fools. "No." She sat up and offered him a wry smile. "But I won't blame you if you cut and run partway through. My aunts are gonna get ideas. And they could convince

Ashwin to tell them all his deepest, darkest secrets if they wanted them badly enough."

Deacon sighed and ran a hand through his hair, which was already sticking out in all directions. "I meant what I said about going out alone. I can send another one of the Riders with you, but..." His jaw tightened. "I don't want to. I want to be there, just in case."

She didn't have a name for the funny tickle in her chest. Warmth that he cared, maybe, or irritation that he felt the need to protect her. Guilt at that irritation—*she* would feel a whole hell of a lot better if she could keep an eye on him, too.

And if Deacon was with her, he couldn't have any second thoughts about charging off to sacrifice himself.

"Okay. You shower. I'll grab some gear and a walkie and meet you by the bikes in twenty. I'll let Zeke know where we're going, too."

He grunted and rose. "Got it. And Ana?"

"Yeah?"

"I can control myself." He swept up his boots with a look of determination. "Your aunts will never know."

Ana went up on her knees and grabbed his shirt, pulling him to her for a brief, glancing kiss. It had to be glancing, or she'd drag him back down into the bed with her and finish what had been interrupted last night.

Her lips still tingling from his, she grinned up at him. "Keep telling yourself that."

"Have a little faith, woman." But he was smiling and rubbing his mouth as he slipped out the door.

Flying high on the adrenaline, Ana washed and dressed in record time. Zeke answered her firm knock with a sleepy mumble, so she stuck her head into his room. "Hey, wake up."

His blond head poked out from under the quilt. "Is

something on fire? Something better be on fire."

"No." She tossed one of the walkies onto his bed. "Deacon and I are going to be at my aunts' place this morning. If anything happens, call us."

He gave her a thumbs-up as he disappeared back under the quilt. Hiding a smile, Ana started counting down from ten.

At four, his head shot out again. "Hey, bring me donuts."

"If they have any to spare, I guess."

This time she got his middle finger, and she laughed as she hauled his door shut and headed for the parking lot. Deacon was already there, freshly scrubbed, with his beard neatly trimmed again. She took a moment to admire him in his denim and riding jacket before hauling her helmet off the back of her bike. "You ready?"

"Yep." He flipped his helmet up in the air and caught it. Then he grinned as he slid his helmet on and threw his leg over his bike.

Ana decided she liked that—grinning Deacon.

The way his jeans hugged his ass wasn't bad, either.

Ana donned her helmet and slid onto her bike, savoring the first rumble as it roared to life. She peeled out of the parking lot and let Deacon follow, and the thrill of the wind rushing past her and the wide-open road ahead of her still felt new, even after all this time.

She'd been seven the first time her father had let her climb behind him on this bike. Their brief, exhilarating ride around the neighborhood had addicted Ana and resulted in the first and only screaming match she'd witnessed between her parents.

William Jordan didn't take orders from a lot of people. But Fiona's prohibition against letting their daughter on his bike had held for two long years after her death. At twelve, Ana was better equipped to take the responsibility—and the lessons—seriously. She'd learned to ride on this bike. She'd learned to *love* riding on it.

And when her father had died, she inherited it.

A few hundred yards down the winding road through the orchard, Deacon roared up next to her. It was safe to ride side by side out here, especially this early in the morning. They took the slow, wide turns together as the sun rose high enough to break through the trees in dappled light, and finally turned toward the center of the sector.

Ana's aunts' shop was on the western side of the sector, in the shadow of the large apartment buildings that had gone up in the first years of the Prophet's reign. Plenty of people were out and about here, heading to jobs on various noble estates or to the market shops where they plied trades or sold services. But they jumped out of the street with alacrity at the rumble of the bikes, with waves or greetings or blessings.

The parking space behind her aunts' duplex was tiny, with just enough room for both of their bikes next to the space marked off for delivery vans. Ana hauled off her helmet as she dismounted, and waited for Deacon to do the same. Then she quirked an eyebrow at him. "There's still time to chicken out. My family was never overly impressed with my dad's lofty status, so don't expect them to be awed by you."

"I'll manage," he told her dryly.

She was starting to suspect Deacon had a sense of humor buried under all his brooding. Maybe even that it had been there all along, so deadpan that no one ever noticed because no one expected him to be joking.

But there was a glint in his dark eyes, the one he had when he teased her. She was still pondering how to coax it closer to the surface when she pushed open the back door to the bakery and stepped into controlled chaos.

Olivia was tall and willowy, with deep-brown skin, impossibly sharp cheekbones, and dark eyes framed by long lashes. A brightly patterned scarf held her hair out of the way, the vivid reds and golds repeated in the apron she'd tied over her black dress.

She turned toward the open door with a huge metal tray in her hands, and beamed. "Perfect timing, Ana. Can you...?" Her voice trailed off as her gaze drifted past Ana's shoulder.

Oh God, here it goes. Ana stepped aside, giving Deacon space to stand beside her as she tilted her head toward him. "Hey, Aunt Olivia. I brought a friend this morning. You know Deacon, right?"

"By reputation, of course." Olivia offered him her most brilliant smile, the one people had started writing poetry about by the time she was fifteen. "What an honor to have you visit. And a stroke of luck. Here." Olivia thrust the tray toward Deacon. "Is it okay if I use his muscles?"

Ana didn't know whether to laugh or cover her face with her hands. "I don't know, you should probably ask him."

"It's fine." He took the tray, surveying the room. "You're filling orders for bread?"

"Yes, the first van should be here any minute." She nodded to a tall tray rack near the door. "I have to get all the orders for the market vendors organized and ready to go. They need bread for their sandwiches and lunches and, well..." She wiped flour from her hands and winked at Ana. "I am the best. It's the secret family recipe."

Deacon took her words seriously. He nodded, then

slid the tray onto the rack. "Just tell me what I need to do."

"Excellent." Olivia engulfed Ana in a hug that left flour scattered all over her T-shirt and jeans, then swatted at her with a towel. "Go help Naomi. We'll be fine here. We'll even bring over breakfast when we're done."

Leaving Deacon alone with her aunt felt a little like abandoning him in the midst of battle. But he just rolled his eyes at her hesitation, so she obeyed and slipped through the swinging door to the front of the shop.

The front room of the bakery was bright and open, decorated in cheerful golds and bronzes. At one side stood a long counter with glass display cases and baskets that would soon fill up with fresh baked goods.

The rest of the space was cluttered with tables and chairs and couches grouped for easy conversation—and Ana knew *those* would be filling up soon, too. Most of the neighborhood found a reason to stop by during the day, whether it was for a bite to eat, a cool drink, or to pick up the evening's baking.

Mostly, they were there for the gossip. Today was going to be a *really* good day for that.

The west wall was a giant open archway. Ana ducked through it and into the other side of the duplex. "Aunt Naomi?"

"Back here!" She emerged from the stockroom, dressed in her customary overalls, her arms loaded with bottles of shampoo and conditioning cream. "You're late. I thought you might not make it."

"Things have been hectic." Ana patted the walkie-talkie on her hip. "We may still have to bolt out of here."

Naomi made a skeptical noise in the back of her

throat. "If you brought Reyes, you tell that boy to mind his manners today. Eliza's coming in later."

Somehow Ana doubted the presence of Naomi's wife would deter Reyes's flirtation—not when Eliza still flushed pink at his effusive compliments. "No, Deacon came with me. And about two steps through the door, Aunt Olivia hijacked him. He's loading bread into trucks by now."

"Good," her aunt replied absently as she placed bottles around the wash and style stations. "She can use the help."

"Here, give me some of those." Ana rescued half the bottles from the precarious pile and crossed to the opposite side of the room. Mirrors set on the deep-red walls reflected the whole room back a hundredfold. Paintings of saints set in between them amplified the dizzying effect. Ana tried not to look as she placed the bottles. "How's Eliza doing?"

"She's doing well. Busy, but aren't we all?" Naomi turned and propped her hands on her hips. "What about you?"

Most of the things she'd done over the past week were restricted information. The rest were so deeply personal, her cheeks warmed at the thought of them. "I'm okay. I've been focused a lot on training."

In the mirror, Naomi tilted her head and narrowed her eyes.

Yeah, this wasn't going to work any better than *I couldn't have broken the mirror, I was in my room reading.*

Ana put the last two bottles in place and turned to face her aunt. "Maybe I've been having a little fun, too. Is that a problem?"

"Not at all, I just expect details. Unless..." Butter wouldn't have melted in her mouth as she jerked her thumb toward the archway. "Unless the details happen to be next door right now?"

Ana had always assumed she would reach an age where she could stare down Naomi. Someday. Maybe if she made it to fifty. Her cheeks burned hotter as she dropped into one of the swivel chairs and bumped her heel against the footrest. "It's not a thing, okay? Don't make it a thing. Riders don't get to have *things*."

"Your mother would have begged to differ."

"Riders didn't exist when Mom and Dad fell in love." With one boot planted on the floor, Ana swiveled the chair back and forth, not quite meeting her aunt's eyes. "I barely even remember it, you know. When we all lived together. I was so young when he had to leave for the compound."

Naomi walked over and stroked a familiar, soothing hand over Ana's hair. "They both loved you more than anything else in this world. That's all you need to remember."

"I know." But sometimes she wished she had more than fuzzy, half-imagined memories of their house with its tiny garden, and her parents' big bed that always had room for a little girl who'd woken up from a scary nightmare. "It couldn't have been easy on Mom when he left. I know she believed, but..."

"She believed," Naomi said firmly, then snorted. "And your mother was far from the first person to go it alone while their spouse was off fighting for something. There used to be entire armies before the Flares, and plenty of those soldiers left families at home. But you're too young to know what it was like back then." Her eyes lost some of their sharp focus, like she was caught up in a memory too strong to escape. "Seems like everyone these days is too young to know."

Sometimes Ana forgot that Naomi, the eldest of

the three sisters, had been close to twenty when the Flares happened. The silver twisting out from her aunt's temples was a little thicker every year, but her skin was still smooth, the crinkles at the corners of her eyes barely visible.

In spite of Ana's determination to stay alive long enough to do some good, some part of her had always thought that she would go down fighting before she had to face a future without her family.

A different future bloomed in her imagination now—her, alone. Hard, like her father after he'd lost Ana's mother. Walled off. No Naomi or Olivia to remind her why the fight was so important. No lover, because she couldn't afford the distraction. Just the job, day after day, until she finally missed her mark or stumbled or simply met a monster she couldn't slay.

That couldn't be what their God wanted. That couldn't be what *Gideon* wanted. "Do you remember?" she asked softly. "Why the Riders don't have families? We never even talk about it, it just...*is*."

"Surely you know better than I ever can." She sank into the chair beside Ana's. "But I imagine it must be simpler, not being pulled in two different directions—duty or family. And that's not even taking into account how young some Riders are when they die. There's a price for that, Ana. Widows and orphans. I don't think Gideon Rios can stand to have either on his conscience."

She'd thought the exact same thing before, but today it felt...wrong. She'd seen the cracks in Deacon's armor. The exhaustion, the solitude. The tiny glimpses of someone else, of the someone he might have become if he'd been teased and loved for the past twenty years instead of left in solitude to turn to stone.

"What about when we don't die?" She thought about the night she'd sparred with Deacon. *Three days is a long time to be alone.*

He'd been alone for *twenty years.*

"That—" Naomi's voice cracked, and she smiled. "That's why you have each other."

That worry was back in Naomi's eyes. It was one thing to say *fuck you* to the assholes, but family was different. Family was *hard*, because Naomi's disapproval sprang from deep, unshakable love.

Ana had to swallow to keep her own voice from cracking. "I know this isn't the life you would have chosen for me—"

"Hush." Naomi rose and turned to the counter, where she busied her trembling hands at sorting through the bottles. "It's your life. No one gets to choose it but you. If you're happy, that's all that matters to me."

She watched her aunt in the mirror, hating that there were no easy words to bridge the space between them. Naomi had offered her the truth, all Ana could do was give her the same in return. "I am. Not every day, but way more days than not. And I don't just have the Riders. I have you, and Eliza, not to mention Olivia and those impossible flirts she calls husbands."

Naomi paused and looked up to meet her gaze in the mirror. "Always, Adriana. You will *always* have us."

Tears stung her eyes, and Ana blinked hard as Deacon appeared through the open archway, saving her from throwing herself into her aunt's arms and bursting into sobs.

Except when she spun the chair to face him, her heart kicked.

Deacon looked...adorable. Harried and a little rumpled, sure, with flour dusting his T-shirt and beard. He even had a smear of it high on his cheekbone, and

Ana curled her fingers toward her palm to keep from reaching out to brush it away.

"We brought breakfast." He slid the tray he was holding onto a table that her aunt had quickly cleared of books and tablets.

"That was fast." Naomi beamed up at him. "You must have loaded those orders in record time."

"He did," Olivia said, coming in behind him with a wide smile. She paused to pat Deacon's cheek and brush away the flour on it. "And no whining, not like when I make the boys help me. He's even faster than Zeke."

Ana froze. "Zeke? Zeke loads trucks for you?"

"Oh, not often. Just a few times a month, when he comes by to do repairs on the tablets and download the new books and movies to the network he set up for us."

Ana had known about the network. Zeke had come with her to install it in the first chaotic month after the war, while she was still grieving her father and fighting for the right to take his place. She'd never been sure if Zeke's gesture was that of a Rider caring for the family of a fallen brother...or a quiet statement of support for Ana's petition to join them.

But she hadn't realized the relationship was ongoing. That was Zeke, down to his bones—quietly helping people whenever he had the chance. If she confronted him, he'd laugh it off and claim he was in it for the free donuts.

Impossible idiot. "Well, you guys spoil him with all the baked goods. How could he stay away?"

"Why would he try?" Deacon pulled out a chair for Naomi, who raised both eyebrows at Olivia as she sank into it. Olivia's return smile spoke volumes, and Ana resolved to pretend they weren't having a whole silent conversation about Deacon as he held a second chair for Olivia.

At least they weren't having it out loud.

Ana took the third chair before he could do the same for her, but once he was seated next to her, she couldn't look away from his jaw. Flour still dusted his beard, and her fingers itched impossibly the longer she stared at it.

Ah, fuck it.

His beard tickled her fingertips as she gently wiped away the flour, and the perturbed look he shot her only made her giddier. His oh-so-stern eyebrows drew together, and she could almost *hear* his exasperation—*I was trying to be cool, woman. Now you're groping my face.*

She was, and she didn't give a goddamn. Because her aunts were exchanging meaningful looks, and joy had replaced the worry in Naomi's eyes. Ana licked her thumb and cleaned the last remnants of flour from his cheek before grinning at him.

Ana wouldn't have fucked Deacon to make her aunts happy any more than she would do it to piss off the jerks. Whatever this was, it was about them and only them, whether it fizzled out by tonight or lasted as long as they both survived.

But as added bonuses went...enraging assholes and pleasing her family didn't suck.

sixteen

Reyes wouldn't stop pacing.

Or maybe he *couldn't* stop pacing. Deacon watched him go from one end of the common room to the other, then shook his head and went back to brushing out the gun barrel in his hand. Trying to settle him down when he was already gearing up for battle wasn't just useless, it was a good way to get sucker punched in the nose. Reyes would gladly start a fight to relieve some tension, and Deacon didn't plan on indulging him.

Reyes stopped beside a window, stared out of it for a moment, then turned and pointed at Gabe. "Best way to die. And make it better than your last answer, for Christ's sake."

Gabe glanced up from the knife he was sharpening, though his hands continued their slow, steady movements. "With honor."

"Goddammit, Gabriel, I said a *better* answer, not the same one. You fucking sound like Ivan."

"Now that's not fair," Zeke argued without looking up from his computer. "Ivan would have gotten *really* specific. Like..." He lowered his voice to a terrible impersonation of Ivan's tersest growl. *"The best death is dying while protecting Maricela from stubbing her toe."*

"Oh, are we taking potshots now? 'Cause I've got a few for you." Hunter kicked Zeke's chair, nearly rocking it back on two legs. "Worst death. Go."

Zeke glared at him. "Trapped in a room, forced to listen to Reyes talk about his sex life."

"No cheating," Lucio reminded him mildly. "Deflection is against the rules."

"Fine, being buried alive. With Reyes."

Reyes pressed both hands together like he was getting ready to pray. "If that ever happens, Zeke, I promise I'll kill you quickly."

"Love you, too." Zeke blew him a kiss and turned to Ana, who was seated across the table from Gabe, sharpening her own knives with slow, graceful strokes. "What about you, Ana? Worst way to go out."

She didn't look up. "With unfinished business," she said softly. "Knowing that whoever I was trying to protect didn't get to safety."

No one had any smartass comments to make about that one. It was the closest you could get to the universal truth of the Riders, the one thing they all feared—failing those who depended on them.

It still hurt to hear Ana say it out loud.

"What about the best?" Deacon asked her quietly.

She stole a glance at him so fast the others probably didn't even see it. Then her lips quirked up. "Having a heart attack during a sexual marathon."

Lucio looked up from the reloading press he'd clamped to the edge of the table. "I can't tell if she's joking or not."

Zeke squinted at her suspiciously. "Neither can I. Reyes, you're the sex-marathon expert."

"What does that have to do with Ana's fucked-up sense of humor?"

"You know." Zeke waved a hand. "Takes one to know one, all that."

From the corner of the room, Gabe snorted. "Reyes would never have a heart attack during sex," he said, his face utterly serious. "Talk about dying without honor. His ego would keep him going until his partners had finished coming."

"Zombie dick," Hunter chimed in solemnly.

Laughter rippled through the room, a comfortable, comforting sound, and even Reyes—who, for all his faults, never took himself too seriously—joined in. Deacon still wasn't sure how all this shit with the Kings would end, but he knew he would miss these bastards.

And, for the first time, he thought maybe they would miss him, too. Even Gabe, who still couldn't quite look at him.

Deacon had always known that his death would be deeply felt in Sector One. Hell, half the artists in residence at the temples probably had his memorial iconographies painted and stored away, waiting to be finished off based on how much gray needed to be added to his beard, how many wrinkles to his face. It would be a production, *days* of feasting and celebration—Saint Deacon, first of the Riders, martyred defender of the faithful.

In the past, he'd thought the remaining Riders would mourn the loss of his service, but not *him*. He figured that would be left to Gideon, some small bit of truth his best friend could keep for himself. That was enough, being remembered well by a person like Gideon. More than most people ever got.

Now he knew better. There would be other Riders. New ones, full of jokes he would never hear, with faces he would never see light up with laughter. But none of them would ever be *Deacon*, just as none of them would be Jaden McKinnon or Will Jordan or any of the other painted-in portraits that graced the wall of the Riders' Temple.

Gabe slid his freshly sharpened knife into its sheath and gathered up his collection of weapons. "I'm heading to bed," he told Ana. "Just leave the whetstones on the table."

"Got it." She smiled at him. "Sleep well."

He hesitated by the table where Deacon sat, oiling the now-clean gun barrel. But then he kept walking, the set of his shoulders tense as he disappeared down the hall.

If Gabe got any sleep at all, Deacon would eat his bore mop.

The soft, repetitive sound of steel against stone resumed as Ana sharpened her final knife. It joined the crackle of the fire in the hearth and the rhythmic tapping of Zeke's fingers on his keyboard.

Lucio rose. "Does anyone mind if I leave this? I want to finish tomorrow."

"Nah." Zeke closed his computer with a sigh of frustration. "I'll help if you want. I can't do anything useful until that drone gets back with the surveillance video."

Hunter eyed him appraisingly. "Want to go upstairs and knock each other around?"

"Only if you promise not to break anything I'll need."

Reyes held out both hands, but he didn't speak until all three men had left the room. "What am I, invisible? No one's inviting me anywhere."

"They probably figure you have plans." Deacon started slipping the tools back into his cleaning case.

"Yeah," Ana murmured, glancing up at Reyes with one eyebrow raised. "What happened to Davin?"

He narrowed his eyes as he turned a chair around and straddled it, but his expression cleared as he folded his arms on the back and gazed innocently at Ana. "I don't know what you mean."

Ana's cheeks flushed, but she held Reyes's gaze stubbornly. "Go ahead and do it. I know it's been killing you not to say it."

"Fine." He waved a hand between Deacon and Ana. "You two, together. It's cute."

"Cute," she echoed flatly.

"Yeah, cute. Sweet, adorable. It's nice." He scoffed. "I'm not an asshole *all* the time, you know."

Ana glanced at Deacon. She looked so *worried*, like he might have some sort of macho meltdown at being called adorable. So he winked at her. "Thank you, Reyes."

"You're welcome."

Ana was still watching him, her lips slowly curving up until she was looking at him the way she had in her aunt's salon, all big brown eyes and soft smiles.

"All right." Reyes stood with a laugh. "I'm not an asshole, but I'm also not a voyeur. Not tonight, anyway." He left, and his last words drifted back up the hallway. "You kids have fun."

When he was gone, Ana gently slid her knife back into its sheath and tossed her braids over her shoulder. "So." Her voice held a note of teasing flirtation wrapped up with something even hotter—anticipation and certainty. "Are we gonna have fun?"

"I think that depends."

"On?"

"Whether you trust me."

Both of her eyebrows lifted. "So we're gonna have a *lot* of fun."

He rose and offered her his hand. "Come on."

Losing him would be tough for the Riders. But Ana was a different story entirely. He could see it in her eyes, feel it in her touch as she folded her hand in his and followed him to his room.

The other Riders would grieve, but Ana would be heartbroken.

It was his bitterest regret, the one that threatened to twist arousal into dark melancholy. So he pushed the thought away as she closed his bedchamber door behind her and leaned back against it, her dark eyes bright. "I trust you, Deacon."

"Uh-uh." He dropped his hands to his belt, lingering over the buckle when she drew in a sharp breath. "Show me."

She'd come down to the common room barefoot, dressed in the same clothes she wore to work out. Her simple tank top clung to her curves as she peeled it slowly up her body, revealing a lacy bra with a little black bow between her breasts. Her underwear matched when she kicked her pants off, and she paused to run her fingers along the lace at the waistband. "Do you like them?"

"I do." They fit like they were made for her, and maybe they were. "I promise I won't rip them."

"Good." Her finger toyed with the clasp between her breasts as she took a step closer. "If you did, I'd make you buy me new ones. Do you know how frivolous it is to own lacy underwear you never show to anyone?"

"Nope." He couldn't tear his gaze away from that clasp. "Never tried it. Should I?"

"Maybe I'll buy you something." Her fingers twisted, and the fabric eased aside, revealing the firm, sleek curves of her breasts.

His mouth started to water. "You know, I think it looks better on you. Looks better *off* of you, too."

"Yeah?" Mischief glinted in her eyes as she slid her fingers inside the waistband of her panties and beneath the silky fabric. "You probably want me to take these off, too."

Two could play her game. He moved his hand from his belt buckle down to his fly, where his aching cock strained against the denim.

And then he waited.

Her gaze fixed on his hand. Her tongue darted out over her lower lip, like she was remembering the taste of him. Seconds ticked by in a silence broken only by her quickening breaths.

"Fuck." In a sudden burst of movement, Ana shoved her panties down her legs and kicked them away with so much force they flew across the room. She stood in front of him naked, and he drank in the sight of her.

He could do it all night, if only he had the patience. But there were other things he wanted, things that were just as good or maybe even better—like listening to that first shaky breath when he put his hands on her.

He stripped his shirt over his head. "On the bed."

She didn't challenge him this time. She crossed the room and slid onto the quilt, stretching out on her back with her upper body propped up on her elbows so she could watch him.

"I have plans for you." He moved slowly, giving

her all the time in the world to watch as he unbuckled his belt and pulled it free of its loops. He folded the warm leather between his hands, just long enough for a spark of curiosity—and hunger—to light her eyes.

Every emotion played nakedly across her face. She was wondering if he'd use it on her. *How* he'd use it. And she wanted him to use it, to bind her wrists or slide the supple leather over her skin in a million other ways.

Not tonight. He tossed the belt aside and popped open the top button on his jeans. "Plans," he said again, putting a hint of steel into the word this time, just to watch what *that* did to her flushed, expressive face.

She shifted restlessly on the bed, her gaze following his fingers. "You're good at plans. Strategy. Tactics." She wet her lips again. "Conquering."

"Usually." The second button gave way, and he left his jeans hanging low on his hips. "You make me forget."

"Sorry," she murmured, then flicked her gaze up to his. Mischief and satisfaction shone from her eyes now, and an utter lack of regret.

"No, you're not. But that's okay." He knelt at the end of the bed, just one knee, and trailed his fingers over the inside of her ankle. "I don't want you to be sorry. About anything."

Goose bumps dotted her skin, and she sucked in a breath. "That's why this is so good. You're not trying to get me to be something I'm not."

"Never." He eased his hand higher, up her calf to her knee, urging her legs apart as he moved.

She shivered under his touch, but her knees fell open readily. "I used to think you were a wall. This immovable stack of bricks I could throw myself against over and over, and I might get banged up but at least

I'd be tougher."

He stroked his fingers up her thigh. "And now?"

"You're a wall." She relaxed back to the bed and spread her arms wide as she closed her eyes. "But you can lean against walls when you're tired of being tough. You can put a wall at your back and know you're safe."

The words sparked another sort of ache, this one somewhere in the vicinity of his heart. "Then lean against me for a while," he whispered. "I've got you."

"I know." Her fingers curled into the covers, and her hips lifted, quiet entreaty instead of impatient demand. "Show me."

He slipped off the rest of his clothes and joined her on the bed. Instead of his hands, he rubbed his jaw over the inside of her knee. She laughed, low and warm, and squirmed under the touch. "Your beard tickles."

"Uh-huh." A little higher, and her laughter subsided. Higher still, and it melted into a rough moan.

This was the key to Ana—a slow build with committed follow-through.

He pushed her thighs wider, opening her to his gaze as well as his touch. Her hips arched again, bringing her just close enough so that his lower lip slicked over her clit.

"God." She released the blankets and slid one hand into his hair, fingers tangling in the short strands until his scalp burned. "Please, Deacon."

Just one hitching syllable, but it rocked his self-control. He slipped both hands beneath her and lifted her to his mouth. Her moan of gratitude was immediate, and her hand tightened in his hair. "*Yes.*"

He went slowly—not a tease but a promise, that every careful caress and flick of his tongue would lead to *more.* And he gave it to her, rewarding each gasp and moan until he had to clench his hands on her hips to hold her when she tried to squirm away.

When his tongue grazed her clit again, she gave a full-body shudder and jerked at his hair, dragging his head up to meet her eyes. "Your mouth," she panted, "is *dangerous*."

"I've barely gotten started." Another promise, this one breathed across wet, aroused flesh, and he affirmed it by thrusting his tongue into her. She was melting for him, soft and sweet, burning so hot that she began to move her hips, rocking up to meet him. Fucking his mouth.

And she didn't hold back this time. Not with the hungry, focused movement of her body, not with her moans and whimpers that grew in volume, guiding him to her most sensitive places. She wasn't trying to be quiet, wasn't trying to hide.

But she needed more.

He let go of her hips. When she rocked up again, he pushed two fingers inside her—just far enough to elicit a husky sigh of pleasure, but not enough to satisfy the driving hunger. He wanted her on this edge, drawn and tight, balanced so carefully that one tiny thing—*any*thing—could send her tumbling over it.

"Deacon—" Her thigh moved restlessly against his shoulder, her voice breaking as she rolled her hips up, chasing a harder touch. When he retreated to keep her on that edge, she made a desperate noise and threw her arm across her eyes. "If you don't fuck me into the mattress after this, I'm gonna strangle you."

"Lies." He turned his head and bit her thigh. "But if you don't like it..."

"Fuck you," she groaned, but a shudder went through her and her pussy clenched around his fingers. "C'mon, Deacon. You know you wanna be inside me when I come. All hot and wet, riding your cock."

The words slithered down his spine, evoking a memory vivid enough to make his balls tighten. He'd never forget what she felt like, gripping him in the throes of desperate pleasure.

With a snarl, he pulled away and flipped her over on her knees. She laughed in victory and bowed her back, offering him a mouthwatering view of her ass as she stretched her arms out and pressed her forehead to the mattress. "Yes. Do it. Fuck me."

He bent over her, sinking his teeth into the back of her shoulder. It would be so fucking easy to give her what she wanted—

If it was what she truly craved.

He traced his tongue over the hollow of her lower back instead. "You're used to that, aren't you? You say jump, and the men just ask you how high."

She glanced back at him, her eyes still sparkling with laughter and hunger. "No, I say *fuck* and they ask *how deep?*"

"Ah, there's the difference." He drove his fingers into her, curling them to stroke her inner walls as she fluttered around him. "I don't have to ask."

"Oh *fuck*—" Ana buried her forehead against the quilt as her hands fisted around the fabric. "God, right there, right—*fuck*."

"You just have to trust me, Ana." He bit her again, this time on the luscious curve of her ass. "And I'll get you there."

"I know," she whimpered, rocking back against him. "I know. I trust you."

He stroked her faster, harder, filling the room with the slick sound of his fingers fucking in and out of her. Her legs started to tremble, and he pressed the heel of his other hand hard against her clit.

A keening noise escaped her, sharp and desperate.

Her pussy gripped his fingers tight, and her muscles tensed. She teetered on the edge, utterly attuned to his touch, caught in that moment before orgasm.

"Go on." He kissed her back, then kept his open mouth on her damp skin. "Come."

She did. *Hard.* It started with a shudder beneath his lips, and then a groan of helpless relief. She clenched around his fingers as her hips moved, grinding down against the heel of his hand in rhythm with the pulse of her body. His name escaped her, low and hoarse, broken by little moans as he raked his teeth over her skin.

When her quaking subsided into delicious little tremors, he pulled her body up against his chest and wrapped his arms around her. Her heart thumped under his palm, so loud he could almost hear it, and he closed his eyes as he drank it in.

This was Ana—stripped down, naked in ways that had nothing to do with clothes. Vulnerable. Open.

His.

She turned her head, her cheek brushing his lips. Her voice trembled. "Deacon."

"Anything you want. Everything." A promise that didn't come close to repaying her for her precious trust, but it was all he had. "I swear it, Ana."

She opened her mouth, and he captured it, licking the words from her tongue. When she shuddered in his arms, he pressed her down to the bed once again, following her to draw his tongue up the sleek line of her spine. She shivered when he nudged aside her braids to kiss the vulnerable spot at the base of her neck, and her response came as a breathy sigh. "Everything. I want everything."

He straightened. Her thighs were slick, and he rubbed his thumb over the inside of one. "Be careful with that word, princess." He slowly slid his thumb up over her pussy to tease at her ass, holding her hip when she squirmed. "Make sure you know what it means."

"I know what it means," she said hoarsely, her back bowing. *"Everything."*

"You mean this?" He took his cock in hand and stroked the blunt head between her pussy lips. "Or this?" He flexed his hips, pushing forward just enough to make her jerk and shiver.

Then he gripped her hips and drove forward, burying his cock in her impossibly hot body with one long, ruthless thrust.

She cried out as he gritted his teeth and struggled to maintain a shred of control. But her pussy clasped around him, tempting him to abandon his intentions, his plans, everything but the pounding need to *take*.

She was still moaning when he spread his hand across her lower back. He skimmed his thumb, wet with her arousal, down between her ass cheeks to test the tight ring of muscle there. She gasped, and he growled and pressed his thumb deeper. "Even this?"

"Everything," she whispered hoarsely. "Fuck, Deacon—"

The husky plea rocketed through him like an electric shock. Trust wasn't a one-way street, something he could demand from her and refuse to give in return. She deserved this, all of him.

All of him.

"You want it rough, don't you?" He ground against her, driving deeper. "No holding back."

"Yes." She stretched her arms above her, bracing her hands against the headboard. "I want to—" He rocked his thumb deeper, too, and the words broke on a moan. "I want to feel alive."

Her words throbbed in his veins, pure, undiluted

fire. Hungry for sensation, the kind of pleasure maybe only he could give her. He pulled back as far as he could stand and began to thrust into her—forceful, fierce, holding her against the onslaught with his hand on her lower back.

I want to feel alive. He'd never felt more alive than this, with the fire burning away the straining threads of his self-control, one by one. She met him thrust for thrust, holding nothing back, and he drank in every harsh breath and helpless cry. He fucked her hard, *harder*, until every pounding movement carried them farther up the bed.

Her hands slipped off the top of the headboard, and Deacon caught her, cupped his hand over the top of her shoulder and bowed her back. With a desperate noise, she slid her hand down her body, fingers slipping over her clit as her pussy pulsed around him.

The last of his self-control dissolved as she came with a hoarse cry, and the almost undeniable need to follow her into oblivion washed over him.

Almost. The one thing he needed more was to give her the uninhibited lover she yearned for. So he clenched his jaw and kept going, pounding into her until the slap of flesh on flesh nearly drowned out her cries. And she kept coming, kept screaming, until not even the fucking roof caving in around his ears could have stopped Deacon's headlong rush toward pleasure.

He came with her name on his lips. The world went hazy, like it didn't fucking exist anymore. Nothing did, except for Ana, her cries and her pleasure and the hot, sweet clasp of her body.

I want to feel alive. It was some sort of miracle, a twist of fate, that they should both be in the world at the same time, in the same place. Some cosmic hint that maybe he didn't have to be alone, after all.

Deacon had never believed in the god that folks in Sector One trusted and worshipped, but Ana could change his mind.

She sagged in his grip, still whimpering softly as the aftershocks of pleasure drifted through her. He eased away, then helped her to the mattress before curling up behind her. She shivered under the quilt he pulled over them, and Deacon petted her as she settled down.

After a few minutes, she snuggled back into him with a sleepy sigh of contentment. "I am the definition of well-fucked."

If he was an asshole, he'd feel smug. Hell, he felt smug anyway. "Don't forget exhausted."

"That's implied." She wriggled around onto her back and shook a stray braid out of her face. Her lips curled into a soft smile. "Hi."

Her blissfully satisfied expression was contagious. "Uh-huh."

She leaned up to nuzzle his cheek, then found his lips for a slow, lazy kiss that ended with her tongue teasing across his lower lip. Then she kissed the tip of his nose. "You should smile more. You have a beautiful smile."

"Don't let any of the others hear you say that. You'll ruin my hard-ass image."

Ana's laughter tickled his cheek as she kissed her way back down his jaw. "Small chance of that." She settled her head on his shoulder and her hand over his heart, but her fingertip traced in a slow, restless circle against his skin. "Can I ask you something?"

"Sure."

"For the longest time I felt like..." She hesitated, something so out of character that he tensed in anticipation of her words. "I was sure you disapproved of me.

That you didn't want me to be a Rider. Because I was a girl, or because...I don't even know why."

"What? No." It hadn't been that long, but it was already hard to remember back before the end of the war, when the barracks had overflowed with Riders, but Ana wasn't among them. "Your dad and I, we didn't see eye to eye on some things. He trained you, you know? Not just to fight. He trained you *for the Riders.*"

Her nervous finger stilled. "Is that...bad?"

"It's not fair to you." Christ, he wasn't making any sense. "This isn't a job, Ana. We trade our lives for this—*give* our lives for it. You know that now, but did you know it when you were eight? Ten? He should have given you a chance to figure out if there was something else you wanted more."

"I knew that. I've always known that." She spread her fingers wide on his chest, over his heart. "The sacrifice of it, at least. I always knew the moments he had with me were stolen. I knew every time he left that he might not come back. But my dad didn't have to give up his life outside being a Rider. We all made the sacrifice together, because it was worth it."

That was part of the problem, the fact that her tiny, not-quite-fractured family was the exception. The reason for the rule. "I don't know if joining the Riders should be a legacy."

"Maybe not." She sighed. "I'm not Ivan, you know. No one ever told me this was my path. My dad gave me a choice, but he never sugarcoated shit. And it's not..."

"Not what?"

"Being what I am? The first? It's not something that happens to you. Every day of my life since I decided to try, the world's been pushing back. Sometimes it's obvious. Sometimes it's so subtle, people act like I'm crazy if I call them on it. Sometimes people pretend they're trying to help me. Maybe they really are. But it adds up. If I had any doubts, if I ever wanted out..."

Her voice drifted off before returning, softer. "This is the path of most resistance. Maybe my dad wanted it for me, but if it wasn't my dream, too, I would have quit years ago. Sometimes I want to quit anyway, because it's so fucking hard. But I can't now. If I flame out...I won't just be the first woman. I'll be the last."

She sounded so worried, so full of doubt—and that much, at least, he could fix. "That's bullshit. You're good, Ana. Better than you realize. You belong here. But even if you didn't, if you felt like you wanted to go, you wouldn't be the last woman in the Riders. Gideon wouldn't shut that door, and neither would I."

Ana turned her face to brush a kiss to his shoulder. "Thank you."

"Shit, thank me for anything but that. It's just the truth."

"Maybe." She snuggled back down against him and closed her eyes. "Still feels like a fantasy. Maybe it would be easier to believe if I wasn't the only one."

That would take time. "If you know anyone who wants to sign up, let Gideon know."

"Mmm. I'll think."

But not right now. She was falling asleep in his arms, which was as strangely moving as it was adorable. Intimate, something he might not have asked for—

But it felt right. God help him, it felt *right*.

ivan

Maricela's sitting room was nineteen feet across and twenty-seven feet wide. There were three windows that overlooked the courtyard, floor-to-ceiling glass that made Ivan nervous, even though he knew the royal guard would be doing regular patrols around every interior courtyard tonight and every night until the threat of the Suicide Kings had been neutralized.

The sitting room had only one interior door. It opened to the antechamber where Ivan waited, pacing off the width of the long, narrow space. Eight feet across. Fifteen long. One end had been transformed into a cozy nook with a soft chair and footstool, a side table, and a pretty stained-glass lamp. A quiet place to curl up with a book.

Or a good place for a guard to get lazy.

Ivan frowned at the chair before pivoting on his

heel and starting back in the other direction. As he reached the double doors to Maricela's bedroom, the breathy sighs coming from within turned to giggling moans, and he hastened his stride.

The opposite side of the anteroom was more to his taste. A utilitarian table held the weapons he wasn't wearing, as well as a walkie-talkie he could use to raise an alarm within moments. A simple cot was folded up in the far corner.

When the time came to rest, he'd lay it out in front of Maricela's door. Anyone who wanted to get into her bedroom would have to go through him.

Satisfied, he paused and picked up the walkie. "All clear?" he asked, just as he'd asked once every fifteen minutes since Maricela had disappeared into her bedroom with her...guest.

"All clear," came the immediate response. Johan's voice was unmistakable, and unmistakably exasperated. But the captain of the guard would hold his tongue and tolerate Ivan's check-ins, because an enemy had walked up to a Rios under the oblivious eye of the royal guard, and the shame of that wouldn't wash away overnight.

With his check-in complete, Ivan set the walkie-talkie back down and resumed his pacing. The muscles in his shoulders tightened as he drew closer to Maricela's door. Two steps away from it, Maricela's voice drifted out to him. "Wait—"

Ivan froze, his fingers flexing. She didn't sound distressed, but if he could say he *thought* she'd sounded distressed, he'd have an excuse to kick in the door and haul Colin Visscher out of the royal bed by the scruff of his neck.

Maricela's tone turned into husky, liquid command. "Use your tongue."

The low, masculine laughter in response grated on Ivan's nerves.

There was nothing *wrong* with Visscher. On paper, he was an ideal dalliance for a member of the royal family. His father was a competent and loyal member of the royal guard. His grandfather had served the Prophet as a personal bodyguard. He was young, personable, trustworthy—and, Del had assured him, possessed of a rather formidable reputation amongst the acolytes as a considerate and enthusiastic sexual partner.

Ivan regretted asking.

Pivoting sharply, Ivan retreated to the table and picked up one of his new throwing knives. The blacksmith had copied the design of Ashwin's to produce these sleek, expertly balanced beauties. Over ten inches long, it still rested lightly on the tips of his fingers, thanks to generous cut-outs along the blade and in the handle.

Of course, the blacksmith hadn't left it there. Whereas Ashwin's knives were plain, utilitarian steel, Ivan's had been delicately engraved with climbing vines and elegant flourishes. The crafters of Sector One appreciated function, but they worshipped form. Nothing that passed through their hands remained unetched, ungilded, undecorated, or unadorned for long.

As a weapon, Ivan related more to that cold, utilitarian steel.

The radio crackled, and Johan's tense voice filled the silence. "We have movement at the south wall. Stand by."

Ivan moved.

The handle on Maricela's door liked to stick. Ivan slammed it down and threw his weight against the solid wood. It sprang open, crashing against the wall and rebounding to bounce off Ivan's shoulder as he strode through. "Maricela—"

He caught sight of the bed and stopped abruptly, spinning on his heel so fast he wobbled. But even with his back to the bed, he could still see her in perfect, snapshot clarity—

Her head thrown back, face flushed with pleasure. The bodice of her dress pulled low enough to bare her breasts, and her fingers clenched in Visscher's hair as he obediently made use of his tongue.

Ivan had to force out the words between gritted teeth. "Visscher, get dressed and go home."

Fabric rustled, and Maricela swore. "Ivan, what the hell are you doing?"

He reached for his belt and realized that, in his haste, he'd left the walkie-talkie out in the antechamber. "There's been movement outside. For your safety, I need to secure this room."

He chanced a glance over his shoulder in time to see Maricela slip from the bed. She'd fixed her clothes in record time, and her bare feet whispered over the rug as she approached. "If something's going on, he should stay here."

Ivan shot the boy a commanding look that had him scrambling out of the sheets and back into his clothes. Then he returned his attention to the far-less-biddable princess. "He'll be fine. Nobody's after him."

"*Ivan*—"

The radio crackled out on the table, and Johan sighed across the channel. "False alarm. One of the kitchen staff was sneaking off to a secret rendezvous in the orchard. The perimeter's secure. All clear."

Dammit. With his pants on but unbuttoned, Colin froze, as if unsure of what to do, and somehow even *that* irritated Ivan. If the boy had given him attitude, he could have booted him out of the room, guilt-free.

Now he'd just look like an asshole.

His displeasure must have shown on his face, because Colin hastily did up the button and dragged his shirt over his head. "I should go anyway."

Maricela pressed her lips together and nodded. Her expression stayed fixed in a polite mask, but as Colin pressed a fleeting kiss to her cheek and retreated toward the antechamber, Ivan caught a telling glimmer in her eyes.

Anyone who hadn't spent years watching her would have missed it, but Maricela was on the verge of tears.

The door snapped shut behind Colin, and Maricela flinched. Tiny, barely perceptible, but guilt settled like lead in Ivan's gut. "What's wrong?"

"Nothing," she answered immediately. Automatically.

He'd never dealt well with other people's emotions. He'd never had any reason to. Growing up, he'd had trainers and teachers instead of friends. And after he joined the Riders... Well, they accepted his taciturn silences and idiosyncrasies without question or judgment. No one made him guess what they wanted from him.

But Maricela was hiding her needs, and he had to try to figure out how to fix this. "I'm sorry I ruined your..." He couldn't quite bring himself to say the word *dalliance*, not about the Rios princess. "Your evening. I can't take any chances with your safety right now."

"No, it's not your fault. I just..." Her shoulders slumped. "I didn't want to be alone tonight."

Of course she didn't. That mercenary had stepped up to her and slid his threat right into her hand. He'd probably touched her. Smiled. He'd been close enough to *hurt* her, and if the thought made Ivan tremble, he had no idea what it was doing to her.

"Get back in bed," he told her gruffly. It was seven long steps to the door, even with his ground-eating stride, and seven steps was too far tonight.

In the antechamber, he retrieved the walkie-talkie and his spare knives. Then he hefted the folded cot on one shoulder and hauled it back into Maricela's room. She turned at the sound, surprised, as if she'd expected him to abandon her after her confession.

Even Ashwin was better at soothing scared women than he was, and Ivan didn't have the Makhai soldier's excuses.

"Look," he said, snapping the cot open. He dragged it to the foot of her bed and pointed. "I'll be right here. No one can get past me."

"I know that." She sank to the bed, her dress tangling around her legs as she drew her knees up under her chin. "No one could get past you out there, either. That's not exactly what I meant."

"So tell me what you need." He crouched next to the bed, bracing one hand beside her. Her rumpled dress brushed his thumb, the expensive silk soft against his skin. "I can't read your mind, but if you need something, I'll make it happen."

She worried her lower lip between her teeth for so long he thought she might not answer. But eventually she said, "Will you talk to me? It doesn't have to be about anything important."

If only she'd asked him for something easy. Build something, destroy something. Kill someone. Find a rare fruit she craved. Hell, as blasphemous as putting his hands on her would be, crawling into her bed to take Colin Visscher's place would be preferable.

He knew a lot of ways to make women happy with his mouth. Talking had never been one of them.

But she looked so vulnerable like this. Hunched and small and nothing like the proud, fearless princess who walked among her people, easing their fears with a gentle touch and a kind word.

"Okay." He slid his hand over hers, hoping the contact would reassure her. "Deacon and I have been working on a cottage for George Cook and his wife. Now that she's pregnant, he wants to move into someplace big enough for a family."

Maricela lay down on her side, still curled up, smiling as her cheek nestled into her pillow. "I'm happy for them. They've been trying for a long time."

"They have." Ivan twisted to sit next to the bed, stretching out his legs in front of him. Her side table made for a suitable backrest, and the thick carpet was probably more comfortable than the cot. "We may have to clear some of the pine trees on the north side of the property to make room for more cottages, at this rate. Seems like now that the war's past, everyone's pregnant."

"Mmm. The war was hard on everyone." Maricela spoke slowly, her words slightly dreamy. When he glanced over at her, her eyes were closed, and the rise and fall of her chest had slowed.

However inane, the talking was working. "It was. But it's behind us now. And we'll do whatever we have to do to keep the peace."

She made a sleepy noise of agreement. Then, "Ivan?"

"Yeah?"

"I'm glad you're here."

It was a soft, sweet confession, and it warmed something in his chest. From the time he'd been old enough to understand words, his mother had made it clear that the greatest honor available on this earth was service to the Rios family, and an eventual glorious death in their name.

Growing up, Gideon had been an ideal to Ivan. Larger than life, especially when hazy childhood memories painted him in a heroic glow. The day that Gideon had come to take them to a safe home with solid walls and a roof that didn't leak had sealed Ivan's devotion. He trained every day of his life, willing and eager to walk into fire for the Rios clan.

But it was different, living here amongst them. Gideon and Isabela had presences that seemed almost otherworldly, but Maricela was young, untested. Still growing into her power and her position, harboring a streak of idealistic vulnerability that ran deep—a weakness her elder siblings didn't share.

Dying in a blaze of glory might bring Ivan honor, but a dead Rider—even a sainted one—would be of no use to Maricela.

If he wanted to keep his princess safe, Ivan was going to have to stay alive.

seventeen

The blare of the Riders' emergency alarm shattered the most blissful sleep Ana had enjoyed in months. Groggy and disoriented, she tried to bolt upright but found herself pinned to an unfamiliar bed by a heavy arm.

In the next moment Deacon rolled over, freeing her. He rubbed both hands over his face, then sat up. "Shit. Clothes."

"I think yours are at the end of the bed." Enough early dawn light filtered through the windows that Ana didn't knock into anything as she rolled to her feet and went hunting for the underwear she'd kicked off last night. "Fuck, I'm usually smarter about this."

"Here." He tossed her bra and shirt to her, then stepped into his pants and jerked them up.

She knew how to dress fast. But the tickle of her

braids against her skin was new—it had been over a year since she let Naomi do anything but braid her hair tightly to her scalp in a carefully strategic attempt to deprive an enemy of a convenient handhold. It had seemed important to live in that tiny box. To minimize anything that made her different, that could be pointed to as a vulnerability.

Ana was over living inside other people's boxes. If anyone wanted to make a try for her hair, she'd be happy to remove their hand for their trouble. She'd fucking do it, too. Because Deacon was right. She'd earned her place.

And she was damn good at her job.

Deacon already had the door open, so Ana scooped up her socks and boots and followed him into the hallway. Zeke was in the common room, standing over the big table and staring mournfully at a mangled pile of tech parts.

He glanced up when they entered. "Ashwin's going to murder me."

Deacon glowered at the table. "Is that...?"

"The drone," he said sourly as Ana slid into a seat and started to pull on her socks. "I got a ping that it was on its way back and opened the door and..." He waved at the mess on the table as Reyes and Hunter arrived, looking rumpled but awake. "And I'm not saying it crash-landed. Someone fucked this thing up and left it for us like a disemboweled squirrel."

Deacon's glower deepened into a scowl. "Can you pull anything off of it?"

"I'm trying." He waved his hand at his tablet, which had a cord coming off one side leading to a flat box about an inch tall. Some sort of tech chip was resting on top of it. "I jumped the gun and called Gideon. If it turns out to be nothing and he gets mad, you can blame me."

"Doesn't look like nothing." Hunter nudged the shattered edge of the drone's exterior shell.

No, it really didn't. Ana pulled her other boot up onto the edge of her chair and focused on tying the laces securely. Lucio arrived looking serenely composed, followed closely by Gabe, whose hair was unusually mussed and face sported three days' worth of scruff.

Ana had straightened her clothes and tied her front braids back from her face by the time Gideon arrived. The leader of Sector One had clearly rolled out of bed, into his boots, and out the door. His belt was undone and his shirt buttoned only halfway, revealing light-brown skin covered in vividly colorful ink.

"What do we have?" he asked Deacon as he slid his belt into its buckle.

"A smashed drone on our doorstep," he answered dourly. "And it didn't get here on its own."

"Got something!" Zeke gestured at the wall in front of the couch. "Lucio, can you...?"

Lucio reached up and dragged down the white screen that covered about six feet of wall. Zeke tapped something on his tablet that activated the projector embedded into the ceiling, and the screen filled with a man's face lit by the soft light of dawn.

He was handsome, Ana supposed. His face held the lines of hard living, but the streaks of silver in his light-brown hair were distinguished, and his crystal-blue eyes were striking.

But they were cold, too. Hard. Mean. So was his smile as he held the camera out at arm's length and made a *tsk*ing sound. "Deacon, Deacon, Deacon. Sent your pretty toy out and didn't even have the guts to follow it. I'm disappointed."

His voice was gravelly in a way that could have

been sexy if the words hadn't been so utterly mocking—and if Deacon hadn't gone rigidly still at the first syllable.

The camera swung in a dizzy turn, and Ana's blood froze as a building came into focus—the front door of the Riders' compound. "But time's up, old friend," that voice rumbled. "You come home to the Kings, or the next time we visit, we're not gonna be this nice."

The audio crackled, and Ana caught a glimpse of the stone pathway rushing toward the camera before the video went staticky and then cut out completely.

Reyes rubbed his chin. "Well, fuck."

Ana glanced at Deacon, who didn't move or even blink until Gideon put a hand on his shoulder. "That's Seth?"

"Yeah." The word ripped out of Deacon's throat. "That *motherfucker*."

Hunter shook his head. "You can't be thinking about going."

"I don't know if any of us have a choice, not anymore." Deacon took a step forward and turned around to face them all, his shoulders square with resolve. "Some of you think I have a death wish, some guilt-driven desire to sacrifice myself on the altar of my past deeds. Well, that's bullshit. I don't want to die." His gaze tracked over the room, lighting on each one of them in turn. Lingering on Ana. "I want to live."

It was a fight to keep her expression composed. Her heart lurched dangerously, not just because his brown eyes seemed to soften whenever he looked at her. The words *I want to live* had fallen from his lips with the ring of undeniable truth.

Then he looked away, and her skin crawled in warning as her heart lurched in the opposite direction.

"But I know the score. We all do. Gideon makes

sure of that before we take our vows and the priest-
esses draw us on that goddamn temple wall. We're
Riders, and Riders don't get old and die in their beds.
That's not fatalism or giving up. It's just fact."

She could have spoken the words herself, so they
shouldn't have raised the hair on the back of her neck.
But her awareness of Deacon had mutated into something more. At some point over the past frantic days,
she'd wriggled through the fractures in his armor.

She *knew* Deacon. And she knew where this was
going.

Zeke didn't. Oblivious to the slow-building tension
in the room, he flopped into a chair and glared at the
mangled pile of equipment. "I don't give a shit about
facts. I give a shit about murdering these motherfuckers for high crimes against technology."

"*Zeke.*"

Deacon's voice snapped through the room, edged
with a growl and rough enough to make hardened soldiers piss their pants. Zeke slumped lower, looking
momentarily chastised for once in his life. "Sorry."

"It's fact," he repeated. "And you have to give a
shit, all of you, because I need you to listen to what I'm
about to say. That's non-negotiable." His gaze focused
on the busted drone. "I've been a Rider for a long time.
I've fought my way through bad patches and made it
through every battle alive, somehow. But I've seen lots
of Riders fall. Good people, the best. And I can't let that
happen, not this time. Not over this."

Uneasy silence wreathed Ana, and she dug her
nails into her palms until the sting burned, fighting to
hold back the words that would stop what came next.
The quiet had grown oppressive when Lucio spoke.
"What does that mean?"

It pulled Deacon from his reverie. "I'm not heading

out there alone. We're all going, but if it looks like this is gonna get ugly, then *I'll* handle it. Just me. I may not make it back, but at least I can take the Kings down with me. That's more than most people get on their way out."

He refused to meet her gaze. Her nails broke the skin. Her tiny box closed around her, claustrophobic walls pressing inward. A perfect Rider wouldn't interrupt. A perfect Rider wouldn't disobey. A perfect Rider would accept the word of their leader, as well as his sacrifice. Grieve it, certainly, but also honor it. Celebrate it.

"What I need from all of you," he continued, "is a promise. I'm not looking to die. But if it comes to that, I need your word—no, your *oath* that you won't try to stop me."

The words settled like a fist at the small of Ana's back. She barely heard Gabe's murmured assent or Zeke's subdued, "You're the boss."

She was waiting for him to look at her. To have the courage to meet her damn eyes.

It took forever. One by one, the Riders offered their promises. Their oaths. Obedience to their leader, who they worshiped but didn't know, because no one really knew Deacon except Gideon. And now Ana.

When she was the only person who hadn't responded, his dark-brown eyes finally sought hers. She consciously relaxed her hands, and her palm throbbed with the imprint of her fingernails.

"Fuck no," she said, calmly and pleasantly.

Deacon didn't look surprised. "Like I said, it's non-negotiable. An order, if you want to call it that."

"Well, it's a stupid one—"

Gideon slapped his hand down on the table hard enough to rattle the drone. He pinned Ana with the harshest look she'd ever seen on his face, and her blood ran cold.

"Disobedience gets Riders killed in dangerous situations," he said in a voice so slashing, Ana felt flayed. "If you can't respect the chain of command and obey your leader's orders, you'll be staying here."

For a few terrifying seconds, Ana couldn't breathe. Her lungs had seized, and trying to make them expand was impossible.

She was staring at her nightmare. Not an enraged Gideon—even now, the leader of Sector One was above such petty emotions as rage. No, his usually gentle eyes stared at her with disappointment so withering, her little box felt enormous.

Because she felt so, so small.

This was it. The stumble. Her pedestal crumbling beneath her. She'd allowed herself a tiny bit of space for something other than the mission, and the penance she paid wouldn't just fall on her own shoulders. The next woman who tried to join the Riders would be judged by Ana's failure. *Too emotional. Too hysterical. Too irrational.*

Not good enough.

"No." Deacon stood there, shaking his head, his arms crossed over his chest. "She goes. We need her there."

No one said *no* to Gideon. Ana's shock melted into the dizzy feeling that Deacon had extended a hand to catch her before she could fall.

Gideon released her from the weight of his gaze and turned to Deacon. "It's your call," he said finally. "Outline your plan and let me know the details. I'm going to warn the other sector leaders."

The uneasy tension was back, reigning in a strange silence that made the whole room feel frozen in time.

Then the door slammed open, and everybody moved at once.

Ana sprang out of her chair, tensed on the balls of her feet. Hunter suddenly had a gun in his hands, and so did Lucio, both trained on the door and the woman standing framed by it.

She was tall, almost as tall as Kora, but that was where the resemblance ended. Instead of soft smiles and curly blonde hair, this woman was all leather and hard angles and dark-brown hair edged with violent shocks of pink.

And guns. She was covered with guns.

"Jesus." She held up both hands, palms open and empty. "Am I that scary, or are you guys just twitchy?"

Gabe froze with a knife balanced on his fingertips. "Laurel?"

"In the flesh." She raised both eyebrows. "Maybe I should have knocked."

"Maybe you should have," Gideon said mildly. He gestured to Lucio and Hunter, who lowered their weapons. "Laurel. You're Six's girl, aren't you? Did she send you?"

"Not exactly, but she knows I'm here." Laurel hefted a large black bag from the ground beside her, walked in, and dropped it on the table, rattling the smashed remains of the drone. "I had a couple of beers with Goose last night. He said you've been gathering intel on the Suicide Kings."

Zeke's mouth dropped open, then snapped shut as he glowered. "I'm gonna fucking kill that little—"

"No, you're not. He idolizes you, and that's a hard thing to come by." She paused and looked around the room. "Well, maybe not around here. Anyway. From the sound of things, it's just about go time, so here I am." She held out both arms and bowed with an almost formal flourish. "I want to go."

That said, she crossed her arms over her chest and stood there like she had every expectation of the men simply shrugging and letting her come along.

The perverse need to laugh added a new dimension to the aching pressure in Ana's chest, and she decided she liked Laurel.

A lot.

Gabe still looked perturbed, but Gideon's expression had grown thoughtful. He stroked his chin idly and glanced at Deacon, who nodded almost imperceptibly.

"All right. I just have one question." His next words felt like a slap across Ana's face. "Can you take orders? Because if you risk them by going rogue..."

Every trace of easygoing humor vanished from Laurel's face. "I don't take chances with other people's lives. And I can follow orders."

Deacon looked around. "Anyone have any objections?"

Nobody murmured a protest. With Gideon standing next to him, the memory of his harsh words to Ana still hanging in the air, who would dare?

"Okay, then. Get your gear. We're leaving in fifteen minutes."

The Riders broke apart, and Ana slipped from the chair, still too raw to deal with Gideon. She kept her gaze averted as she edged around the room, but she felt Deacon fall into step behind her as she headed to change.

She expected him to follow her into her room, but when she reached her desk and turned, he had planted himself in the doorway, his face serious, his eyes dark and wary and...

Not disappointed. Not quite. But there was a hurt in them that cut deeper than even Gideon's disapproval, because that had been a professional catastrophe, but this?

This was so, so personal.

And there was no escaping it. Bracing herself, Ana crossed the intervening space between them, sure that the only thing that could make what followed worse was forcing Deacon to raise his voice loudly enough for everyone to hear. "I know I fucked up. But I'm not sorry for not being able to give up on your life."

"That's not your decision, Ana. And if that's what you think I'm doing, then you weren't listening." He shook his head. "I couldn't let Gideon make you stay behind because I know how much you need this. Being a Rider. But you don't get to make this call."

"I was listening," Ana replied, her voice wavering with the struggle it took to remain calm. If she blew up, if she was emotional, he'd never hear her. "I caught the part that matters. You can't let us risk our lives *over this*. You're not strategizing to win. You're trying to figure out how to avoid losing any Riders, because you'd feel guilty. You still think this is all your fault."

His hand tightened on the doorframe. "Seth hand-delivered a message addressed to me right to our fucking doorstep. How much clearer does it need to be?"

"Yeah, some sick asshole is gunning for you." She started to curl her hands into fists and flinched as her nails scraped her raw palms. "That doesn't make it your fault."

"Say it all you want. It doesn't change anything." He took a step back. "Get your shit together. Twelve minutes."

The coldness in his voice hurt. Her defiance had shut down something inside him, killing the softness in his eyes. She wanted to force the fight, to make him say all of it—that this was over. That he'd liked her fine when she wasn't challenging him on anything that mattered, but trusting her only went so far.

A woman could have fought, but a Rider had to turn off personal feelings and obey. And Ana had already fucked up her duties as a Rider enough for one day. "Fine."

"It's *not* fine." Deacon pinned her with a hard look. "I overruled Gideon, but not because he was wrong. I won't be put in that position again."

He closed the door, and irrationally the quiet *click* of the latch was the part that upset her the most. Something this final should resonate with raised voices and slammed doors, not this chilly, perfectly controlled silence. Mechanically, Ana turned and began to strip. The usual bubbling anticipation that accompanied pulling on her work clothes was nowhere to be found.

Deacon hadn't used the words, but he'd just ended things between them. That was the curse of understanding him now. Of having seen past the cracks in his wall.

Not that there were any now. He'd mortared that shit down. His walls were twelve goddamn feet high, impenetrable and unshakable. Ana could throw herself against them until her bones were dust and never get to the other side again.

Assuming he didn't martyr himself before sundown.

It hurt, being shut out. It hurt more knowing she'd asked for it. She'd gotten careless and sloppy. She'd let Deacon convince her that it was safe to carve out a little breathing room, to be human. That had been her first mistake—how the hell would Deacon understand the pressure to meet some perfect, impossible ideal?

Ana's father had understood.

William Jordan wasn't a saint yet, but as Ana

laced her boots, she offered a silent prayer to him. *Help me get through this fight. Help me be smart. Help me get us all home alive.*

And when we are, help me figure out how to be strong enough to live my life alone.

Her father's voice didn't answer.

Ana supposed that shouldn't surprise her. She'd never really believed her father had ended up in some eternal purgatory, damned for his crime of trying to make a world a better place. The God Ana believed in—the one who told her to love fiercely and proudly— would have recognized the honor and loyalty in her father's heart.

When Ana closed her eyes to pray, she didn't imagine her father floating in darkness. She imagined him where he belonged after all those years of sacrifice—with her mother. Reunited. Happy. At peace.

They'd never offer their blessings on a solitary life for their only daughter. They'd want her to fight, the way she'd always fought—to believe she deserved everything she wanted and not stop until she had it firmly within her grasp.

But she wanted...love. Not just the big, obvious parts. The filthy ones. She wanted the tiny moments. Deacon watching her with a secret smile. The flour on his cheek and his willing submission to her aunts' teasing. The warmth of him at night when they curled around each other in bed. The way he asked her advice, and seemed to listen.

The way he'd leaned into her, vulnerable and tired, and let her see the parts of him no one else ever got to see.

The way he'd let her lean against him.

Her throat stung like she'd swallowed glass, and she laughed so she wouldn't cry. She didn't want love.

She wanted Deacon.

Too fucking bad. She'd fucked up, and apparently Deacon wasn't gonna offer her any second chances. And why would he? The rest of the world never had.

Ana swallowed past the lump in her throat and checked the clock over her desk. Six minutes left. Not enough time to cry. Not enough time to grieve. Just enough time to bury this pain so deep that all she could feel was a numb ache. It might fester there and poison her heart, but Ana didn't have the luxury of giving a shit.

It wasn't like her heart had done her any favors lately. Maybe if Deacon broke it badly enough, she could sweep away the unmendable pieces and live inside this numbness forever.

Then she'd be the perfect Rider.

eighteen

Some things never changed.

The Suicide Kings' compound wasn't one of them.

The surrounding terrain was the same, familiar enough that Deacon had slowed his bike even before reaching the well-hidden turnoff from the main road that led down into the canyon. He'd had to remind himself to keep the wheel straight, to drive past the turnoff and up into the hills beyond.

But now, as he stared down at the façade of the Kings' compound through the scope of Lucio's favorite rifle, he felt...nothing. No hint of recognition or familiarity.

The old man had taken possession of a pre-Flare bunker built into the canyon wall, the kind of place where paranoid people had once prepared for the coming apocalypse. Too bad they usually picked the wrong kind of apocalypse. The ones who built this bunker had apparently been braced for a full-scale nuclear conflict.

When the solar storms fried the electrical system responsible for their air and water filtration, they abandoned the bunker entirely. But it had suited the old man's purposes just fine. He rewired the systems for solar power, reinforced the entrance, and painted the whole thing to blend in with the craggy walls of the canyon. No one who didn't already know where it was could find the Kings' compound.

It looked different now, starkly visible in the morning sunlight. The entrance had been expanded, the small, squat vault replaced by a gray concrete building. A fence surrounded it, wicked wires he had no doubt were electrified.

Ana's voice came from just behind him. "Zeke says he found a signal, but their network is locked up pretty tight. He thinks he can get in, though."

The sound of her voice *hurt*. Not just his head or that vague place in his chest where his heart was supposed to be. He ached all over, like he'd trained too hard and then collapsed afterwards with innumerable bruises.

He couldn't flinch every time she spoke to him. But he couldn't quite face her, either. "The Kings want me in there, so Hunter and Gabe will find an access point. But Zeke'll have to work harder if he wants to breach their systems."

"Then any access point they find will be a trap."

He finally looked at her. She was calm, unruffled. Half a foot away, but she may as well have been on the other side of a whole fucking ocean. "We knew that already. But I made a promise not to go in there without the other Riders at my back, and I plan to keep it."

She stared at him in silence for a moment and

then looked away.

Lucio took the rifle from Deacon's hands and peered through the scope. "No guards stationed outside."

Laurel was kneeling behind a cluster of scrub a few yards away, a pair of binoculars around her neck. "I saw two, but they didn't seem to be patrolling. They came outside, had a smoke, and went right back in."

Lucio tilted his head—hesitant, though his expression didn't change—and gestured toward the opposite ridge. "Some well-placed explosives could bring the walls of the canyon right down on the complex. We could bury it without having to risk engagement."

Even if they knew for certain that only Kings were inside that bunker, the lingering questions, the possibility that Seth may have escaped, would haunt Deacon. But that wasn't the only reason the idea turned his stomach. "We have to assume there are noncombatants in there. Domestic workers, maintenance staff. Children."

"Yes." Lucio rubbed his chin. "Reyes?"

"You know me," he drawled, both thumbs hooked into his belt loops. "I never take the easy path if there's a rougher one available."

"So we're going in," Ana said quietly.

"Not all of us," Deacon told her.

Her brow furrowed, and she started to open her mouth, but her gaze shifted at the soft rasp of boots on gravel.

Hunter and Gabe crested the ridge behind them. They'd circled around the long way, making sure to stay out of sight of any lookouts or surveillance. Deacon turned away from Ana and raised one eyebrow. "Well?"

Hunter's expression was grim. "We found a defunct ventilation shaft. It's big enough to rappel down, no laser grid. We should be able to get into it easy enough." He shook his head. "In other words, they left a door open for us."

"Wouldn't be the first trap we've sprung," Gabe countered. "Nobody's ever really ready for us."

The Kings might come close, but the Riders had advantages. They trusted each other, and they knew how to get shit done. But, more than anything, they were fighting for something bigger than money.

"We'll be fine," he told them. "Reyes, Gabe, Hunter, and Lucio—grab the gear you need. You're with me. We'll get down there, see what happens. Ana? Zeke and Laurel will stay here with you."

He saw the questions piling up behind Ana's eyes. The stiffness in her muscles. But she remained rigidly, coolly controlled. "What's our objective?"

Her doubt hurt more than her chilly regard, but in a different way. A less personal one. So he embraced it, facing her squarely as she glared at him. "The most important one. Zeke will keep trying to bust into their network, and you'll work on contingency plans. If the mission goes sideways, your job is to get the rest of the Riders out."

"The rest of the Riders," she echoed, each word precise.

He couldn't slip it past her. She was too ready for him to pull some supreme act of self-sacrifice. And it was tempting, really, to go ahead and embrace his destiny. To stop fighting the fact that the whole goddamn sector was just waiting to turn him into paintings and prayers and tattoos. A sainted martyr.

Except that somewhere along the way, this had stopped being about him, about vengeance or settling old scores or cleaning up what was left of his guilty past. When he closed his eyes, all he could see was Seth surviving. Sector One in danger.

Ana in danger.

No. He had to finish this.

"You have your orders," he whispered.

Her eyes blazed. She hated him for doing this to her, but she kept it from her voice as she replied just as softly, "Yes, sir."

If they listened hard enough, could the others hear his heart break?

He spun around. "Everyone on comms. Let's move."

Lucio, Reyes, and Hunter fell in behind him. Gabe took the lead, tracing a path back past the line of sight of the surveillance cameras. When Deacon glanced back, Zeke was bent over his portable laptop, intent on whatever had his fingers flying over the keys and screen. Laurel had unzipped the massive bag she'd insisted on bringing, and Ana—

Ana was staring after him, just as focused as Zeke, as if fixing the image of their retreating forms into her brain.

"Worst way to die," Reyes said brightly. "Who's up? Lucio?"

For once, he didn't rattle off fifteen carefully researched historical tortures like scaphism or waterboarding. "In an obvious trap we walked right into, knowing full well it might get us killed."

"Oh, ye of little faith."

"Shh." Gabe scrambled over a boulder and glared back at Reyes. "Stealth. You understand the concept."

"Gallows humor," Reyes shot back. "You understand the concept."

"If you both don't shut up," Hunter muttered, "the Kings won't have to kill you."

The top of the ventilation shaft looked like any other kind of aging access door—plain, unmarked steel, five feet across, with peeling paint and pits of rust dotting its surface. There was a slot for an old-fashioned padlock to secure it, and the broken lock lay on the rocky ground nearby. The rusted hinges shrieked as Deacon pulled open the door, and he cringed before stepping back to let Gabe go to work on cutting the bars across the top of the shaft.

Lucio handed out the rigger's belts as Gabe fired up the tiny oxy-fuel cutting torch. Then he glanced over at Hunter. "Best way to die."

Hunter pulled away the first bar as Gabe freed it. "Starting to think maybe there isn't one."

"Hmm. Reyes?"

Reyes didn't answer until the final bar had been detached and tossed aside. In fact, he was uncharacteristically quiet as he fixed his belt in place, checked the retracting wire mechanism, and smoothed his gloves.

Then he winked at Lucio and grinned. "With your boots on."

"Notice he said boots, not pants," Gabe murmured.

Reyes waggled his eyebrows. "No tengo pelos en la lengua." With that, he clipped his carabiner to the solid steel frame ringing the ventilation shaft and lowered himself in.

Lucio froze, his brow furrowed in confusion. "Did he just...say he doesn't have a hairy tongue?"

Hunter snorted out a laugh and clapped Lucio on the back. "It's an old saying. It means he's not afraid to tell it like it is."

"Maybe the rest of us should stay up here and let him talk the Kings to death." In spite of his words, Deacon fixed his carabiner in place and dropped down into the abyss.

The ventilation duct felt smaller on the inside. Deacon cut on his light so he could see the bottom, but it seemed dull and dim, unable to penetrate the gloom. His ears rang from the harsh sound of the rappelling wire spooling free as he sank into the darkness.

A few feet from the rough concrete floor, he flicked the switch on his belt and shuddered to a halt. He released the buckle on the belt and dropped the last bit of distance to the floor, landing with a soft thud.

Deacon activated his earpiece as the others slid down behind him. "You got me, Zeke?"

"Loud and clear, boss."

"We're in. Stand by."

The hallway dead-ended beneath the shaft. The other disappeared around a single corner, and Deacon motioned for Gabe and Reyes to take point. The familiar rhythms of working as a team, moving as one unit, were taking over. It didn't matter that his thoughts were somewhere else, lingering up on that ridge with Ana. This was his job, his life.

The only thing he'd ever been any damn good at.

Reyes flashed the all clear, and Deacon flowed forward with Hunter and Lucio at his heels. They rounded the corner, and all he could see was red as laser sights splashed through the darkness and off the walls before honing in on his chest. A quick glance at the others revealed *dozens* of them, trained squarely on each of them.

"Lights." Seth's voice was still echoing around them as electricity clicked and buzzed, chasing away the darkness.

They were in a huge, cavernous room lined with catwalks—and men bearing rifles. Completely surrounded, and all Deacon could do was give the order. "Stand down, Riders."

Next to him, Gabe tightened his grip on his weapon, his eyes feverish. Wild.

"*Montero*." Deacon waited until Gabe looked at him, then repeated his words through gritted teeth. "Stand. Down."

The others were already lowering their weapons to the floor. After a tense moment, Gabe exhaled and followed suit with tense, jerky movements.

"Nice," Seth drawled, clapping his hands together mockingly. "You always were good at that, weren't you, old friend? Finding obedient puppies to follow you around and only piss when you tell them to."

He didn't have much time before they were disarmed, stripped of their equipment—and checked for communications devices. He had to make these words count. "Six-to-one odds, Seth. Not much choice in the matter."

Seth strode forward until he was nose-to-nose with Deacon. Still smiling that mocking smile, he reached up and plucked the communications transmitter from his ear. Seth turned it over in his fingers, examining it for a moment, then dropped it to the concrete and crushed it under his boot.

"Sweep them," he ordered.

nineteen

She'd probably never see Deacon again.

For long minutes after Laurel returned to her surveillance, Ana watched the spot where he'd disappeared into the trees, trying to reconstruct her last sight of him.

He'd looked back at her. Their eyes had clashed. He'd looked away.

Maybe, in the lonely days to come, she'd be able to augment the memory, make it more than it was. She would close her eyes and pretend they'd stared at each other for endless, breathless seconds. That she'd seen futures that could never be in the darkness of his gaze, words he couldn't say. Promises he wished he could keep. His apology. His regret. His love.

Goodbye.

Instead, she'd seen his unyielding acceptance

of his own death. And what had he seen in her face? Nothing soft, that was for sure. She hadn't sent him into the beyond with sweet smiles and tender goodbyes. She should have, even as she hated him for leaving her behind. She *should have.*

But she couldn't.

It didn't hurt yet. It would, eventually, she supposed. But the only thing she could feel now was chilling, icy numbness and resolve to do the job she'd been given. To obey her orders.

To be the perfect Rider.

Turning her back on the path the others had taken, she glanced at Zeke. "What's the status on their network?"

"I'm trying," he muttered, a warning sign even without the deep furrow between his brows and the tense set of his shoulders. Zeke never *tried.* Zeke just *did,* usually with plenty of boasting and bravado along the way. The lack of either signaled significant trouble.

Another reason to keep her cool.

Ana crouched next to Laurel. "Notice anything else?"

"Just the obvious." The woman gestured down into the canyon. "Still no patrols, so they're not worried about security. Which means they're locked up tighter than Grandma's good silver."

Ana dug her binoculars out of her pocket and unfolded them. The approach was steep and offered next to no cover. Undoubtedly every inch was covered by cameras and motion detectors. The fence would be a bitch to climb and the razor wire at the top discouraged it. Cutting through wouldn't be so bad—if the thing wasn't electric.

Behind her, Zeke said, "Loud and clear, boss." Awareness tingled along her spine, making all of her distant numbness a lie. Deacon's voice was in Zeke's earpiece, and she was hungry for it in a way that had her gripping her binoculars too tightly. One more bit of him, before he threw his life away like it was worthless. Just one more—

Fighting back the ache, she shifted her surveillance to the doors. "How'd those smokers get in and out? Keycards or codes?"

"Definitely a code, but I didn't catch it. The panel's half-hidden behind that little tree, of all damn things."

Of course it was. Even if they could get past the cameras, and the motion sensors, and the fence...how did you get into a door you couldn't hack and didn't have the codes for? "Zeke," she said, "how's—?"

"*Shit.*"

The panic in Zeke's voice had Ana on her feet and halfway to his side while the blond was still fumbling at his keyboard. "Deacon told them to stand down," he said, still typing frantically. He smashed a final button, and a familiar, gravelly voice spilled out of the small speakers.

"—weren't you, old friend? Finding obedient puppies to follow you around and only piss when you tell them to."

Seth's voice. The mockery was unmistakable. So was the satisfaction.

"Six-to-one odds, Seth," came a just-as-familiar voice, and Ana's heart and stomach leapt in opposite directions. "Not much choice in the matter."

Deacon sounded so calm, still in control, passing them the information they needed to arrange their plans. Five men had gone in, which meant Deacon had eyes on at least thirty Kings.

Her whole body ached, helplessly tensed for his next words. But all they got was a muffled noise and a crackling sound, followed by static and then silence.

"Zeke—" She gripped his shoulder too hard. "What happened? Can you get anyone else on comms?"

"I'm trying." He worked rapidly, swearing under his breath in increasingly colorful language as words scrolled across his screen too fast for Ana to read. "Shit, they're going offline one by one. *Shit.*"

He looked panicked. Ana didn't have that luxury. She forced herself to relax her grip on his shoulder until it was encouraging instead of frantic. "That's okay, Zeke. We knew this could happen. We're Plan B, right? So focus and get us into their security system."

"Right, right." Zeke exhaled roughly and drove his fingers through his hair, a nervous habit that had become a tic since Jaden's death. She squeezed his shoulder again and returned to Laurel's side.

Part of Ana curled in on herself, clutching her shredded, bleeding heart. But the rest of her—the woman trained by William Jordan—surveyed the compound as her father's voice drifted through her memory.

Don't get ahead of yourself, girl. Work the problem. What do you have? What do you need? How can the things you have get you what you need?

She needed information. She needed a way in that wasn't a trap. She needed to find the Riders, get them out, and kill every last King she encountered along the way.

One problem at a time, babygirl.

She had a jumpy hacker and a clear-eyed Sector Three sniper who'd arrived with a bag of toys. Ana nudged it with her foot as she squinted at the fenced-in entryway. "You've been watching a while. Have the smokers come out more than once?"

"Twice. Ten minutes apart." She glanced at her watch. "If it's a pattern, we have about two more minutes until we see them again."

Ana had gone through Laurel's bag when they'd first arrived to categorize the various tools. Apparently, some part of her brain had already started working the angles, because the idea came as easy as breathing. "Don't you have something in here that can shoot darts?"

Laurel nodded and reached for the bag. "It'll shoot just about anything you want."

Ana retrieved Zeke's bag and dug through it until she found one of his tiny listening devices. "Hey," she told him, poking him to get his attention. "Pair this up. Fast."

In a few seconds, it was done. Ana surfaced with the quick-drying adhesive and took a dart from Laurel, affixing the tiny bug to the end. "Can you compensate your aim for this weight?"

Laurel took it back from her, testing its weight by bouncing it in her hand. "Yeah, no problem."

Easy words, but then Laurel loaded the dart, stretched out on her stomach at the edge of the ravine, and braced the gun on her arm. After two seconds— and one slow, deep breath—she fired, and the dart vanished.

Ana lifted her binoculars and scanned the area near the door. Most of it was unrelieved concrete and steel, and she was about to ask Laurel where she'd aimed when her gaze passed over the tiny potted tree placed specifically to hide the entry panel.

A tiny black dot was barely visible against the dark bark of the trunk—a trunk all of two inches wide. Admiration momentarily overrode everything else— Lucio and Ashwin were both *good*, with the mental agility to perform complex calculations in their head. But she wasn't sure either of them could have hit a target that small, from this distance, even without an awkwardly weighted dart. "Nice shot."

They both ducked back behind cover as the door opened a moment later. Zeke turned up the volume on his spare tablet and pushed it toward them before returning to his computer.

The bug worked perfectly. They heard the snap of the door and the scrape of boots over concrete, even the click of a lighter. Then, "Fuck, shit's getting stupid in there."

It was a smooth voice, deep and pitched low. A second voice—higher, with a hint of a drawl—replied, "Getting?"

A snort. "Seth's around the bend on this one," Low Voice said. "It could have been over weeks ago."

"Seth lives around the bend," Drawl replied. "I'm telling you, he hasn't been right since the old man kicked it."

"Because there's no one left to rein him in." A pause, presumably to take a drag on his cigarette, and Low Voice continued. "But this is a new low. We had them in a fucking kill box. That should have been the end of it. *Again.* Taking captives is always stupid, but trying to hold goddamn Riders?"

Ana closed her eyes and let out a breath, dizzily relieved. They were still alive—for now.

Seth was still an idiot.

The drawler agreed. "You know they're gonna bust out of there, sooner or later. And more of us are going to die because of Seth's vengeance boner."

Ana resolved to make that happen.

Deep Voice groaned. "What *is* it with him and Deacon, anyway? The bastard's been gone for how many years?"

"Twenty, at least. But I guess that's the point.

He went AWOL on a mission, then turned around and started protecting his damn mark. Anyone else, they would have tracked down and ended." The drawler's voice dropped to a whisper, but Zeke's bug still picked it up. "I heard from Haze that when Seth inherited the old man's files, he found proof that the bastard knew where Deacon was the whole time. Was even checking up on him. Like he missed him."

"Shiiiiit." Deep Voice huffed. "So we're all fucked. Maybe we should go downstairs and shoot the Riders before Seth's daddy issues get us all killed."

"Be my guest, but you better be willing to run afterwards. Seth'll make you wish a Rider had gotten you."

"Fine, but if the one with the crazy eyes comes at me, I'm shooting to kill. I don't care what our orders are."

The sound of boots scraping on the pavement followed—probably someone snuffing a cigarette—then the beep of the panel next to the door. Ana turned the last statements over in her head as she sat back on her heels, trying to tease useful intelligence from angry ranting.

The Riders were being held somewhere inside. Seth's stupidity would keep them alive—for now. They were resourceful and had planned for a trap, so there was a good chance they'd find a way out of their cell.

But if Ana hadn't cleared a path for them by then, a bunch of antsy mercenaries sick of Seth's bullshit would shoot the hell out of them. And if it took too long, those mercenaries might not wait for the Riders to make their escape attempt.

Zeke hacking their network was Plan B. It was time for Ana to come up with Plan C.

twenty

The Kings had prepared a heroes' welcome for them, all right—the drunk tank.

The old man had put the holding cell together out of necessity. Mercenaries weren't exactly known for their universal lack of vice, and Sand Harbor was close enough to the compound for a quick visit. Flush with cash and credits, they'd roll out to raise a little hell on a fairly regular basis. Problem was, they never seemed to leave *hell* where they found it. They'd come back drunk, spoiling for a fight, and the old man needed a place to put them while they cooled off and sobered up.

Deacon had wound up here exactly once before. He couldn't remember the insult that had sparked his rage, or even who its target had been, but he remembered the old man snatching him up by the back of his shirt, dragging him down the hallway, and tossing him onto the single stained, lumpy bunk.

The bunk was gone. Everything else had been stripped out, as well, leaving behind stark walls and a bare floor. Only the smell remained—decades of piss and puke and blood that no amount of scrubbing could erase.

"Watch the goods, asshole." Reyes stumbled across the threshold and smacked into the wall.

The man who shoved him laid a hand on his side-arm. "What did you say?"

"You heard me. I said watch it." Reyes's lip had been split, and he bared his bloody teeth in a feral grin as he added, "Asshole."

The King barked out a laugh, a scornful sound full of angry promise instead of amusement, and stepped forward.

Hunter urged Reyes back with an arm across his chest, but he shook his head. "No way, man. He wants to get rough, I'll get rough. I'll rip his fucking head off."

It was no use fighting, not until they had a handle on their situation. Deacon reached for him, as well. "Reyes, no."

"Better listen to Daddy." Seth filled the wide doorway, stretching his arms across it as he surveyed his captives. "Now, tell me—where are the rest of the Riders?"

A chill shivered up Deacon's spine. "What you see is what you get, Seth."

"Bullshit. By my count, there should be at least twice as many of you. Maybe you left the important ones at home." His eyes glinted. "Or maybe they're right outside."

Deacon bit his tongue so hard he tasted blood.

Seth shrugged. "Eh, we'll find out." He gestured vaguely as he turned away. "Grab one of them, will you?"

The man headed towards Reyes, who was already stepping forward to meet him with murder in his eyes.

Before Deacon could intervene, Seth stopped. "No, not him. We want information, not blood. Well, not *just* blood." He glanced back over his shoulder, his gaze lighting on Gabe. "Bring him."

Gabe glanced at Deacon. Just for a few seconds, his lips parting as if to speak. But the guard grabbed his arm, and Gabe's expression shut down as he shook off the grip and walked forward on his own.

No. Not Gabe, and not like this, when they still hadn't settled their uneasy business. Deacon dove for the door. Two of the Kings intercepted him and tried to haul him back, but he stood his ground. "Cut the shit, Seth. We're way past playing games. We both know why I'm here, so take me instead."

"Don't be greedy, Deacon." Seth arched an eyebrow as his men pulled Gabe from the room. "Your turn'll come." He started whistling, a haunting tune that echoed through the hallway as he receded into the shadows.

One of the Kings slammed an elbow into Deacon's jaw, and he reeled, almost falling into the wall before Lucio caught him. He steadied himself and turned just in time to see the door slide shut, to hear the deep, metallic clang as the lock engaged.

God-fucking-dammit.

Reyes growled and whirled on Hunter. "*Tell me* you did the thing with the thing."

"Of course I did." Hunter propped his right foot on Reyes's knee and pulled at his boot laces. "I'm not stupid." With his boot loosened, he reached in and pulled out his comms device. "I switched it off before I socked it away so they wouldn't pick it up on a sweep."

He handed it to Deacon, who flicked the tiny power switch as he raised it to his ear. Instead of the soft chirp of the device attempting to make contact with the monitoring station, it emitted a shrill, strident tone of feedback that had him jerking it away again.

Seth must have made improvements to the drunk tank before inviting them over. "They're jamming the signal," he told them.

Hunter laced his fingers behind his head. "*Fuck.* Then it's useless."

"Perhaps not." Lucio stood by the door, running his fingers along the nearly seamless edge. "It's a magnetic lock, probably controlled electronically. If we can—"

"Get it open," Reyes finished, already digging in a hidden pocket on his cargo pants. "That's what we're gonna do, right? Get the hell out of here and rescue Gabe, preferably while shooting every last one of these repugnant bastards in the face along the way."

The stone wall was cool against Deacon's back, and he leaned against it for a heartbeat. Lives were riding on what he did next, whether he could marshal his wits and all those years of training and make it *work.*

He straightened. "That's what we're gonna do," he assured Reyes. "But first, we calm down. Take a breath. We inventory what resources we have and lay out what we know—quickly and quietly. Nothing to arouse suspicion until we're ready to move. Got it?"

Hunter nodded, and Lucio murmured his assent as he continued to study the door. Only Reyes hesitated, and Deacon took him by the shoulders.

"We can do this. We can save Gabe, but we can't do it without you." He kept his voice low and even, though his thoughts whirled and his chest ached. He wanted to *unleash*, to bang on the door until someone—anyone—came running, and then loosen his tight hold on control and just...make the Kings pay.

Soon.

The smokers were punctual as hell.

Ana used their appearance to track time as an increasingly harried Zeke struggled for a way past the apparently robust security the Kings had installed.

The first time the men reappeared, Ana had paused to listen to their conversation, hoping they would drop more information. But their bitching followed a similar path, interspersed with complaints that they could be balls-deep in hookers down in Sand Harbor if Seth would move it the fuck along.

Charming. And useless.

So Ana tuned them out, except as a measure of time slipping through her fingers. Instead, she focused on the puzzle of the fence, the cameras, the motion detectors, and that fucking door.

She and Laurel had identified a few of the cameras by sweeping for signals with another of Zeke's toys. Ana quickly discarded the idea of shooting them to disable them. She had confidence in Laurel's ability to snipe small targets in rapid succession, but the chances of getting *everything* were slim to none—and the Kings would be on alert from the first shot.

Work one problem at a time.

This had always been easier in theoretical exercises. Lives rested on her shoulders now—Hunter, Gabe, Reyes, Lucio...

And Deacon. Deacon, who didn't care about his own life. But she did. God, she cared so much it burned in her gut and bled through her best attempts at numbness. The thought of leaving him to die in a hole in this

mountain, locked away from sun and fresh air, knowing he'd never get a proper funeral, knowing he'd die
alone.

*If you can't see a path through, change your per-
spective. It's like one of Eliza's balls of yarn, Ana. When
it gets knotted up, you have to find the right string to
pull first.*

Fine, forget the cameras and the fence. Even if she
circumvented all of them, she'd still be on the wrong
side of that door. She'd gotten a glimpse the last time it
had opened—a solid six inches of steel at least. No one
was cutting through that.

If Zeke couldn't get into their security system,
having him attack the keypad wouldn't be much
easier—and they'd be sitting ducks the whole time,
obvious targets trapped in the canyon with no real
cover, waiting to get shot.

Trapped...

A memory tickled at her. She ignored the sound of
Zeke's cursing and closed her eyes, struggling to chase
it down.

Trapped. Electronic doors and trapped.

Her eyes snapped open. "Oh God, I'm an idiot."

Laurel glanced over from the spot where she was
hunkered down, surveying the opposite ridge. "What's
that?"

"Deacon said they refurbished this place after the
Flares, right?"

"Yeah, it's some kind of old bunker." Laurel rubbed
her temple. "What are you thinking?"

Ana crouched next to her, excitement making the
words tumble out as fast as her tongue could manage.
"There's one change just about everybody made to high-
tech buildings after the Flares. They were so reliant
on technology back then that when all the power went

down and the circuits overloaded, people in bunkers like that? They got trapped behind steel doors they couldn't open, and suffocated."

"So if we cut the power, the doors will open." Laurel nodded, then grimaced. "How, though? They're bound to have all the access points secured."

"We don't need an access point." With her blood pumping faster, Ana turned. "Zeke—"

"I'm trying," he growled. "This shit is so far past military-grade security. Military-grade security wishes it was this impenetrable."

"Leave it," Ana ordered, and his gaze snapped up from the screen. "I need you to build me something."

Both of his eyebrows swept up. "Build what?"

She turned back to the Kings' compound and imagined it without power. Without cameras, or motion detectors, or a charge on the fence. The front door unlocked. The interior doors unlocked. The Riders free. The Kings rushing to evacuate—right into a hail of bullets.

Total chaos. And the perfect trap.

"I need you to make me an EMP bomb." She grinned at him. "A big one. Let's give the Suicide Kings the full Flares experience."

twenty-one

"Hold it still," Lucio whispered. "I think I can boost the signal output, I just need to connect these two—"

Reyes hissed out a curse and yanked his hand back from the tangle of wires sprouting from the transmitter. "Fucking thing shocked me."

"Good. That means there's still juice left."

Hunter waved at them from his position by the door. "Someone's coming."

It reached Deacon's ears a moment later, the murmur of voices, the shuffle of soft-soled boots on concrete. "Hide it," he ordered, then faced the door so the first thing they would see would be him.

The lock disengaged, and the door slid open. As it did, a battered and bloody Gabe fell inside.

Deacon caught him, quickly cataloguing his injuries. A split lip. An eye rapidly swelling shut. Shallow slashes along his arms. At least two dislocated fingers. And that was just what he could see.

As the door slammed shut, Gabe sagged against Deacon. "I need..." a low groan, "...to sit down."

"Over here." Deacon helped him to the back corner of the room, bracing his weight until they reached the wall.

Gabe slid down it, wincing as Hunter took his hand and prodded it. Gabe's jaw clenched as he stared up at Deacon. "They haven't found them yet. They don't even know how many Riders are out there."

"Are they listening to us?"

He shook his head slowly. "I don't think so."

"It's possible that whatever they're using to jam communications in here makes it impossible to bug." Hunter's expression was grim. "I need to set your fingers."

Gabe took a deep breath, then another. Then he nodded abruptly.

Hunter made quick work of the dislocations. Gabe gritted his teeth but didn't utter so much as a curse as Hunter popped the joints back into place. Deacon wiped away the sweat beading on Gabe's forehead as Hunter tested the swollen digits by flexing them.

"They asked a lot of questions, mostly about where the rest of the Riders are. They know names. Details," Gabe said, his voice still edged in pain. "I didn't say anything."

"I know you didn't." Seth probably would have been disappointed if Gabe *had* broken, because then he'd have no excuse to torture everyone else—not that he needed an excuse.

Too bad for him. Riders didn't break.

A moment later, Lucio shattered the thought. "The next one of us to go may have a unique opportunity," he observed quietly. "It wouldn't be difficult to disarm a guard, take his weapon. It could very well lead to escape."

"No," Deacon grated. "You'd be killed by the other guards before you even got your finger on a trigger."

Lucio just shrugged. "As we've already determined, there are worse ways to die."

"I said *no*." Deacon rose. "Your orders are to stay alive—"

The door clicked and slid open again. Seth stood there, grinning and expectant. "Have y'all decided who my next guest will be?"

Dark rage seethed under Deacon's skin, so strong that his peripheral vision actually wavered. His hands clenched into fists, and his muscles trembled under the effort it took to relax them. He didn't hate Seth enough to kill him, not anymore.

Now, he hated him enough to keep him alive. To make it last, to turn that satisfied grin to a rictus of pain and terror.

"Me," he answered softly.

Seth groaned impatiently. "Come *on*, we've been over this—"

"And I'm tired of waiting, so let's fucking *do this*, already."

"Holy Jesus." Seth scrubbed both hands over his face with another groan. "I'm gonna fucking kill you."

Deacon was grateful for the numb acceptance that settled around him. Reyes was behind him, saying something, but he couldn't make out the words. There was only one path, one way out of this mess, and he focused on it.

He took a step forward. Starting down that path. "No, you won't. Because you're a coward."

Seth drew a pistol so fast it might have appeared

out of nowhere. But time was slowing down, stretching around Deacon until every heartbeat took an eternity. A trick of the imagination, surely, that when his time was at an end, it seemed to go on forever.

The pistol barrel wavered between his forehead and his mouth before Seth managed to steady it. "You are such a self-involved *prick*," he spat. "You can't even see what's really going on here because you can't wrap your goddamn brain around the fact that it's not about you. It's a job, man. It's a fucking job."

Deacon froze. "It's what?"

"You heard me." Seth scowled, hatred burning from his eyes, giving lie to his next words. "I don't give two shits about you. The Kings were hired to eliminate Gideon's Riders, and that's what I'm going to do." He gestured with his gun. "Starting with you. Say goodbye to your boys."

It's a job. The words bounced around in Deacon's head, echoing over and over until they weren't even words anymore, just sounds, each syllable drowning out the ones around it.

All this time, he'd assumed the Kings were after him, and everything else was just a distraction. His history with them, the timing, the way Seth had taunted him—it was always the only thing that made sense. But if someone had hired the Kings to target the Riders, that meant *Deacon* was the distraction.

He could work with that.

He turned to Reyes, who immediately grabbed his arm. "Don't do this. We'll figure something out."

"Yeah, you will." He almost smiled at the stern, serious expression on the man's face. "Reyes, it's okay."

"No, it's not, goddammit." He turned to Hunter for backup. "Will you tell him?"

But Hunter remained silent. He stared at Deacon

for what felt like minutes—hours, even—then nodded once. "You've got this. Walk with God."

"Motherfu—" Reyes whirled and slammed his hand against the wall, and Hunter stepped closer, speaking to him in low, unintelligible tones.

Deacon moved on. Eventually, the others would help Reyes understand.

Lucio faced him squarely, his eyes clear and wide. Then, bafflingly, he hugged Deacon, drawing him close with both arms wrapped around him. The embrace put Lucio's mouth right next to his ear, and he whispered, "The voice of the righteous will always be heard."

Deacon's confusion melted as he felt Lucio slip something into his front pocket—the tiny transmitter Hunter had hidden away in his boot.

Gabe's face locked in harsh lines of pain as he pushed himself to his feet. He stood a pace away from Deacon, the silence full of all the words they'd never gotten a chance to say—the air they would never clear now.

Then Gabe extended his uninjured hand. "Brothers in this life, brothers in the next."

Deacon grasped his hand. "Deliver a message for me?"

"Of course."

Saying the words out loud hurt, like someone stomping on his chest with their full weight. But he could do this. He had to. "Tell her I didn't run away. And that I'll see her again...someday."

Gabe pulled him closer, into a swift, hard hug. "I will."

"That's heartwarming. Now get your ass in gear." Seth jerked his head toward the door, and Deacon obeyed without argument.

For a moment, fear gripped him, a certainty that

Reyes would rush Seth because he couldn't handle what had to happen now. Deacon held his breath, and he didn't let it free until the door clanged shut behind them without incident.

"Don't do anything until I get back," Seth commanded.

"But, sir—" one of the guards began to protest.

"Lock it!" Seth roared. His rage filled the hallway, bouncing off the walls like a tangible thing.

"Yes, sir." Resentment seethed under the words.

Seth prodded Deacon down the hallway with the muzzle of the pistol pressed between his shoulder blades. He could fight him, grapple for the gun, but the odds weren't in his favor. The only thing Deacon had going for him right now was Seth's single, terse instruction.

Don't do anything until I get back.

If he played this right, Deacon could buy them something more precious than gold—*time.* He had to use what he knew of Seth, because every moment he kept him occupied was a moment his Riders had to think, plan, strategize, escape.

Live.

"You've made a mistake," Deacon said finally.

"Oh, okay." Seth jabbed him harder. "Turn right. And shut up."

"I'm serious, Seth. You fucked up."

Seth thumped him on the back of the head with the barrel of the pistol. "I said *shut it*. End of the hall."

There was nothing at the end of the hall except a blank stone wall. Deacon stopped at it, tensed to move if Seth planned to murder him where he stood.

But Seth just reached out, keeping the muzzle of the gun pressed tight to the base of Deacon's skull as he flicked open a concealed panel on the short wall at the end of the hall. There was a mechanical door handle inside, and Seth used it to haul the wall open, revealing a hidden space behind it.

The gun barrel jabbed Deacon again. "Go."

He stepped into a medium-sized room, about twenty feet square, puzzlingly empty except for the rows of lights on the ceiling. He'd expected torture, or even a summary execution staged for the amusement of the other Suicide Kings. But this was a complete mystery.

At least until he heard a *beep*, turned, and caught sight of Seth just inside the door. He was *disarming*, placing all of his weapons into a biometric safe built into the wall. And then Deacon understood what Seth had planned for him.

He wanted him to hurt before he died.

"Fife said it wouldn't work, you know." Seth chuckled. "He said you were too smart to fall for the vengeance thing. I told him it'd work like a charm. And you know how I knew?" A pair of brass knuckles hit the top of the pile. "Because you've always thought you were the fucking dead center of the whole goddamn world."

"Says the man who's getting ready to beat me to death when a bullet would get the job done quicker." Deacon shook his head. "That was your second mistake—falling for your own con. You can say it 'til you're blue in the face, that this isn't about me, but you're proving something different right now."

The safe closed and locked with another quiet *beep*. "Humor me—what was the first mistake?"

"Taking a contract on the Riders."

"You think so?" The corners of Seth's mouth pulled down, as if in thought or consideration, though Deacon knew he could be giving neither to his warning. This was all a show to set up his next verbal jab. "I'm pretty satisfied with how it's going so far."

"They're not soldiers or mercs who just happen to work for Gideon and live in Sector One." Deacon watched as Seth flexed his fingers. "They're part of that place. Of its religion."

"Uh-huh." Seth stretched his neck and rolled his shoulders. "Then why would someone hire me to kill them all?"

His words were still hanging in the air when Seth shot across the room. There wasn't enough space to avoid his grapple, but Deacon dug in his heels to keep Seth from using the momentum to slam him against the wall.

Seth recovered quickly, wrapping an arm around Deacon's neck to hold him still for a solid punch square to the nose.

Deacon staggered away, pain blossoming through his head, and Seth drew in a deep, satisfied breath. "Yep, this is gonna be fun."

Deacon interrupted his celebratory moment with a feint left that turned into a hard right hook. The force of it snapped Seth's head to one side, and blood splattered from his busted lip.

Seth touched his ravaged lip gingerly, then smiled at him through bloody teeth. "If you think this is gonna stop me from beating your face in—"

Deacon danced away. "Trust me, I don't."

"Good." Seth bent his knees, lowering his center of gravity as he began to circle Deacon. "I knew this wouldn't be easy. Might have to get regen afterwards, but you know what?" He shot forward again, landing a sharp jab on Deacon's chin before quickly drawing back. "It'll be so, so worth it."

twenty-two

The smokers had stopped coming outside.

As hour two ticked down, Ana paced a safe distance from the terrifying tangle of wires, steel, and God-only-knew-what that Zeke was methodically assembling. He'd stripped parts from two of their motorcycles to put with half the tech gadgets in his *and* Laurel's combined stash.

Ana had to trust he knew what he was doing. And pretend he wasn't muttering, *capacitor, transformer, trigger* over and over in a voice that reminded her of the mad scientists in the old movies he liked to play in the common room sometimes.

The fact that the smokers hadn't returned bothered her. It could simply mean their shift was over. Or something could have gone down inside that building— an escape attempt or a murder or just Deep Voice and the Drawler finally working themselves up enough to risk Seth's wrath by shooting the Riders.

She wouldn't know until she got inside.

A rumble behind her heralded Laurel's return. Ana turned in time to see her lifting a bulky bag off the back of her bike. "Got the thing you wanted." She was panting as she delivered the bag, as if she'd ridden so hard she hadn't had time to breathe. "It wasn't cheap, either."

"I gave you enough cash to buy Sand Harbor," Zeke retorted, unzipping it so fast the bag tore. He lifted out a large coil of copper tubing thicker than Ana's thumb and moved to the front of his device, where long metal spikes stuck out like the skeletal structure of an enormous megaphone.

Ana started to follow him. "Do you need—?"

"*No*," Zeke barked, throwing out his hand. "Stay back. I'm only about fifty percent sure I'm not going to electrocute myself before this is over."

Ana obediently took two huge steps back, until she stood next to Laurel. "Don't listen to him," she told the other woman under her breath. "I recognize that tone of voice. He's got this, but he wants us to properly appreciate how amazing it is."

"If he pulls this off, trust me. I'll be properly appreciative."

In spite of the stress of the moment, Ana found her lips curving. Few people could resist Zeke. "They have their moments. After we rescue everyone, you should come back to the barracks with us and hang out. Some of these jerks can be downright charming."

"If my heart can take it."

Thinking about the common room was a mistake. If they didn't manage to pull Deacon out of there alive, Ana didn't know how she'd ever set foot in her sanctuary again. Or her bedroom, where the memory of those last angry words would always battle the memory of his warm skin gliding over hers as pleasure broke over her.

Or the workout room, where he'd knocked her on her ass a few hundred times—and she'd only done it to him once. Just the one time, because she'd never have another chance.

And the armory. Sweet fuck, the armory. The saints didn't have enough mercy between them to erase that memory. She'd have to start every fight for the rest of her life staring at her locker and remembering how it felt to have Deacon pin her up against it.

"Okay," Zeke said, interrupting the miserable spiral of her thoughts. "I think I got this."

Ana turned and painstakingly kept doubt from her face. The contraption looked...

Ridiculous.

Zeke had coiled the copper tubing around the protruding metal rods in a loose spiral. The mess of wires and metal behind it looked like a contained storm had whipped through a room of old tech and left everything in a tangled heap.

"Don't look at it like that," Zeke chided as he herded them back. "It's a fucking masterpiece. People are gonna write ballads about the time I pulled this off."

"If it doesn't kill us," Ana reminded him.

"Well, obviously." Once they were a sufficient distance away, Zeke drew a pellet gun from his belt and handed it to Laurel. "See that little metal plate I drew the X on? Can you hit it to close the circuit?"

Laurel lifted the gun. "I'll pretend you didn't ask me that."

Ana pulled out her binoculars and sought out one of the cameras, watching its slow movement as it swept in a wide arc. "Okay," she murmured. "If this works, we have to move fast. Make sure you're ready."

She heard Zeke's calm voice over the soft *click* of a magazine sliding into place. "Got it, boss."

"Okay, Laurel. Do it."

Ana didn't know what she expected. An explosion, or at least some crackle of electricity. But the *clink* of the metal plates slapping together faded into silence so intense her nervous breaths echoed loudly in her ears.

The camera stopped.

"Move!" she ordered, already charging forward. She swept up the bolt cutters on her way and skidded down the dirt and gravel incline, comforted by the sounds of Zeke and Laurel hard on her heels.

"Zeke?" she shouted as they bolted across the road and toward the fence.

He had one of his multipurpose gadgets in his hand already, held out at arm's length. "It's still dead, no electricity."

Ana didn't waste time. If she were the Kings, she'd have a backup generator inside with at least enough juice to keep the air flowing and light the emergency evacuation routes.

And to keep the perimeter fence hot.

The cutters sheared through the steel like butter. Zeke hauled at the fence as she cut, until they'd opened a hole wide enough for Laurel to wiggle through. Ana dropped the cutters and followed her, the back of her neck crawling as they darted across the open space to the door.

But no sniper shots cracked out. No alarms went off. Laurel skidded to the front door, and Ana drew her gun to cover her as she swung the heavy door wide.

Laurel went in firing. Screams echoed through the dark room, quickly drowned out by return fire. Bullets whined through the air, one passing by Ana so closely that she could *feel* its heat on her arm.

She ducked inside and put her back against the wall. Time had slowed again, giving her that sweet edge—but satisfaction and anticipation didn't follow. The stakes were impossibly high, and the cost of failure—

Please be alive.

The thought came as she lifted her arms and focused on her first target. The light spilling through the door was just strong enough to outline vulnerable spots—heads, throats, unarmored chests.

As she'd hoped, the blackout had sent the Kings surging for the exit. They flooded into the atrium like unusually violent lambs to the slaughter, and the ones Ana didn't get went down from Laurel's efficient headshots.

It was easy. Almost too easy. She'd crafted a flawless plan, drawing their confused enemies out in total panic. They couldn't organize themselves, because every time one opened his mouth to shout an order, he drew Laurel's deadly attention.

It was beautiful, perfectly executed violence, and Ana should have been high on the taste of victory in the face of such impossible odds. Zeke sure as hell was—his exhilarated laughter rang out as he fired his semi-automatic pistol, the sound reverberating through the concrete atrium.

Ana had no problem pulling the trigger. She did so easily, automatically, again and again until the floor was strewn with bodies and blood—

But this wasn't victory. Nothing about this bloodbath was winning. She hated them for making it necessary. And today, she didn't feel all that great about herself for being so *good* at it.

Victory would come when she knew her people were safe. That was the only part of any of this she could take pride in.

The final body fell, and Ana waited, her gun trained on the darkened hallway as Zeke dragged his final two kills out of their path.

Laurel waded through the carnage and crouched beside a groaning man who was clutching his shoulder. When she drew close, he swung a wicked-looking knife up from his side. Before Ana could shout a warning, Laurel snatched his wrist and twisted—*hard*.

The knife clattered to the floor as he screamed, but Laurel didn't flinch. "Where are they?"

He played dumb. "Wh-where's who?"

She held on to his wrist, but gripped his shoulder with her other hand. "The Riders," she said calmly, then pressed down, digging her thumb into the bullet hole in his shoulder.

He screamed again, and Laurel leaned closer, whispering to him. Ana couldn't hear what he said in return, but after a moment, Laurel stood and wiped her bloody hand on her shirt.

"You made a good choice," she said, then drew her pistol and shot him in the forehead. She stepped over him and nodded to Ana. "They're one level down. Some kind of holding cell."

"Then let's go."

Ana followed Laurel into the hallway, and Zeke fell into step beside her, his gun pointed toward the floor and his gaze on Laurel's back. "Okay, so...she's fucking insane," he said in a stage whisper. "Reyes is going to love her. Or they'll wind up killing each other."

They drew close to the stairwell, and Laurel shrank back against the wall, her rifle at the ready. A moment later, heavy footsteps pounded up the stairs, and Ana glanced at Zeke, who moved to cover from the opposite angle.

Pistol in hand, she swung around the corner and nearly sagged in relief.

Hunter stood three steps below her, with Lucio and Reyes helping Gabe, who looked like he'd been beaten half to death. But the stairs behind them were empty, and Ana's momentary relief shattered.

She tried to hide her panic as she lowered the barrel of her gun. "Where's Deacon?"

Hunter grimaced. "Seth took him. We don't know where."

Lucio pushed forward. "Hunter managed to keep his comms transmitter, and I gave it to Deacon. If you can pick up the signal—"

"Zeke?" Ana cut in, turning.

He'd already pulled out a handheld tablet and was tapping furiously. "Nothing's popping up yet. I can keep trying, though."

"Then we look the hard way. Except you, Gabe." She pointed at him as he tried to straighten, but one eye was swollen shut and he could barely stand upright. "Reyes, get Gabe out of—"

"No," Gabe interrupted, shaking free of Reyes's supporting arm. "You need everyone to clear this place. I'll get to the door and hold it down. I just need a gun."

Ana hesitated, but only for an instant. If Gabe said he could get it done, he'd get it done. "Okay. Laurel?"

She nodded and pulled a 9mm from her thigh holster. She checked it, pressed it into Gabe's hand, then draped a bandolier of spare magazines around his neck. "Be careful."

"I'll be fine—"

"I mean it," she cut in. "You can't afford any more whacks to the head."

He almost smiled, though it had to sting like a bitch with his split lip. "You'd just rescue me a third time. Now go rescue Deacon."

Gabe disappeared around the corner, and Ana turned to Zeke. Even though Hunter was standing next to her—even though she was the newest Rider—all eyes were on her.

Getting everyone out was her job.

Deacon had laid this responsibility on her shoulders, and Ana suddenly understood why her normal exhilaration was nowhere to be found. Striding into battle was easy. She could test her wits against the world, knowing the penalties for failure would always fall most heavily on her. Leading other people, on the other hand...

The weight of it was unfathomable. But Ana was used to carrying people's hopes and dreams. Now she just had to do it with their lives.

She was meant for this.

"Come on," she said, starting down the stairs again. "Let's find Deacon and get the fuck out of here."

twenty-three

Deacon fucking hated getting hit in the face.

He couldn't really avoid it. He wasn't fast enough to get out of the way of every swing, and since he was a built like a tank, people expected him to take it, shake it off, and swing back. And he did—but he still hated it. It was something about the juxtaposition of the sick, sudden shock of pain and the gut-churning ache that spread in its wake. Two different sensations, so discrepant they made his head spin.

Most of the time, he dealt with it by ending fights quickly. He usually outmatched his opponents in size or skill or both, so it was easily done.

Not with Seth. They were roughly the same size, and they'd trained with the same grizzled old mercenaries. But even if Deacon had wanted to end it fast, he had to drag it out.

He had to give his Riders more time.

So he took every hit—all the pain and the sweat and the blood—and came back for more.

Not that Seth would have let him do anything else. This wasn't a normal brawl, one that would end with a couple taps and some busted knuckles and blood smeared on the ground. This was a fight to the death— and Seth meant business.

Even when the overhead lights flickered and died, he kept swinging. Deacon took advantage of the momentary darkness to get in a flurry of punches, ones Seth wouldn't see coming and couldn't block. But he took every hit like it was feeding his bloody obsession, until he roared and grappled Deacon to the floor.

When the emergency lights came up, Deacon caught a glimpse of Seth's eyes—burning with rage, molten with the kind of hatred that would never stop hungering for death and destruction.

Deacon almost shivered.

"Your men have been busy," Seth hissed. Blood and sweat dripped from his face as he edged his arm up under Deacon's chin, across his throat. "But they'll never find you. This room doesn't just have a hidden door. It's shielded. They could scan it with infrared, x-ray, anything your hacker could get his hands on. Nothing."

He said it with such *pride*, like he knew with iron-clad certainty that was what Deacon was waiting on— some majestic rescue where his Riders swooped in and carried him home.

Deacon would have laughed, except for the heavy press of Seth's forearm, cutting off his breath.

"Ask me," Seth commanded, his hand twisted in the front of Deacon's shirt, ripping into the fabric. "Ask me who hired the Kings for this job. I want you to know before you die."

A wave of dizzy, giddy power swept through Deacon. He had something Seth wanted right in his grasp—the helpless pain of knowing who wanted his Riders dead and yet not being able to do anything about it.

Well, he'd be goddamned if he was going to give it to him. The moment Seth relaxed the pressure on his throat, Deacon shuddered, heaved in a breath—and used it to spit in Seth's face.

Seth reared back, swiped a hand over his face with a harsh laugh, then rammed his elbow down toward Deacon's head. He barely had time to jerk out of the way, and Seth's elbow bashed down into the concrete hard enough to split skin and crack bone.

He roared with pain, and Deacon rolled away, scrambling for distance. Prolonging the fight meant more than not beating Seth's face in too soon. It meant not getting his *own* goddamn face beaten in, either.

Except now the man was really pissed off, sputtering and hissing as he clutched his bleeding arm. "You fucking bitch-ass son of a whore."

Panting, Deacon tried to stand, but one leg collapsed beneath him. The best he could do was get to his knees and clutch at his side. It hurt, and he wasn't sure if the pain was because he still hadn't caught his breath, or if one of Seth's lucky kicks had broken a rib. "We don't have to be fighting at all. This is your show."

"Shut up!" he thundered. "I'm talking right now, not you. *Not you.* You know, your real problem isn't that you think you're God. It's that people treat you like you are. That's fucked as shit, man. It's screwed your head all up."

The one thing he hadn't banked on with this plan—how *tired* he would get of having to listen to this motherfucker's voice. "What are you really mad about, Seth?" The pain in his side flared brighter. Hotter. "Is it that I left? Or that the old man let me?"

"He didn't just let you," Seth shot back. "That bastard was proud of you. *You*."

Him—and not Seth. "That's what this whole fucking thing is about? You're upset because a dead man respected me?"

"Because he loved you!"

Seth was blind to everything but vengeance, oblivious to all but his own jealousy. Even in his wildest moments of fancy, Deacon would never say that the old man had loved him, or Seth, or *anyone*. He was a fair man, sometimes even a kind one, but Deacon had never glimpsed real love in him. And now Seth was ready to kill a man who had once stood as his brother...all because he believed Deacon had something he didn't.

A loving father.

Deacon didn't need for his memories of the old man to include that. He'd *had* a dad, a real one, a long, long time ago, and that was enough. Knowing that the old man had respected his integrity was merely a bonus.

And, just like that, he wasn't ashamed anymore. His past was his past—it would always exist, and he would always remember, but it couldn't hold him down. Because when he knew he couldn't do it anymore, when Gideon had offered him another path, he'd taken it, and that was something only a strong person could do. Too many people would just keep going, bound by fear or inertia, terrified of making the difficult decisions. Scared to change.

"It's over, Seth." Deacon's vision started to blur a little, and he struggled to remember if Seth had hit his head against something. "I'm not going to fight you anymore."

"Oh, yeah?" Seth reached into his pocket, and metal flashed in the dim light. It looked a little like an egg, a rounded aluminum cylinder with a hinged top. "Walk away from this."

Deacon was already lurching across the room, pulled forward by instinct and sheer, icy dread, when Seth flipped up the top of the remote switch and pressed the red button with his thumb. Deacon slammed into him a moment later, knocking the switch from his hand. It skittered across the concrete and bounced off the wall, and Deacon dove after it.

"What is it?" he demanded. "What the fuck did you do?"

Seth beckoned him closer. Blood soaked his right sleeve now, and he'd gone so pale that Deacon wondered if maybe he'd critically wounded himself, bashing his elbow. But when Deacon bent over him to listen to his fitfully whispered words, Seth heaved up and headbutted him.

Pain seared through Deacon's skull, rattling him with the sheer force of the agony. A moment later, a deeper agony bloomed between his ribs, a piercing fire that sucked away what was left of his breath. He put his hand to his side, and it came away coated with blood.

The motherfucker had stabbed him.

Seth chuckled as the knife clattered to the floor, but both sounds echoed like they were far away, drifting to Deacon's ears from the other end of a long tunnel. Only Seth's words were sharp. Excruciatingly clear. "Self-destruct sequence. Only one way to reverse it, and you'll never get there in time. Five minutes, and we'll all be dust under the rock."

Time's up. No reason to drag out the fight now. Deacon gripped Seth's face, his bloody fingers making it hard to hold the man still. And when he tried to whisper a soft prayer of forgiveness, he didn't have enough breath to do it.

His strength was slipping away, too. Before it could desert him completely, Deacon wrenched Seth's head to one side with a sharp crack that reverberated through the room.

Or maybe just through Deacon. Seth's sightless eyes stared at him, and he fought a shudder. There was no satisfaction in this moment, and no time for mourning.

On your feet, soldier. He tried again to stand, but his legs would only respond sluggishly, and it seemed to take hours for a single step. He was tired, so tired, and all he wanted to do was close his eyes and rest, like the Riders they lost during the war. Like Jaden. Like the dead man watching him now, silently beckoning him to follow.

Part of Deacon wanted to give in, *give up*, drift off into the endless sleep all the temple priestesses would say he'd earned a hundred times over. But the rest of him—

dear Lord, blessed savior of all sinners

The rest of him wanted to see Ana, just one more time.

He staggered and went down—or did he slip? The urge to fade into the welcoming blankness nearly overwhelmed him, but he gritted his teeth and shook his head.

fold me in your loving arms as I face my destiny with a glad heart

Deacon Price didn't give up. He'd crawl if he had to. He was still one of Gideon's fucking Riders. *The* Rider. He didn't fear death, but he'd be damned if he let it take him easy.

He reached for the door handle, watching his own hand move as if it belonged to someone else, and used it to pull himself up again. He half-expected the handle to hold fast, but it creaked and finally gave under his weight. The door opened, and Deacon spilled into the hallway.

fold me in your loving arms

His shirt was wet now, warm against his clammy skin. If he didn't get up now, if he didn't manage it somehow, then this would be his end. It wasn't a bad one, as far as deaths went. He'd won his fight. Done his job. He even had his boots on.

He laughed, and the sound followed him down into the darkness.

The Kings' underground lair was a fucking nightmare.

For every three rooms, only one had access from the main hallway. And half of those rooms had smaller rooms hidden off them, like a never-ending rabbit warren carved into the mountain.

And then there were the secret rooms. They discovered them when a King had charged out of one, bullets blazing. Reyes took a graze across the arm protecting Lucio before Laurel managed to shoot the bastard, but at least the Riders' gear was in that secret room.

Being armed made this safer, but it didn't make it faster.

And they *still* hadn't found Deacon.

The emergency lighting down here was eerie. Ana swung around the door in the final room and squinted into the shadowed corners, clearing the left side as Hunter cleared the right.

Nothing. *Fuck.* "Zeke, any update on that signal?"

"No." Zeke sounded irritated. "But half the rooms we've been in have basically been low-rent Faraday cages."

Whatever that meant, it sounded bad. Ana pivoted and froze, her instincts screaming. The wall directly across from the door was dimly lit, but amongst the other shadows was one long, thin, far-too-even line of black.

"Hunter," she said softly, raising her gun again and gesturing toward it.

He slid his hand along the wall until his fingers met that imperfection. As his fingers curled around it, his brow furrowed. Then he moved, hauling open a door that blended so completely into the wall that Ana might never have noticed it.

Ana tensed for a hail of gunfire.

Instead, a child let out a pitiful, hastily silenced whimper of terror.

"Shit." Zeke pulled out a flashlight and clicked it on, illuminating a huddle of children, a handful of women, and one grizzled, gray-haired mercenary with one hand wrapped around a shotgun and the other resting on the neck of a growling old pit bull.

The noncombatants. Fuck.

Moving slowly, Ana held both hands out at her sides. "We're not looking to hurt anyone who isn't hurting us. You should get these people out of here. We won't stop you."

He sized her up, studying her with his faded blue eyes. He opened his mouth—

The shrill screech of a sudden alarm was almost deafening. The silence that followed echoed with the sound, and after another few seconds it repeated. It took all of Ana's self-control not to cover her ears. "What the hell is that?"

The elderly man's eyes went wide. "It's the count-down. Self-destruct sequence. It'll bring the whole god-damn bunker down around our ears."

Reyes cursed. "How long?"

The dog tried to lunge, and the man tightened his grip on its collar. "Five minutes."

Saints have mercy.

The weight of leadership bore down on Ana, brutal enough to bow her shoulders. She didn't even have to wonder what Deacon would have told her—weighed against the lives of a room full of scared innocents plus all of his Riders, he would have considered his own life inconsequential.

But it was easy to be the one who didn't make it out alive. As her eyes burned with tears she refused to shed, she hated him all over again for taking the simple way out—and handing her the impossible task of being the one to walk away and leave him to die.

Pain lent her voice a raw edge as she waved at the door. "Get them the hell out of here," she snapped at the old man. "Lucio, clear a path for them. Reyes, bring up the rear. Zeke—"

She turned and saw her own guilt reflected in his eyes as he looked up from his tablet. This would break him, too, right along all the jagged lines carved out by Jaden's death. Zeke might walk out physically whole, but he'd never forgive himself for not finding Deacon in time.

"It's okay," she told him as the women herded the children past them. A lie, and they both knew it, but Zeke jerked his head in a rough nod and joined the rush for the door.

Then it was just Hunter, watching her with too much understanding and too much compassion, and she almost shoved the burden of leadership back onto his shoulders. Let him get the others out, and she could die down here searching, but at least *knowing* she'd tried—

Deacon would never forgive her if she spent her life on something so futile.

"Go," she told him hoarsely. "I'm right behind you."

The stairs were a nightmare. The emergency lights cast threatening shadows. The alarm had terrified the children, and some were too small to go fast. Hunter hefted one onto each hip, and Reyes hoisted a young boy on his back.

Ana swept up a little girl with frightened eyes who wrapped thin, trembling arms and legs around her like a climbing vine. She hid her face in Ana's braids, her rapid breaths falling quick and hot on Ana's neck as she took the stairs as fast as she could.

She'd forgotten about the bodies in the atrium. One of the kids whimpered. Another one let out a scared yelp. The Riders hustled them to the door with the help of an older woman wearing a cook's apron. She was still trying to pry the little girl off of Ana when Zeke shouted.

"I have him!" He raised his voice wildly to be heard over the alarm. "Fuck, the signal just popped up. I have Deacon."

Ana's heart leapt. She unhooked the little girl's feet from behind her back and ignored her pitiful cry as Ana left her in the arms of the cook and whirled on Zeke. "Where?"

"One level down, at the end of the hallway."

She didn't know how much time they had left. A minute or two at most, and Deacon would be *furious* at the idea of it. It was disobedience to the spirit of his orders, if not the letter.

And Ana didn't give a fuck.

Clarity filled her for the first time since their fight, so bright and warm and *real* that it felt like the touch of a higher power. She'd been wrong to tell Deacon he couldn't risk his life to protect his fellow Riders, because no chain of command superseded your right to decide the worth of your life.

She'd been wrong. But so had he.

"I'm going," she announced, already whirling toward the stairs. "Hunter and Zeke, with me. We may need to carry him out. The rest of you find us a quick way out of here."

She took the steps two at a time, so fast she slammed into a wall on the landing. Ignoring the pain, she wrenched her body around the turn and raced down the final steps, leaping over a dead body sprawled across the bottom of the staircase.

The hallway spread out before her, lit ominously by the strips of safety lighting. At the end, she could dimly make out a dark shape on the floor. Her frantic heartbeat ticked off the seconds they had left as she flat-out sprinted down the hallway and skidded to a stop next to Deacon's still form.

Seth lay inside the room, his eyes open and unseeing, his bloody face canted at an unnatural angle. Deacon must have finished him off and then crawled out of the protective shielding of the room before collapsing—but at least getting free had allowed Zeke to find him.

And he looked like hell. He was bruised and bloody, his shoulder dislocated. The quick rise and fall of his chest told her he was breathing, but the tortured sound of it made her wonder how much internal damage he had—and how much more she'd cause by moving him.

But they had no choice. She moved aside so Hunter and Zeke could lift him between them, her whole body aching at his hoarse, pained groan.

She had to be imagining that the wail of the alarm was growing more insistent. Her internal clock had never been as precise as Ashwin's, but she *knew* they were cutting it close as they bolted back toward the stairs. Maneuvering Deacon up them ate away precious seconds, and she winced at every jostle, every bump.

Saints, what if they didn't make it? What if this building collapsed in on top of them? The dilation of time was a curse now—it gave her all the time in the world to second-guess her decision.

The future of the Riders sprawled out before her. Half of their numbers fallen in action. Their morale decimated. And their leadership... Hunter was the most obvious successor to Deacon. *Why* had she grabbed him instead of Reyes or Lucio? He wasn't that much bigger, and *someone* with training in tactics and leadership needed to make it out—

No. Stop.

They would make it out. They would get Deacon to Kora. She'd fix everything wrong with him, and this risk would be worth it.

They burst through the front doors in time to see a huge cargo van backing toward them. As the back doors swung open, the alarms abruptly stopped, the sudden silence more chilling than the sound had been. Lucio shoved the last child into a second van and slammed the doors shut before bolting for the driver's seat.

"Come on!" Reyes shouted, reaching out. He guided Deacon's body into the van, leaving room for Hunter and Zeke to hop in. Zeke reached out for Ana and hauled her in just as Laurel slammed her foot on the gas.

The van shot forward, careening straight for the fence, and Ana dropped to Deacon's side and covered his body with hers as they crashed into it. Metal gave way with a screech. The van shuddered, and Deacon groaned again.

"I know," she whispered, though she knew he couldn't hear her. God, his face was a bloody mess. His nose was broken—again—and one of his eyes had swollen shut. He had gouges on his cheek, and his throat bore bruises as if someone had tried to choke him. She didn't want to guess at how many ribs were broken, or how much *pain* he was in.

But he was alive. And Kora could heal anything.

Lucio's van followed them through the hole in the fence and skidded out onto the cracked asphalt. They were picking up speed now that they were on the open road—and just in time.

A muffled explosion sounded. The road began to tremble beneath the van, and Ana twisted to look through the back doors.

The side of the mountain just...caved in, like someone had pulled the lowest card from a precarious tower built of them. It sank in on itself, an eye winking shut, and every trace of the Kings' bunker simply vanished beneath a wave of rock and sand.

"Jesus Christ," Hunter muttered. "Jesus fucking *Christ*."

"I guess that's the end of Seth," Zeke muttered. "No one's coming out of there."

"Deacon had already ended Seth," Ana said, lifting herself gingerly away from him. Her hand was steady as she wrapped her fingers around her boot knife and used it to slice open Deacon's shirt, but underneath—

Oh *Saints*, his skin was nothing but a patchwork of darkening bruises and split skin. The first-aid kits were back with their bikes, but even those would have been insufficient to deal with the inevitable internal injuries. "Zeke—"

"I'm on it." She heard rustling, and Zeke knelt at Deacon's other side. He thrust a roll of duct tape at her before stripping off his shirt and ripping it to make a bandage for the wound on Deacon's side. "We'll deal with what we can until we get him to Kora. He's strong, Ana. He'll make it."

"I know." She stroked the hair on his forehead—the only part of him that, though bruised, didn't seem terrifyingly fragile—and knew that if he was awake, he'd be furious with her. She had risked her life, along with Hunter's and Zeke's, to go back in after him.

But the writhing shame she'd felt at Gideon's reprimand was nowhere to be found. They could shout at her, punish her, strip her of her place in the Riders, and she wouldn't regret her choice. She'd make it again, every damn time.

Deacon's life was worth the risk. Even if he never spoke to her again, never forgave her...

That was better than having to live the rest of her life never being able to forgive herself.

twenty-four

Deacon wasn't scared of pain.

He wouldn't call it an old friend, but it did firmly qualify as his frequent companion. He'd known it in all its forms—the sharp pierce of loss, the gnawing ache of hunger and hopelessness. The dull grind of bruised flesh and fractured bone.

But he'd never known it like this, screeching and dissonant, a thousand tiny, raking claws ripping him apart from the inside, sheltered and fed by the darkness he couldn't seem to escape.

Is this hell? He tried to form the words, screamed them into the perfectly black abyss that surrounded him. Trapped him.

"He's coming around." Light stabbed at his eyes. "The anesthesia must be wearing off. Increase the dose—carefully."

Deacon fought—he wasn't sure why, because he didn't think he could move or speak. But he fought all the same.

Strong hands pressed down on his shoulders. Ashwin's face swam into blurry focus. "It's okay," he said firmly. "Deacon, you're all right. Everyone got out. Everyone's safe."

Safe. He clutched at the word, carried it back down with him as he slipped into the gloom once more.

Safe.

A gentle, steady symphony of whooshes and beeps lured Deacon out of the darkness.

He fluttered his eyes open, braced against the discomfort, but it hurt less this time. So he pressed his cheek harder into the soft pillow under his head and opened them again.

Gabe lay in the bed beside his, utterly still except for the slow rise and fall of his chest. A woman slept with her face pillowed on Gabe's unmoving hand, dark brown hair streaked with pink spread over the colorful blanket.

Laurel. Deacon's brain automatically identified the visitor. Then, as if even that had exhausted him, he fell unconscious again.

"...going to be okay. So is Gabe."

Ana. Soft, familiar fingers stroked over his forehead, tangling with his hair.

"I'd do it again, Deacon. I don't care what happens. You were worth the risk."

Now, for the first time since he opened his eyes and saw Ashwin, it hurt to fall away into nothingness.

Twenty years of friendship closer to brotherhood had taught Deacon many things about Gideon, but nothing more than this: his taste in literature could best be described as eclectic.

Put plainly, sometimes it was essentially shit.

It was pretty good reading today—Shakespeare, which Deacon usually enjoyed. Except that Gideon liked to choose his material like he was wielding a hammer.

"For it falls out that what we have we prize not to the worth whiles we enjoy it, but being lacked and lost, why, then we rack the value, then we find the virtue that possession would not show us while it was ours."

Deacon managed to speak. "Subtle. Real subtle."

Gideon glanced up with a soft smile. "You know, this was always my favorite of Shakespeare's comedies. Most people wouldn't believe it, but Beatrice always reminded me of Isabela and the way she and John went at it when their courtship started. His parents commanded, and so did ours—and neither of them appreciated commands."

"Your hell-raising sister and Gabe's hell-raising brother?" Deacon's throat was dry and raspy, and he licked his lips. "Never."

Gideon picked up a glass of water with a straw and leaned forward to offer it to him. "Nobody remembers them that way anymore. Sixteen years of longing looks and wise leadership and wedded bliss tend to change the narrative, I suppose."

"We still remember." The word snagged on Deacon's consciousness—something else he was supposed to remember. "Seth."

"Ana said she saw his body." Gideon paused. Sighed. "Hunter told me the rest. What he said to you."

"Someone hired them to kill off the Riders." Deacon could barely believe it himself. "It could be bullshit, some line he was using to taunt me."

"You'd know better than anyone. Do you think he was taunting you?"

No. Seth could lie as easily as most people breathed, but when he spoke about the contract on the Riders, the words had sounded...sincere. Real. "I think...we should be sure."

"Then we will be. After you've recovered." Gideon set the water down, picked up his book, and tapped his fingers on the cover. "I sent Ana to clean up and get some rest. She wanted to wait until you woke up, but I know you two have had some tension. I thought it best to give you a little time."

Deacon didn't have to ask to know what had happened—the rest of the Riders had disobeyed his orders to keep themselves alive, even if it meant sacrificing him. "Was it her?" he asked. He didn't want to, but he had to. "Was she the one who wouldn't leave me behind?"

"I haven't accepted her mission report yet. But, according to Hunter, yes. Zeke managed to pick up the tracking signal from your comms unit once you got outside the door, and Ana brought him and Hunter with her to retrieve you."

"I asked them not to. *Ordered* them not to."

"She made a judgment call. It turned out to be a smart one. But I understand it could have gone the other way, as well." Gideon caught his gaze. Held it. "You have to decide how you feel about that, professionally and personally. I can't decide for you."

Someone had to. Deacon had been so prepared for the end that he still wasn't one hundred percent sure he wasn't imagining all of this. That the Suicide Kings' compound hadn't fallen down around him, after all. The only thing tripping him up was the question of where he could possibly be. It wasn't hell, surely, because apparently Ana existed.

And it couldn't be heaven, because she wasn't in his arms.

"I was ready, Gideon." He could barely grind out the words. "I was *ready*, and now I don't—I don't know if I can ever be okay with it again. Not if I have to know this—that Ana would walk into a building that's about to blow just on the off chance that I'm not already dead."

"Yes," his friend replied softly. "It's a lot harder to die when we know we have something to live for. Someone to live for."

Harder, he called it, as if it was something that could be done at all. "So how do I do it?"

"Deacon..." Gideon leaned forward, and there was a sadness in his expression that Deacon had never seen before. "Maybe you don't. There's a difference, you know. Between being willing to die, and being ready to die. Facing their death on the wall seemed like a good way to make sure people understood the gravity of their oaths. But I never wanted you to be eager. To be ready. To spend yourselves as if your lives aren't the most precious commodity this Sector has."

There was a difference, maybe, but you couldn't slide a knife between *willing* and *eager*, not in Sector One. Gideon's grandfather had taught his people to sacrifice gladly, readily. Zealously. It was impossible for that attitude, an attitude that Gideon was still battling, not to rub off on other things.

"It's easy to forget," Deacon told him. "Especially

when all you see is sacrifice being revered because of the shit the Prophet pounded into people's heads. That old bastard's been dead forever, and he's still pulling their strings. Mine too, I guess."

"And mine." Gideon rubbed a hand over his face and sank back into the chair. "Isabela is officially sainting Ana's father at the midsummer festival. Thirty years he served this sector, and the moments we'll glorify are the last ones he drew breath. But what do I do, Deacon? Deny him that honor? That won't change what they revere, it will just take away a reverence he earned a hundred times over."

"Shit, no. It's just…"

"Tell me."

Deacon met his gaze. "Maybe wait until we *are* dead. You can't tell me that I'm not meant to embrace my death when all of my memorials are already half-finished."

Gideon made a choked sound caught somewhere between a laugh and a sigh. "I know. I *know*. I've avoided that mess for far too long, because honestly? It makes me uncomfortable. The commodification, the opportunism…" This time his sigh was weary. "I don't know how to untangle it or where to start. It isn't as if the Prophet kept his hands clean in that regard. Maybe it's baked into our bedrock."

"It doesn't have to be. Some things have already changed. Just not *these* things."

"You're right. But Kora will murder me if I wear you out with debates over the ethical ramifications of dismantling capitalism." Gideon lifted the book again with a smile. "Get some rest, Deacon. I'll stay here, if you don't mind. I'll even read to myself, if you want."

He *was* strangely exhausted, but the last thing he wanted was to slip back into the darkness, alone. "I don't mind listening."

"All right." Gideon opened the book and skimmed a few pages before settling back, his voice falling into a warm, easy rhythm. "When he shall hear she died upon his words, the idea of her life shall sweetly creep into his study of imagination, and every lovely organ of her life shall come apparelled in more precious habit, more moving, delicate and full of life..."

Deacon listened for a while as he drifted, enjoying the cadence more than the words. "You know I hate this play, right?"

"You do?"

"Everyone thinks Benedick is such an asshole, but Claudio is the *real* dickhead."

"Because Benedick *knows* he's an asshole." Gideon's voice was wreathed with wry amusement. "Never trust a man who thinks he's good and noble."

"Truth."

twenty-five

Ana heard Zeke's bitching while she was still twenty feet from the common room. "...makeshift, corner-cutting shortcuts. He should know better." A pause. "But it's brilliant. Totally fucking reckless and probably unstable as hell—like, I don't even know how the fuck this algorithm *works*—but... Brilliant."

"He doesn't have access to all the stuff he would need to do it straight and proper," Laurel protested. "Surely you remember what that was like. Goose makes it work."

"Yeah, yeah." Ana turned the corner and found Zeke seated at the table with Laurel leaning over his shoulder, watching as he poked at a tablet. "Maybe you should grab the brat up by the scruff of the neck and drag him out here so I can teach him to respect

Dijkstra."

Reyes looked up from his book. "Respect who?"

"Edsger Dijkstra. Some ancient computer—"

"Okay, never mind," Reyes interrupted. "I've realized I don't care."

"Asshole." Zeke looked up as Ana straddled one of the benches. "Hey, you finally get some sleep?"

"A little bit." She hadn't thought she'd be able to, but her body had given up somewhere around forty-two hours of being awake, and Ashwin had made it clear that she was going back to her room under her own power or over his shoulder, but she was putting her ass in bed one way or the other.

Seven hours of restless dreams about running through dark corridors while alarms wailed in warning hadn't been particularly peaceful, but she supposed it counted as sleep.

Zeke took the words at face value as he flipped Laurel's tablet back into its case. "I was looking at some of the custom software our mutual friend programmed for Laurel. She has some pretty sweet toys, I gotta admit."

"A person needs more than weapons of opportunity to crawl the sectors, stamping out injustice." Laurel ruined her solemn statement by winking at Ana.

"Watch it. We've got permanent dibs on the hero gig." Reyes eyed her over the top of his book. "Maybe you should stick around. Help us out."

Laurel laughed.

The first spark of something warm kindled in Ana's chest. She liked Laurel's laughter. She liked her sarcasm and her humor and the way she kicked through doors and demanded to be taken seriously.

She liked having another woman around.

"Let's not be hasty, laughing this off." Zeke stroked his chin and studied Laurel. "I mean you're nuts, but that's more of a feature than a bug. You're a hell of a shot. How do you feel about impossible odds and certain peril?"

"That's all that exists in Sector Three." She glanced around, then stopped and wrinkled her nose. "You guys are serious."

"Ignore them." Ana leaned forward and folded her arms on the table, and it felt *so* good to lower her voice to a conspiratorial whisper. To joke. "Instead, think about how much fun we could have kicking their asses together. I don't have nearly enough time to keep them humble all by myself."

Laurel raised both eyebrows and made a soft noise, like she was considering the possibilities. Then she turned her attention to the corner where Gabe sat silently, an open book ignored in his lap. "What about you?"

Gabe had shadows in his eyes. He'd been cleared to leave the infirmary, but his exhaustion showed in the slowness of his smile. But it *was* a smile, one of Gabe's rare, genuine ones—the kind he rarely offered to anyone outside the Riders. "I thought you liked saving my ass. Now you want to kick it?"

She shrugged. "I'm a complicated woman."

The front door swung open, and Ashwin stepped through. All eyes landed immediately on him, and he inclined his head in acknowledgment. "Deacon's awake and doing all right. Kora's run some tests and thinks she'll be able to release him by tomorrow."

Relief fluttered in Ana's chest. But before she could

voice it, Ashwin turned to her. "And Gideon wants to see you in his office. Now."

Oh, shit.

Facing Gideon was the hardest thing Ana had ever done.

No, she amended, planting her boots and lacing her fingers behind her. Facing the possibility of leaving Deacon behind would *always* be the hardest thing she'd ever done. But holding steady while her leader watched her with serious brown eyes was firmly in the top ten.

Then he gave her that *look*—the one that made believers out of skeptics. The one that made you feel stripped naked, your flaws and faults identified, weighed, and measured.

But not judged. Gideon rarely judged. He *understood.*

"All right," he said finally. "I've heard Hunter's version of events. Now I want yours."

Ana swallowed hard. It was tempting to unleash her fraying temper, to empty herself of the exhaustion and nerves and stress and grief that had built as the aftermath of this battle—and what it could have cost— hit her.

But she was a soldier, one who'd been asked to report. So she did, picking each word with care, describing the situation and Deacon's orders and her decisions. Gideon's eyes narrowed as she continued, so she flattened her voice even more, trying to wipe emotion from her tone.

Then she reached the point where she'd had to make the call to leave, and no amount of clenching her hands behind her back could keep the soft tremble from her words. "I knew he'd want us to leave," she said. "I ordered the noncombatants and the Riders out. But when we reached the top level, Zeke got a hit on Deacon's location."

"And?" Gideon prompted, when her pause went on for too long.

"And I made a choice." Her voice steadied as she remembered that moment of clarity, and she met Gideon's eyes squarely. "Returning for Deacon was an acceptable risk."

"Is that why you did it, Ana?"

God, she hated this question. She'd turned it over a thousand times by now, picking at the edges of it. Doubting herself. Wondering if her feelings had overshadowed her common sense, or her grasp of tactics, or her ability to see the risks clearly.

Because she loved Deacon. And they all assumed love made her weak.

"I brought Hunter and Zeke with me because I believed it was an acceptable risk. If it hadn't been, I would have sent them out and gone back for him myself."

"Why?"

"Because I love him." She faced Gideon's unblinking gaze defiantly. "That's what you want me to say, right? I love him, and so I let my heart overrule my head and disobeyed orders. But it's bullshit. I *do* love him. Risking my life for him was worth it. *And* it was the smart tactical call, one I would have made for any of the other Riders. It doesn't have to be one or the other. You of all people should know that."

Gideon watched her. His fingers tapped on the desk. Slow, even, from his pinky to his pointer and back until the soft rhythm hypnotized her.

"Do you know why I let you into the Riders?" he

asked finally.

It was such an abrupt change of topic that Ana eyed him warily. "No."

"It's not because you're good at fighting, though you are. It's not even because you're good at tactics." His lips curved in a shadow of a smile. "Though you've certainly proven yourself your father's worthy heir in that regard, too. But there's nothing particularly unique about being good at tactics or fighting."

"Then why?"

"Because I'm tired of watching my Riders die." He turned to stare out the large windows, where the edge of the apple orchards was visible and in full and glorious bloom. "And I'm tired of watching you all settle for a shadow of a life while everyone else enjoys all the bright colors and joy."

They were the last words she'd expected, and she still couldn't see the connection. "I don't understand. Why does that—?"

"Your heart, Ana. I chose you for your heart." He glanced back at her. "In the field, when lives are on the line, we have to use our brains *and* our hearts. And that's what you did when you went back for him. I, for one, am extremely grateful you did. You're right. Love isn't a liability. Your passion is your strength."

A tiny kernel of warm relief unfurled inside her. "Thank you."

"You're welcome." His brief smile crinkled the corner of his eyes before his face grew serious again. "However, Deacon's allowed to feel differently. And you crossed the line in the barracks when you defied him. There are ways to voice disagreement with your leader. Saying *fuck no* is a disrespect I won't allow. Whatever your personal relationship with Deacon, when he stands at the head of that table, he is due the respect of his twenty years of service and experience."

The reprimand, even delivered in a gentle voice, stung—because she knew he was right. "I understand. I made a mistake."

"You did," Gideon agreed. "And you'll learn, just like they all learned. Do you think noble-born sons like Reyes and Hunter and Gabe came here knowing how to obey orders? I had to yell at Reyes three times in the first *week*. And Zeke..." He rolled his eyes skyward. "Maybe someday we can stop yelling at him. Which is to say that making a mistake isn't the end of the world."

Ana tightened her hands again, struggling against a renewed flood of words. They caught in her throat, burning until it hurt...and Gideon was smiling, because maybe this was the one thing he couldn't understand.

Well, he'd told her that passion was her strength. *Be careful what wishes you put out into the world, Gideon.*

"That's more bullshit." The words exploded out of her with the force of all that pent-up repression, and once the dam burst, she couldn't stop herself. "With all due respect, Gideon, I'm not Reyes or Hunter or Gabe. I'm not Zeke. I'm the first woman to ever stand where I'm standing. *Everyone* is watching me. People notice my mistakes. And you and Deacon can say all day long that it doesn't matter, that you're not going to hold it against the next woman—"

Her throat burned. Her eyes burned, as if saying the words out loud finally had brought the weight of their reality crashing down on her. But if she *cried*, her utter failure of self-control would be complete, so she clenched her nails into her wrists until the pain grounded her.

"I can't be the only one," she told him. "It's too much pressure. And you can wave your hand and make a lot of things true, but you can't make it okay for me to make mistakes. Not while it's just me."

Gideon stared at her, his expression utterly unreadable. The seconds ticked on, each one measured by the nervous beat of her heart, and the wild thought intruded that these were surely her last seconds as a Rider.

Had a Rider ever been excommunicated before? Would they remove her ink? Banish her from the sector? Maybe she'd have to track down Gideon's cousin in Sector Four and try to talk her way into the O'Kanes—

"I'm sorry," Gideon said softly. "I had no idea. You should have told me all of this before."

Shock and relief escaped her on a choked laugh, and for a moment she felt lightheaded. "I just yelled at you. It's basically blasphemy. My father would be smacking some manners into me."

Gideon snorted. "If you think your father never yelled at me..."

Ana tried to envision loyal, implacable William Jordan growing angry enough to shout at the man he believed had one foot already in heaven—and suffered an abject failure of imagination.

It must have showed on her face, because Gideon laughed. "Your father understood the true spirit of the chain of command. He expressed his disagreement in private and never undermined me in public. So you're here now, Ana. In private." He waved a hand. "Don't stop. Everything you've been holding in."

It was permission. Freedom to kick restraint to the curb and say the things that had churned in her gut, every word she'd ever swallowed or bitten back or shoved down deep.

At first she didn't know where to start. But when she stopped trying to *not feel*, the pain in her chest bloomed so fast and bright it nearly stole her breath.

"Deacon is broken," she said, softly to hide the tremor in her voice. "For twenty years, he's barely been living. He never let any of us get close. He never understood how much we cared about him. He doesn't even know how to let us care. It's not right that he lives like that. It's not right for *any* of us to live like that. I know that letting us have families can make it harder when we die…"

She swallowed hard and repeated the words she'd said to her aunt. "But it's so much worse when we keep living, alone. It's a stupid tradition, and it should go away."

"I agree." Gideon met her surprise with a sad smile and lifted one shoulder. "Shocked? It's not actually as simple as waving my hand, you know. Belief is like a forest fire. Once it really gets going, the person who started it doesn't have much say in which direction it turns or how high it burns. I've tried this before, remember? The ravens?"

It took a moment for her to catch the edge of the memory. She'd been in her teens or early twenties, totally focused on her training and not much interested in politics. But everyone who lived on the Rios compound remembered those hectic, chaotic weeks.

The Riders might be known for their ravens, but all of the faithful in Sector One marked a life taken with a tiny black bird tattooed to their skin. And there was only one way to remove the stain from your soul, a method implemented by Gideon's grandfather so many decades ago.

Seven years of service to the Rios family.

Penitents eager to wash the stain from their souls labored in the orchards and worked the gardens. They built new additions to the temples, cooked or washed or cleaned or crafted as their skills allowed. The unpaid labor had built the palace they stood in, had lovingly carved the chairs around the room and painstakingly woven the carpet beneath her feet.

The Rios family had gotten rich off repentance.

But when Gideon had tried to end the tradition by offering blanket absolution, the sector had nearly shredded itself apart at the seams. Day after day, people frantic for their souls had arrived on the estate, crowding the garden paths and pleading to be set a task or given a job. They'd cried in their fear of having been forsaken, convinced that any forgiveness that came without toil would endanger their souls.

In the end, Gideon had issued a proclamation, claiming the offer of absolution had been a test. He'd praised Sector One for holding firm in their beliefs and resisting temptation, and in return had offered them a reward—from that day forth, seven years of service would become one.

And the sector had embraced the change. Because Gideon had given it a cost and made them feel like they earned it.

"Yes," he murmured, as if following the path of her thoughts. "It's not a simple thing, changing traditions. They can settle into place in a matter of months, and disassembling them becomes the work of a lifetime. I may have started this one with the best of intentions... but it's grown out of my control. I wanted to protect families like yours, Ana. But I never wanted my Riders to shut themselves off from living."

It was so much to take in. A subtle but earth-shattering shift in perspective, like a flare of light in a shadowed room, illuminating alcoves and corners she'd never imagined were there.

Her box was bigger than she'd realized. And she

could take a full breath, a deep breath, and not feel crushed by it.

So she did. Then she took another one. "Thank you."

"No, thank you for your honesty." Gideon's wry little smile was back. "I have to prod a lot harder to push it out of most people. That's another reason I chose you, Ana. You have passion, and convictions. Your skills in combat are matched by your compassion. You're the future I want to see for the Riders. And you'll keep me honest."

"I could do that," she agreed, answering his smile with one of her own. "In private."

"See?" He leaned back in his chair. "You learn fast."

Yes, that was one thing she'd always had going for her. That, and the fact that Ana never hesitated to push an advantage. "Then, in the spirit of keeping you honest, you should recruit Laurel."

One dark eyebrow lifted. "Six's girl?"

"Yes. She's dubious about the idea. But she's smart, and she's talented, and she worked well with us. The guys like her. I like her." Ana offered him her most wistful smile. "It'd be nice, having her around. I wouldn't feel like everything was riding on me."

"I imagine so." Gideon sat forward. "I'll look into it. Poaching a valued asset from Six might be almost as dangerous as mercenary assassins, though, so I hope you'll understand if I look into it delicately."

Ana had met the new leader of Sector Three only once—but her trips into Sector Three with her father had taught her what sort of hellscape the place had been before its change in leadership. Anyone who'd grown up on the streets of that sector could be a strong ally—or a terrifying enemy.

Which was why Laurel would be perfect. "Of course. I have faith in you."

"So good to hear." Gideon flicked his fingers at her. "Go on. Get out of here. Let me figure out how I'm going to steal a sniper from Sector Three."

Feeling lighter than she had in…ever, maybe, Ana grinned. "Yes, sir."

Euphoria carried her out the door and down the hall, but she was crashing hard by the time she'd slipped through the kitchens and out the door to the little side garden. She took the shortcut through the cherry trees and made it to the fire pit in time to collapse on one of the benches.

Her hands were shaking. Her chest was tight. The itch in her throat turned to a lump, turned to familiar shards of glass that burned as badly as her eyes did.

For as long as she could remember, she'd choked down that feeling. Swallowed tears, blinked them away, stuffed them down into that box that felt like a black hole in her soul. She'd done it because she had to, because being a Rider meant calm and poise and sacrifice—

Or maybe that was just another wall she'd built around herself. Just like Deacon.

God, she was a damn hypocrite.

The first fracture hurt. The tears ripped out of her, jagged, cutting their way free. She covered her mouth and bent over herself, trying to stop the avalanche. But she couldn't. Tears spilled over her cheeks and down, each sob purging a hurt.

Her mother's loss. Her father's grief. Her aunt's worry.

Fighting for acceptance. Fighting to be better and faster. Fighting just to fight, because it hurt so much to know she was good but still never feel she was good enough.

The war. The pain. Her father's death.

Every step she'd taken since then, dragging the enormous weight behind her—everyone's expectations but no one's as much as her own.

She cried until it hurt, until warm arms enclosed her and a gentle, familiar voice murmured, "Oh, my darling."

Soft silk enveloped her, along with the scent of the temple—spices and incense and the lavender Del distilled personally from the flowers that grew around the temple. Shuddering, Ana leaned into the embrace and gave into grief.

Deacon's willingness to die. Their fight. Facing the choice to leave him for dead. Seeing him bruised and bleeding, broken inside and out, and knowing she couldn't fix him. Couldn't fix *any* of it.

"You're all right," Del whispered, her hands stroking gently over Ana's braids. "Let it out. Let this go."

Ana cried until she was empty. Until she was hollow and curiously light, and her eyes ached. She didn't even have the energy to protest as Del coaxed her to her feet and turned her toward the path that led to the temple.

The priestess didn't speak until they reached a big grassy clearing. Instead of going to the main entrance, Del led her around the back to a door framed by an old wooden trellis and climbing ivy. "I want to show you something."

"Okay." Ana's voice was raspy, and her throat hurt. But she followed Del inside the darkened room and waited while the woman moved gracefully from lamp to lamp, lighting each one in turn.

The colorful glass shades illuminated the room in warm, calming light, revealing walls covered in saints murals and stacks of canvases, some covered in paint, some still empty.

A table in the middle held an array of paints. And on the massive easel next to it...

Ana's breath caught.

Her father stared back at her. Del had captured him perfectly—from the curl of his short black hair to the deep, rich brown of his skin. His cheekbones, his chin—*Ana's* chin—his stern brows and his warm, protective gaze. Shadowy wings formed behind him, black and gold, half of the feathers still sketched in outline. And in one hand he held a fiery sword thrust toward the sky, the flames licking their way up the blade toward the heavens.

His official saint's painting.

"I've been working on it for a few months now," Del told her, coming to stand next to her. "I don't usually let people see them before they're done. Sometimes I throw out an entire concept and start from the beginning. But...I've known for a long time what your father would be."

Ana reached out, afraid to touch, but unable to keep from letting her fingers hover over the wings spread out behind him. "An angel?"

"A guardian angel." Del wrapped an arm around Ana's shoulders. "Deacon might be the longest surviving Rider, but your father served the Rios family from the time Gideon was just a child. No one in the history of Sector One has protected us longer, or better."

The tangle of feelings curling around her were messy. Loss and love. Fierce pride and a hint of jealousy. Ana had always been stuck sharing her father with Sector One—a tiny, childish part of her wanted to wrap this painting up and steal it away, so he could be *hers* in death as he'd never been in life.

Then at least *something* would be.

Instead of squashing down the jealousy, she let it breathe. Let it expand. Examined its sharp edges and acknowledged that many of them belonged to her fear and loss over Deacon. Yes, she'd had to share her father—but even with a hundred other duties, he'd always found time to put her first. To teach her and love her.

To build her this reality, where she got to be exactly who she was meant to be.

Ana could share William Jordan with the world. His heart had been big enough, and so was hers.

The tears that pricked her eyes this time didn't hurt. Maybe because she wasn't trying to choke them back. "It's perfect," she whispered. "I love it, Del. Thank you for showing me."

Del turned her and cupped her face, her soft thumbs swiping gently across Ana's cheeks to wipe away the tears. Deep-brown eyes stared down into hers, and Gideon had *nothing* on Del's ability to make you feel like she was staring into the depths of your soul.

"It's time for a tattoo," she said abruptly. "I'll do your new ravens first. But if you're open to it…"

An offer of an original tattoo from Del was an honor few Riders turned down. Del had a knack of diving deep to pull up what you needed to see—whether you were ready to face it or not.

Right now, Ana could use a little guidance. "Whatever you think I need."

"Good." Del set her hands on Ana's shoulders and turned her toward the door. "I know just the thing."

twenty-six

When Kora finally released Deacon from the infirmary, it was with a bright smile—and the warning that, at this rate, he'd never be sainted, because he was obviously too stubborn to die.

He'd take it.

After days of intravenous fluids and soup, he was starving. But the idea of heading to the temple to be fussed and fawned over made him want to puke, so he went to the kitchen in the barracks instead in search of leftovers.

Gabe was already there, digging into a huge bowl of jambalaya. He greeted Deacon with a genuine smile of welcome and tilted his head toward the pot keeping warm on the stove. "Del brought it over an hour ago. We must have really scared her if she's cooking for us personally."

"No shit." Deacon hovered uncertainly in the door-way. "You sure you don't mind?"

"Get some damn food, Deacon."

It was uncharacteristically forceful for Gabe, even considering the circumstances, and Deacon hid a smile as he took a bowl from the cabinet. "Feeling feisty today, Montero?"

"Maybe." He waited until Deacon settled at the table across from him with his own food before inclining his head. "I should have talked shit out with you, even if it hurt and we both hated it. We can't afford unfinished business, and we never know when we're going to have to drop everything to fight and maybe die."

Deacon's appetite wavered. "I changed my mind. You're not feisty, you're a total downer."

"And you're cracking jokes." Gabe frowned. "Trying to crack jokes. We should probably leave that to Zeke and Reyes. I don't think either of us is all that good at it."

"Lies." Deacon toyed with his spoon, spinning it on the table. "We could go upstairs and fight it out, but Kora just got finished putting us both back together. And I don't know about you, but I'm kinda tired."

"Yeah." Gabe rubbed his hand over his shoulder, which obviously still twinged, even after all the care Kora could provide. "Seth was a bastard, but he could land a punch. Not sure I need another beating right away."

Deacon picked up his spoon. "Have you seen Ana?"

"Yeah, she's been around. She spent most of last night over in the temple. I think Del chose a tattoo for her. She seems..."

The muscles in the back of Deacon's neck tensed. "What?"

"Sad," Gabe admitted finally. "She seems sad. And it's weird that I can tell. Nobody beats Ana when it comes to game face."

It didn't surprise Deacon. People saw what they recognized, and he'd never met anyone with more hidden sadness than Gabe. "I have to talk to her. When I can *find* her."

"Deacon..." Gabe trailed off again, his gaze fixed on his bowl as he stirred the contents. "Who am I talking to right now? The leader of the Riders, or my brother?"

"They're the same." Deacon shrugged despite the ache in his chest. "Isn't that the problem?"

"Do they have to be?" Gabe's spoon clinked softly against the bowl. "I'd tell my leader that Ana is good. I know you think you know that, but what she pulled off was something else. Remember how you could set Will down in the most impossible situation and he'd just take one look and somehow see all the angles? He taught her that, somehow. To keep her cool and work any problem, no matter how impossible it is."

"Will was a good man. A great soldier."

"Will would have left you behind. And it would have been a mistake."

"That's arguable." He raised a hand to cut off Gabe's protest. "I'm grateful to be alive. But if something had gone wrong, then three more of my Riders wouldn't have made it out. That's why I gave the orders that I did. So stop with the *all's well that ends well* bullshit and *own it*."

"I didn't say that. *You* did." Gabe looked up at him. "If I was talking to my brother, I'd tell him to pull his fucking head out of his ass and think about the rest of us for two seconds. Not think about our lives. Think about *us*. Ana made the hard call. When we couldn't find you, when it was hopeless—she did what she had to do. She was going to leave you."

Deacon opened his mouth, but Gabe stopped him. "And then we found out there was a chance. And maybe you don't give a shit because you don't think your life was worth saving, but me? I would have spent the rest of my life wondering. Maybe if I'd held out against the torture a little longer. Maybe if I'd said something to distract Seth. Maybe if I'd been tough enough to help them look for you. And Zeke? How do you think Zeke would have coped with being the one who found you thirty seconds too late? How do you think *Ana* would have gotten out of bed every morning, knowing she was the one who decided you just weren't worth the risk?"

It was a different way of looking at the whole thing, but one he understood immediately. Gabe was talking about what the Riders could live with, consequences they could stand to face. Choices they could and couldn't view later without regret.

Deacon had spent half his life struggling with the concept. He'd never ask anyone else to do it. "Okay."

Gabe eyed him warily, as if he didn't quite trust the easy acceptance. "I'd also tell my brother to be careful with Ana's heart. It's the one thing she's never been very good at protecting."

"And I would hope you knew your brother better than that."

"I don't," Gabe said quietly. "But I want to change that."

"So do I." His relationship with Ana wasn't the only one he had to fix, and this was a good place to start. "What's up with you and that lady from Three, anyway?"

"Who, Laurel? Nothing." He said it too fast, and suddenly found his food fascinating. "I mean she saved my ass over in Two, and she seems like a valuable ally.

But nothing's up."

The skin on Deacon's arms prickled, the way it sometimes did when someone was lying to him. "I saw her, Gabe. In the infirmary."

That made him look up. "What?"

"Sitting by your—" Fuck. The bewildered expression in Gabe's face was clear. "You didn't know."

"She wasn't there when I woke up." Gabe's brow furrowed. "Are you sure you didn't imagine it? Kora had you on a *lot* of drugs."

"It's possible." Even without the drugs, Kora had made it clear that Deacon's brain had been only a few knocks short of fully scrambled. "It seemed pretty damn real, though."

"Oh." Gabe gave him a ghost of a smile. "I guess some of Reyes's irresistibility has finally rubbed off on me."

"Or she likes you just the way you are."

"She didn't *seem* stupid..."

"Oh, Christ. Shut up and eat your jambalaya."

It turned out digging holes in the ground was weirdly therapeutic. Even when it was hot as hell outside.

No, *especially* when it was hot as hell outside.

Ana had stripped off her shirt an hour ago and thrown herself into her work with an enthusiasm born of restlessness and avoidance. The small hole in the dirt Deacon had started was turning into a respectable fishpond-shaped crater, and she had the sweat and burning muscles to show for it.

The discomfort was part of the cure. Ana had never really understood that until she'd been under Del's needles again. She'd been punched and kicked and stabbed and even shot one time, so she thought she'd understood the various flavors. Stabbing, sharp, throbbing, aching, grinding...

The sting of her initiation tattoo and her raven couldn't compare to the exquisite burn of Del working line after line across her spine and all the way up her neck to her hairline. The burn had spread into her bones, into the places hollowed out by her crying, as if purifying all of those raw internal wounds with fire.

She'd cried again. Not the deep, wracking sobs of before, but soft and gentle, hot tears tracking silently down her cheeks. Del had stroked her back and murmured quiet encouragement and brought her a damp cloth to wipe her eyes. And Ana had cried without shame as every jab of the needles stole another piece of her pain away.

She'd had a lot of crying to catch up on.

There was catharsis in endurance. The ache in her muscles as she rammed the shovel into the dirt and stomped her boot on it to drive it deeper was a more familiar sort of discomfort—the satisfaction of spending her energy and strength on something productive, something that would make the world a little better.

Even if it was just a fishpond.

"You're getting your ink dirty."

Ana froze, her fingers tightening convulsively around the shovel's handle as the familiar timbre of Deacon's voice scraped raw nerves. "Doesn't matter," she said without turning around. "Del used med-gel."

"You should still keep it clean for a few days." His hand appeared in her peripheral vision, hovering still and steady by her head.

Apparently he wasn't going to go away. Ana forced herself to release the shovel and accept his hand, but she couldn't quite bring herself to look directly at him as he helped her out of the pit. As much as she wanted to replace the memory of him bloodied and clinging to life with the reality of him whole and healthy—

God, her armor was paper thin right now. If she threw herself against the wall that was Deacon, she'd break every bone in her body.

"We need to talk," he murmured. "It should probably be soon. But if you don't want to look at me right now, I can wait."

"It's not—" She swallowed hard and ducked to retrieve the bottle of water she'd brought out with her. The midday sun had heated it to lukewarm, but she still drained the whole thing before turning to face Deacon.

Her heart kicked painfully.

Kora had done her work exquisitely. There was no evidence of the terrible lacerations and bruising to his face, though his nose looked a tiny bit more crooked. He stood in front of her, taking slow, even breaths, and Ana spared a moment to marvel over Kora's gifts. If it weren't for the slight pallor in his face and a bruised exhaustion in his eyes, no one would know he'd been beaten within an inch of his life.

"I'm sorry," she told him softly. "Not for going back to get you...but for before. In the barracks. I was out of line. I should have found a better way to voice my disagreement."

"Yeah, well." He glanced away, then back at her, and away again. "You deserved better than what you got for it, too. I'm sorry, Ana."

It sounded genuine, and Ana didn't know how to cope with it. It was bad enough for Gideon to taunt her with this magical world where her mistakes didn't ruin everyone else's lives. If Deacon started acting like her mistakes weren't the end of *her* life, either...

Crap, she'd probably go make another one. And not even hate herself for it.

Feeling awkwardly vulnerable, Ana wrapped her arms around herself. "We're being very polite and solicitous to each other. This is fucking weird."

"Maybe it's supposed to be. Otherwise, we could just pretend it never happened."

"I wish I could." But the second the words escaped, she knew them for a lie. "No, I don't. I've been shoving everything that hurts down for so long because I was trying to make myself better. The perfect Rider." She finally met his eyes. "You, I guess."

His brows drew together. "What?"

Of course he didn't see it. It was his eternal blind spot. "That's the shitty side effect of being worshipped, Deacon. People try to emulate you, whether you want them to or not."

A sharp breath huffed out of him, and he bent forward at the waist, bracing his hands on his knees as his shoulders shook.

He was *laughing*.

Wounded pride battled with her morbid sense of humor. She wondered fleetingly if the last few days had broken that forever—but the urge to laugh bubbled up, sweet as champagne. She masked it with a growl and swatted at his shoulder. "You're an asshole, you know that?"

"Why?" He straightened, clutching at his side as if the force of his laughter hurt. "Be like me? I thought you, of all people, knew better than that. I'm no role model, Ana."

"That's not true—"

"But I could be." His humor faded. His hands skimmed over her arms, then closed on her shoulders. "I think I can be the man they look up to...but not

318

without you."

Her breath caught. Her stomach flipped. Her heart—

No, she couldn't listen to her heart right now. Not *just* her heart. She grasped desperately for her brain, but her thoughts were skittering in all directions, too. But one remained clear. "I meant what I said. I'm not sorry for going back for you. I'd do it again. If you can't handle that, all we'll ever do is rip each other to shreds."

He gazed at her—intense, focused. "Why did you do it?"

All the bold defiance from Gideon's office had bled out of her over the last twenty-four hours. She could hardly believe she'd faced the leader of her sector—a goddamn saint in human flesh—and proclaimed her love for Deacon.

It had seemed so easy. Loving someone was the highest compliment available in Sector One. She loved her fellow Riders. She loved Maricela and Nita and plenty of the people who worked the Rios estate and had formed a loose, extended family for her as she grew up.

But that love was open and simple and rarely had the power to cut deep enough to leave her bleeding. Her feelings for Deacon were new and bright and still lined with unexpected sharp edges.

And if she got the words out and he bent over laughing again, she'd die. Or murder him.

"I had to," she whispered finally. She wanted to look away, but his eyes held hers, compelling the truth in all its messy glory. "If I'd thought it was too dangerous, I wouldn't have risked the others. I know that mattered to you. I *care* that it mattered to you. But if I hadn't tried—"

Tears filled her eyes, even though she should have

been cried out. Her words came out hoarse. "I know you could die tomorrow. So could I. But you didn't have to die in that bunker. If it had been Zeke down there, or Hunter, or *anyone*—I would have gone back. And no one would be asking me *why, why, why* because they wouldn't be assuming I'm some idiot girl in love who can't assess risks properly."

"Now who's assuming?" But he was smiling as he touched her face, brushing away a tear that had slipped free to track down her cheek. "You did risk, Ana. You and the other Riders could have been long gone before Seth activated that self-destruct. But I understand now what a blow it would have been to the Riders—not just you—to leave without trying, no matter what my orders were."

A blow? It would have *crushed* them. Even now, he underestimated his own value—but at least he knew he had some. A heartbreakingly small step forward, but progress. "You have to decide if you trust me to protect their lives, just like I protected yours."

"You were right," he murmured. "*And* you were wrong. Acceptable risk doesn't exist until it all works out in your favor. Things can go south too fucking easy for it to be any other way. That's leadership."

"I know," she admitted. And because she didn't feel cornered anymore, it was easier to admit the thing she hadn't even told Gideon. "When I was down there and they were picking you up—I realized I'd fucked up. I grabbed Zeke and Hunter because they were the biggest, but if we *had* gone down... You and Hunter and I are the three best trained in tactics and leadership."

His fingers slid over hers, wrapped around them. "I don't know if anyone can really understand it, not until they've made a bad call. Gotten someone killed." He took a deep breath. "My first one was two years in.

Mad was still running with us then. It wasn't bad intel or any kind of conspiracy. I just fucked up. I would have died, but Drake took the bullet meant for me."

It took her a moment to connect the name to a painting. Drake was one of the first paintings on the left wall—not an original Rider, but one of the earliest to replace a fallen member. No one left in the Riders barracks had known him, but there were always fresh offerings and flowers laid at his feet. And now that she thought about it, Deacon always drifted to that corner whenever they gathered in that sanctum.

No wonder this ripped him up. If someone jumped in front of a bullet for Deacon now, Del would be starting sketches for their saint's painting before the body was even burned. But no one remembered Drake.

No one except the man he'd saved.

Ana turned her hands to grasp his. "What do you want us to be to each other, Deacon?"

When he answered, it was slowly—nothing easy, but with the weight of thought behind his words. "We have to find a way that we can be together without sacrificing who we are."

So simple on the surface. Potentially impossible in practice. Deacon would have to order her into danger without flinching, knowing any mission could be the one that killed her.

And if he chose to take his own risks, she'd have to let him.

"It won't be easy," she acknowledged. "It's gonna hurt like hell sometimes. We're probably going to fight. But I was willing to risk dying to keep you in my life. I'll fight for you. But you can't—"

Her voice broke. The tears returned.

"I know." He bent his head and pressed his forehead to hers. "We both had shit we needed to say, things to settle. I shouldn't have walked away, especially when I knew what we were heading into. I'm sorry."

"That was almost the last thing we said to each other," she whispered, curling her arms around his neck. Impossible to remember how close to death he'd come when he was *here*, as strong and solid as ever, and warm against her body. But she couldn't stop crying. Whatever switch she'd flipped to shove the bad stuff down was broken. "I don't know how I would have moved on. It would have been a wound that bled forever."

"Ana—"

She kissed him. Hard, out of control, because it felt *so good*. The warmth of his lips, the scrape of his beard, the way they improbably fit together, like they'd been forged from the same steel. "Promise me," she murmured against his lips in between kisses. "Promise me we'll never go into battle angry."

"Never again." His teeth scored her lower lip. "I promise that the last thing you'll ever hear from me will be how much I love you."

Ana kissed him again, and her heart...healed.

Not like new. It wasn't like Kora and her regen tech, wiping away the damage so completely it was as if you'd never been broken. Ana felt like the pottery her aunt's second husband made by fitting broken pieces back together with adhesive dusted with gold.

The broken places might always be visible, but Ana wasn't ashamed of them. They made her stronger. They made her *Ana*.

And she had never taken the easy way.

Deacon lifted her in his arms, and she wrapped her legs around him. He was as steady as always, like a tree she could cling to in a storm. But the only storm now was the one building inside her as he tilted his head and kissed her deep.

His hands found her back, fingers sweetly gentle as he stroked up the sensitive skin where her new tattoo was. Her sports bra didn't offer much protection as she rocked against him, and the bright little sparks of pleasure distracted her from the fact that they were moving until Deacon lowered them both to a stone bench.

She broke away and got her knees against the stone to give her leverage as she straddled his lap. Then she reached for his shirt. "Take this off. I want to see that you're okay."

He let her strip it over his head. "Everything is healed up. Not a bruise left."

It was true, but she examined him anyway, running her fingers over his shoulders and down his chest. Her fingers lingered over the smooth, pink skin where she'd held Zeke's shirt to his bleeding side while Laurel raced back toward the sectors.

Whole. Alive.

Hers.

She kept touching him, her fingers skating over his skin, inch by inch, as his breathing quickened. Finally, he cupped her face and lifted her gaze to his. "I'm here."

"I know." She told herself she wouldn't cry again. But it wasn't pain that was welling up inside her now as she turned her face into the gentle warmth of his hand.

It was hope. And anticipation. Relief and giddy excitement. Desire. The ghost of sorrow and grief, but so much joy.

It was life.

No. It was *love*.

Her lips found his again, clumsy under the force of

her need. His hands steadied her, tilted her head, and held her still for the slowest, sweetest kiss she'd ever tasted. Lips caressing, tongues teasing, growing deeper and deeper by millimeters until she was rocking her hips, grinding against him right there on a stone bench next to a forest path.

And she didn't really give a shit if the whole Rios estate lined up to watch.

Her hands shook as she got his belt undone and his pants open. But she couldn't get out of *hers* without giving up his mouth, and her frustrated growl had him chuckling against her lips as his hands settled on her hips.

Together they got her naked enough. And laughter shifted to moans as he dragged her back down, his cock sliding against her pussy. She would have taken him then, but he was Deacon, and Deacon *always* had a plan.

A slow, torturous plan.

He touched her everywhere. Legs, hips, arms, back. Sliding her sports bra free to cup her breasts. Ana clung to his shoulders and arched her back, giving him free rein to lick and suckle and nip and stroke until the heat of the sun glaring down on them was eclipsed by their fire.

Only then did he let her lift her hips and take him inside, and she was so close she almost came as she sank down on his cock. His hand gripped the back of her head, forcing her to meet his eyes as he guided her hips in a circling grind that couldn't be doing much for him but hit *every* damn place she needed.

And she took it. Took him. Claimed him with greedy hands clutching his shoulders and hungry noises falling shamelessly from her lips, and when the first orgasm broke over her, she kissed him just to keep from shouting her pleasure loud enough for them to hear it at the Temple.

By the time he ground her over the edge the third time, she didn't care. She cried out, offering her bliss to the bright blue sky, and when he shuddered and joined her, Ana didn't have to hide from the tenderness flooding her. She wrapped her arms around him, cradled his head to her chest, and dared the world to try to take him from her.

If the world tried, she'd fight.

And she'd win. Because Ana was a fucking badass Rider.

twenty-seven

The only thing scarier than facing down an entire company of mercenaries was facing down Ana's aunts.

Though Deacon supposed that wasn't quite fair. They smiled and they laughed and they seemed to like him—and Naomi and Olivia would probably only conspire to murder him if he broke Ana's heart.

Probably.

"Deacon!" Olivia waved an arm at him from beside the buffet, where two men had joined her—one with bright red hair and one with black. When he approached, she beamed up at him. "I want you to meet my husbands. This is Jin, who works as a potter. And Aaron, who was just promoted." She reached up to pat the redhead on the cheek. "He's a supervisor in the Montero textile factory now."

"Congratulations." Deacon shook each of their

hands in turn.

Olivia reached up to ruffle Deacon's hair like he was ten years old. "Deacon helped me load a truck last week without *any* complaints, and he did it faster than you two ever have."

Jin's lips twitched. Aaron gave Olivia a look of exasperated fondness and winked at Deacon. "I'm so glad Ana brought home a *nice* boy who's more helpful than we are."

As if any of Gideon's Riders could be called *boys*. Deacon nodded and looked around the room. "The first temple services must be ending. It's getting busy."

"Oh, this is nothing," Jin said. "Give it another half hour and the whole neighborhood will be in here."

"Yes, they will," Olivia said, clapping her hands together. "You two keep him company. I'm going to make sure we're ready for the rush."

She enveloped Deacon in a quick, fierce hug. "I'll be back! Don't you go anywhere."

Aaron watched her disappear through the swinging doors, a soft smile on his lips. Then he turned back to Deacon. "She makes it sound like a threat, but trust me. She adores you."

"Because you make Ana happy," Jin added. He nodded toward where Ana had gathered a cluster of neighborhood girls around her. "I haven't seen her smiling like that since before we lost William."

She was beaming, kneeling to speak to some of the girls and drawing others into embraces that ended with smiles and sometimes laughter. They obviously looked up to *her*, not her status or position as a Rider.

And who could blame them? The new roses inked on her back surrounded a sword with an unblunted edge, sharp enough to deliver death or salvation with a single blow, and it *fit*. Ana was as formidable as she was loving, as fierce as she was kind.

Everything, in one single, stunning smile.

"I guess we're going to keep you," Naomi said from his right, breaking his attention away from Ana. When he turned, she laid a hand aside his face and stared up at him with deep-brown eyes that looked so much like Ana's. "You look at her like she's your world. You promise me she is."

He quelled a laugh. "You don't mince words, Naomi."

"Not when it comes to family." Naomi dropped her hand and turned to stand next to him. "My daughters are grown and gone. They have their own families now. But Ana... I loved William like a brother, but some days I came close to hating him for taking her from me. I didn't want her to spend her life alone."

"We're each other's world." Deacon found her hand and gave it a quick squeeze. "I promise."

Naomi clutched his hand for a moment. "Good," she whispered hoarsely, before clearing her throat and shooting Aaron and Jin a sour look. "What are you two troublemakers staring at?"

"Nothing," Aaron said too quickly at the same time as Jin said, "Seeing which one of us won the bet."

"Bet?"

"If you made Deacon cry."

Naomi jabbed a finger toward the kitchen. "Go help your wife before I make one of *you* cry."

Jin grinned at Deacon. Aaron tossed him another wink. But they both obeyed, and Naomi shook her head. "This is what you're getting into," she warned him, before waving a hand to take in the people spilling out of the wide-open cafe doors and into the salon. "Them too, you know. They loved William, and they love her. They're proud of her. She's *theirs*. And if you start coming around with her, you'll belong to them as much as she does."

The Riders already belonged to everyone in the sector. But this was a different sort of belonging—these people didn't own Ana or her actions, but they felt responsible for her. Protective of her.

Like a family.

"Excuse me." The conversations around him melted into a vague buzz as he crossed the room. More people were pouring in, and if he didn't steal a quiet moment with Ana right now, it would have to wait.

And waiting was unacceptable.

Ana looked up at his approach, flashing him a quick, brilliant smile before returning her attention to a little girl who was engaged in telling her a very intense story about climbing a tree to rescue a kitten. The rescue had apparently ended with a safe kitten and the cast on the girl's arm, which Ana examined solemnly before commending the girl's bravery.

"But next time you should wait for your parents," Ana cautioned as she rose. "A smart warrior always waits for backup. If I had to rescue a kitten from a tree, I'd bring Deacon here with me. I've heard he's some-thing of an expert at kitten rescues."

He managed to keep a straight face. "The trick," he told the little girl, "is to sing to them while you wait for backup. It keeps them from getting lonely."

"Ohhhh." She beamed up at him with a smile lacking two teeth. "Okay!"

"Yes, that's very good advice." Ana waved them toward the counter across the back wall. "Why don't you guys go see what Auntie Olivia has for temple day treats? I heard a rumor about cookies with real chocolate."

That started a minor stampede. The children

flowed around them like waves rushing back to sea, and Ana grinned at Deacon. "Hunter convinced his uncle to give Olivia a bargain on imported chocolate. Now she's the only person on the block who can afford to sell it."

"Really?" There was a short wall at one side of the bakery, hiding the head of a hallway from the rest of the room. Deacon grasped Ana's hand and began pulling her toward it.

"Mm-hmm." She twined her fingers with his and leaned into him as he tugged her into the shadowed alcove. "How are you hanging in there? I saw Naomi talking to you."

"Your aunts don't scare me."

Ana lifted one eyebrow. "Uh-huh. Sure."

"Fine, they scare me a little." Ana was glowing, and he drank in her smile as he traced the delicate line of her jaw. "What about you?"

"What, am I scared of my aunts?"

"Smartass." He swatted her hip. "The children. Do you still feel boxed in by their...?"

"Their dreams?" Ana wrapped her arms around his neck, her fingers tickling through his hair. "No. I mean, it's still a responsibility. I hope I never forget that. But...Gideon promised me he'll try to recruit Laurel. And if she doesn't want to join us, there will be someone else. He knows now, how much it matters. And..."

He nuzzled her cheek. "And?"

"And I realized I don't have to prove myself." Her voice dropped to a whisper. "I always see everything I do wrong, and then I miss the most important parts. Nothing matters more to you than the lives of your Riders. You wouldn't have put those lives in my hands if you didn't believe in me."

"Nope." He took her face between his hands. "But

I do believe in you. I always have. I hope you believe that, too."

"I'm starting to." Her heart was in her eyes, deep, beautiful brown and shining just for him. "I hope you believe how much I love you."

"Oh, I do." There wasn't much time, only a few more stolen moments before someone would miss them. Deacon took advantage of those moments to kiss her, and his heart skipped when he felt her lips curve into a smile beneath his. "Almost as much as I love you."

maricela

When she was young, no more than seven or eight, Maricela had developed the habit of eavesdropping when her brother held meetings with his Riders in the palace. It didn't happen often, so it was a novelty, a fine way to break the monotony of days filled with dolls and lessons and music and art.

She would hover on the balcony overlooking the second floor. It was close enough to the conference room to overhear, especially if voices were raised, or if they forgot to close the heavy wooden door. She would hover and listen, and marvel over how many people Gideon commanded.

As she got older, it grew into something else. These meetings were important occasions where people discussed important things, vital to the safety and well-being of the sector. No one had ever asked Maricela to do anything more important or vital than choose a wine to accompany the dinner menu. A different kind of novelty, but a novelty, nonetheless.

What would it be like to be *important*?

She didn't have to hide on the balcony anymore, but she also wasn't invited to the meeting. Which was rich, considering the topic of discussion had plenty to do with her life, not to mention her safety. So she stood outside the partially closed door, arms crossed over her chest, and felt not even a twinge of remorse over eavesdropping.

This time.

"We're going to want to gather intel on this *discreetly*," Gideon was saying. "Whoever hired the Suicide Kings to take out the Riders will know they failed. But they don't know what *we* know. And there's no reason to tip our hand."

"How many people could it have been?" Zeke asked. "I mean, let's be real. We were never going to be an easy target. Someone had to have paid *big* money. Noble-family kind of money."

"We can't assume that," Deacon countered. "Seth would have done this job for free. Not saying he did, but I don't think we can count on him having charged full price, either."

"I agree." That was Gabe's voice, solemn and serious. "And not just because I don't want to consider my family working with the people who killed my aunt. Seth was *obsessed*. Half the questions he asked me were about Deacon."

It wasn't cold in the palace, but Maricela shivered anyway. There weren't many reasons why someone would consider the Riders an obstacle in their path, much less want to eliminate them. And the biggest reason was that they were *Gideon's* Riders.

Her family was in danger.

"We'll examine all the options. But in the meantime... Bishop, I'd like you to stay with Isabela until we can come up with a more permanent solution."

"Of course."

"And work with her household guard. I know she'll resist this, because my sister feels strongly that her trust in the faithful will be rewarded in kind...but I want personal guards for *all* her children. Around the clock. This sector is not going to deal with another royal heir held hostage."

A sharp pain splintered through Maricela. Her cousin Mad still carried scars from the kidnapping he'd endured as a child, the same one that killed his mother and father. But what too many people didn't know was that it had scarred Gideon, as well. He would move heaven and earth—even hell—to keep it from happening again to another of his loved ones.

"I'd like to stay with Maricela," Ivan said abruptly. "The royal guard might be fine for the younger children, but they don't have her responsibilities. She's out among the people too much to trust her safety to anyone but a Rider."

No. No, no, no, no. It had already been torturous, having Ivan so close—sleeping at the foot of her bed, for God's sake—and yet so far away. And the way he *looked* at her, like she was already a saintly painting on the temple wall instead of a woman—

Please tell him no. Please.

But her traitorous brother did the opposite. "I agree," Gideon said. "Thank you, Ivan."

Maricela could see Ivan through the crack in the door, and her pulse stuttered when he seemed to sense her gaze. His head turned, and his icy blue eyes caught hers. After a second, he inclined his head in a subtle

nod. A *deferential* one.
Then he looked away.
Oh, shit.

about the author

Kit Rocha is the pseudonym for co-writing team Donna Herren and Bree Bridges. After penning dozens of par-anormal novels, novellas and stories as Moira Rogers, they branched out into gritty, sexy dystopian romance.

The Beyond series has appeared on the New York Times and USA Today bestseller lists, and was honored with a 2013 RT Reviewer's Choice award.

acknowledgments

As with every book, we have an entire team to thank for helping us to the finish line. Our editor, Sasha Knight, our Keeper of Bibles and Timelines, Lillie Applegarth, our sharp-eyed proof-reader, Sharon Muha, our assistant, Angie Ramey, and our community moderators, Jay and Tracy. Without this fabulous group of women, we would be lost and our books would be abandoned manuscripts. Thank you, a million times thank you.

As always, thank you to friends and family, to twitter pals and raptor pals. We want to especially thank the amazing Alyssa Cole, who basically read chapters of this book while it was written, even sometimes via giant text messages at four in the morning, which is absolutely above and beyond the reasonable demands of friendship. She's extraordinary that way.

Finally, as always, thank you to our readers. Your enthusiasm for the Sectors and your willingness to embrace the Riders as you embraced the O'Kanes is a blessing and our daily motivation. We love you and are grateful to you every day.

gideon's riders

Ashwin
Deacon
Ivan *
Hunter *

forthcoming

the beyond series

Beyond Shame
Beyond Control
Beyond Pain
Beyond Temptation
Beyond Jealousy
Beyond Solitude
Beyond Addiction
Beyond Possession
Beyond Innocence
Beyond Ruin
Beyond Ecstasy
Beyond Surrender

www.kitrocha.com